Fool Me Once

Fool Me Once

T. Lynn Ocean

THOMAS DUNNE BOOKS

ST. MARTIN'S PRESS ♏ NEW YORK

THOMAS DUNNE BOOKS.
An imprint of St. Martin's Press.

www.stmartins.com

Book design by Irene Vallye

ISBN 0-312-33669-1
EAN 978-0312-33669-1

First Edition: July 2005

10 9 8 7 6 5 4 3 2 1

For my father,

who always had an answer and was the greatest grill chef in the world

Acknowledgments

To my manuscript readers who offered great feedback: Dave Barnes, Ted Theocles, Rick Storm, and Tracy Kahn.

To those who happily answered hypothetical questions: Steve Lawson, Chief Harold "Buster" Hatcher, the Preservation Society of Charleston, the Historic Charleston Foundation, bird enthusiast Gary Phillips, and attorney Carolyn Hills.

To writers Richard Oliver Collin, Mickey Spillane, and the late Jack Ehrlich for their encouragement.

To my incredible agent, Stacey Glick, who made it all happen.

To two fabulous editors: Carin Seigfried, who tactfully pointed out the obvious and skillfully uncovered the not-so-obvious, and Katherine Carlson, who worked her magic and kept things on track.

And to my husband, who never complains when I bring my laptop to bed.

Many thanks!

Fool
Me
Once

Prologue

Prone on a chaise lounge and squinting through near-blinding rays of sunshine, I watched a bird effortlessly skim the surface of the ocean and tried to figure out what species it was. It had a dark body and a gold neck with a silver stripe, and it seemed to glide forever before it had to flap its wings for momentum. It went up and flew a spiral pattern, like a jet coming in for landing, as I sipped on a frozen drink and wondered where my husband was.

He'd left to cash some traveler's checks more than three hours ago. I'd called our room and checked the swimming pools. I even walked through the resort's sports bar, where he might have been perched in front of a television screen to catch a ballgame score.

The bird suddenly folded its wings and dove straight down, head-first into the ocean. It resurfaced and bobbed in the water, swallowing the fish it had just captured. I realized the bird was a brown pelican and felt a flash of self-pity at not being able to share the moment with someone. The beaches of Belize were beautiful, but I was on my honeymoon and resented having to enjoy the beauty by myself.

"They are funny birds, no? Like dive bombers," a dark-haired server said with a delightful accent. He replaced my empty plastic cup with a full one. The rim was garnished with fresh fruit, and he'd thoughtfully wrapped a paper napkin around the base before handing it to me. Like all workers at the resort, he wore casual shorts complimented by a brightly colored shirt. His gracious demeanor announced that life was good.

I thanked him and returned my attention to the sky, hoping life with my new husband would be good. Two days ago, Robert arrived at our wedding with booze on his breath and a stain of some sort on his shirt, neither of which sat well with Mamma. He made up for his matrimonial faux pas by surprising me with a gold bracelet and airline tickets for our first vacation as husband and wife. But the destination was Belize, not the quaint resort I'd chosen in the Florida Keys. And now he'd disappeared on me, saying he was off to the bank to cash some traveler's checks. Which didn't make sense because the hotel would cash a traveler's check. The guest directory in our room said so. For that matter, there was a bank within walking distance. He could have gone and been back in ten minutes. Fifteen, tops.

The second frozen drink helped ease a tight feeling in my stomach, and as I rubbed sunscreen on my shoulders, I decided that the apprehension I felt was just postmarital jitters. Walking down the aisle had been both thrilling and scary, kind of like watching the pelican hurl itself into the water at breakneck speed.

Although Robert and I had grown up in the same schools and dated briefly in high school, we hadn't spent much time together as adults, and perhaps we shouldn't have gotten married so quickly. On the other hand, getting to know someone is what marriage was all about: sharing moments, creating memories, and establishing a future together. Daddy says he's still getting to know Mamma, and they've been married nearly forty years.

Robert was probably just sightseeing and had lost track of time. I closed my eyes and tried to think of nothing at all except the hot sun on my bare skin and the reassuring sounds of waves gently rolling onto sand just a few feet away.

1

I love you.

Three simple syllables with the capability to set hearts aflutter. Three short words that wield the power to transform lives. One tiny sentence over which futures had been planned, careers had been chosen or discarded, and seeking spermatozoa had penetrated ripe eggs.

I love you.

One second's worth of utterance that bared a soul and meant everything in the world. Or, like the promise of Santa Claus, could mean nothing at all.

I love you.

Words that could melt a heart, or shatter it.

The last time I'd heard those words roll off my husband's tongue, they were so passionate, almost guttural, nearly animalistic. He'd repeated them again and again, intensely, fervently, heatedly, while his hips moved to the rhythm of his words, up and down, up and down, until, with one final "God, I love you so much!" he climaxed with a sepulchral moan, pushed in deeply, then stilled.

Unfortunately for me, Robert's words had been directed into the ear of Corin Bashley, a divorced neighbor who lived two houses up the street. Until that instant, she had also been a good friend.

I'd returned home from the airport after my flight was canceled and simply stood in the bedroom doorway, transfixed, watching, *listening.* I didn't even move when the two of them, sweaty and spent on my favorite yellow cotton sheets, realized that they were no longer alone.

"Oh, no, Carly . . . Oh, God. . . . ," Corin sputtered, undergoing an instant transformation from ecstasy to shame and haphazardly throwing on her skintight jeans and button-down blouse. "I'm so sorry . . . this isn't what you think," she lied, as though I'd believe her words rather than my eyes. As though there could be any explanation.

But Robert had remained quiet. He just looked at me, his bride of less than a year, and sadly shook his head. He couldn't claim that Corin meant nothing to him and he didn't even try. The passion in his voice as he'd repeated those three simple words over and over again from his position on top of her had been too evident. They'd never sounded that way when he'd uttered the same words to me. Or maybe they had, but the scene I'd just witnessed made all his prior declarations of love seem hollow in comparison.

Two days later, as I sat staring at the massive desk that separated me from Robert's divorce lawyer, it occurred to me that I probably would have forgiven Robert if he had bothered to ask. People make mistakes. I would have been willing to do what was necessary to make it work: pay more attention to him, learn to appreciate hockey, act interested in the stock market swings.

Perhaps I'd put a wedge between us by getting so angry when he flushed my birth control pills down the toilet. Maybe I should have given in to his plea for a baby, even though I wasn't yet ready to be a mom.

After all, I'd rearranged my life and moved to New York because he'd asked. And because he was funny and handsome and he made me feel special. We could have made a beautiful child together.

But it hadn't occurred to him to ask for forgiveness. The emotion he emanated at having been discovered with his dick inside Corin Bashley reeked of relief rather than regret. There was no apology, in words or actions, and no talk of keeping our marriage together. His immediate concern was coordinating my schedule with his lawyer's, so we could get on with the apparent divorce.

I should have gotten my own lawyer, and I should have done the filing. After all, he was the party who'd been unfaithful. But I was too stunned by the turn of events in my life to care. And besides, I wasn't sure that I even wanted a divorce. So, like a wounded bird stuck in a rapidly moving undercurrent, I just went with the flow and tried to keep my head above water.

Since I was a kid, I'd always been the logical-minded, easygoing, quiet one. While my twin sister argued her way through adolescence and eventually became the star of her junior high debate team, I put equal energy into avoiding conflict because I saw no gain from it. At school, Jenny enjoyed instigating quarrels just for kicks and was a pro at pushing people's buttons. I, on the other hand, felt a duty to smooth out the situation when a fight erupted on the playground or when a teacher was threatening to give my sister detention. As early as my teenage years, I'd developed a knack for solving everyone's problems and had decided that acting on emotion rather than reason was ridiculous. It simply made no sense. Everyone was surprised when I, not Jenny, applied to law school.

I turned my attention to how Robert and I were going to divide our newly acquired furniture instead of dwelling on the idea of living the rest of my life without him. I wondered if he would consider marriage counseling. I wondered if it would help.

As I robotically scrawled my signature and initials on papers that the attorney pushed toward me to initiate the legal separation, I wondered if my soul mate was still out there somewhere, waiting for me.

Perhaps I only wanted to get married because I was turning thirty-two and figured it was time. Perhaps the fact most every friend from South Carolina was already married bothered me more than I'd thought. Perhaps we just weren't right for each other. Perhaps the mechanical malfunction on the Delta jet was the best thing that could have happened.

Still, I felt as though I'd been kicked in the gut and my self-confidence had been expelled with the resulting breath that was forced out of me. I felt inadequate, foolish, confused. So even though I was keeping the two-story house that I'd bought before the marriage, I picked up the phone and called my folks in Charleston. I was fine, I told them. I just needed a vacation. I'd like to come for a long overdue visit to the Palmetto State, and no, Robert would not be with me.

I could have gone anywhere to get away for a while. But nothing could revive my spirit like a few weeks of Mamma's pampering and home cooking. And, nothing could improve my outlook on things like a few weeks' worth of Daddy's life lessons. I knew that right now, I'd rather be with Mamma and Daddy in Charleston, South Carolina, than anywhere else in the world.

I was ready for an attitude adjustment, Southern style.

2

Cruising the roads that wound through South Carolina's low country acted as a dose of therapy for my wounded soul. Watching the landscape flatten, inhaling the marshy scent of the coast, and admiring the massive oak trees that I had climbed on as a child, I could feel the tension exiting my body. It was the beginning of April and the day was incredible: sunny and sleeveless-top warm, with some fat white clouds slung low in the sky, just to be enjoyed.

As always, I admired the view when I approached the city. The downtown buildings don't stretch higher than the nearest church steeple, and there isn't another skyline like it in the country.

Charleston is one of the oldest cities in America and the oldest city in South Carolina. Evidence of its eventful history can be found everywhere, from the historical buildings to the colorful tales spun by oldsters at the local hangouts.

People waved to me as I navigated the narrow roads that lead to Lowndes Street, and when I pulled into the drive, my limbs aching to move after the long trip, I realized that I'd missed Charleston. It was little more than a year since I'd left, but it suddenly seemed like such a *long* year. I missed the people. I missed the culture. I missed pushing my naked toes into a sandy beach, fishing from the pier, eating shrimp and grits, and wearing sandals year round.

And I missed Mamma and Daddy. I hadn't seen them since my wedding day last June. And that was in New York, not where I wanted to get married to begin with. But it's what Robert had wanted, and I convinced myself that the location of the ceremony didn't matter. So Mamma and Daddy came to New York to see my new house and give their daughter away.

Like me, Robert had grown up in Charleston. We'd played together as children, avoided each other during the awkward pubescent years when hormones caused hair to sprout in weird places, and had become inseparable by our junior year in high school. He was athletic and bright, and all the girls in school thought he was positively *hot*.

But unlike me, Robert couldn't wait to get out of Charleston. Just days after graduation he moved to New Haven, where he eventually earned a bachelor's degree and then an MBA from Yale, while I was busy going through law school at the University of South Carolina in Columbia. He became an investment broker and thrived on the same perpetually moving, high-powered business environment that caused other people to have nervous breakdowns. I, meanwhile, decided that I didn't want to insert myself in the middle of hostile disputes and fight for one side. I chose a career of mediation instead of litigation.

Only by chance did we cross paths a few years later when he was in Charleston for a conference. The youthful attraction we shared in high school materialized into a passionate long-distance affair, and six months later, at Robert's suggestion, I quit my job and moved to Pawling, New York, to live with him. A month after that, I bought a house on three acres. He said it was a great investment and convinced me to go ahead and buy it, even though I was still looking for a job.

A year earlier, on our thirtieth birthday, my sister and I had gained access to a trust that was set up by our grandpa. Overnight, we each became worth a quarter of a million dollars. My money had simply sat in the same account, drawing interest, until I used most of it to buy the house. It was more house than I needed, and even after putting two hundred thousand dollars down, the monthly mortgage payment was more than I wanted to spend on a place to live. But Robert assured me that it was a wise move since real estate in the area was appreciating at fifteen percent a year. Were Grandpa still living, Robert said, he would be very proud of my investment decision.

A week after I became a New York homeowner, Robert broke the lease on his high-rise luxury apartment on the Upper East Side, and we moved into the house together. A month after that, we married, I was offered a job in the city, tried to focus on the plusses of commuting by train, and eagerly stepped into the role of wife.

Despite all the exciting change and palpable energy that radiated from the city twenty-four hours a day, I had never truly embraced the Northern lifestyle. The area was beautiful and vibrant. It had everything anyone could want. But the nearby beaches, like the roads and sidewalks and stores, were insanely crowded and difficult to get to. I suddenly yearned for South Carolina's marshy coast and Charleston's slower-paced lifestyle.

As I stood stretching in the driveway, Taffy materialized to greet me. A five-year-old golden retriever, her long fur vibrated with excitement as she sniffed my legs and demanded to be petted.

The rich aroma of chocolate chip cookies hit my nose when we reached the back screen door, and my stomach responded with an anticipatory growl. Mamma always made them from scratch with freshly shelled walnuts, thick chunks of Hershey's chocolate, and, in Daddy's words, a dollop of love.

She was on the phone with her back to me, and, judging from the decibel level of her voice, I surmised that she was talking to my sister in Georgia. The intensity of Mamma's voice always increased coordinately with the distance of the person she was chatting with. It had been that way ever since I could remember, even after communication satellites and fiber-optic cable brought opposite sides of the world together without a hint of static. If she was talking in hushed tones when I was growing up, I knew that our next-door neighbor, Miss Rose, was on the receiving end. If she was to the point of near yelling, I knew that it was Miss Nellie, a family friend who lived in Germany.

"Hey there, little girl!" Daddy said, surprising me with a bear hug from behind.

It was a term of endearment that he used on both me and my sister, and it always made each of us feel special, even though we were twins and it was a shared nickname.

I happily returned the hug, and we both took a step back to better examine each other. He looked and smelled just like he did the last time I'd seen him. Thick white hair that was shaved to a near crew cut and just slightly thinning on top, closely cropped mustache, dark eyebrows, tanned skin, trim build, and the rich scent of cherry pipe tobacco clinging to his clothes.

He'd recently turned sixty and was the only person I knew who looked forward to his annual physical exam. It wasn't going through the motions of the doctor's visit that he enjoyed but rather bragging to Mamma about all of his numbers afterward. He could talk cholesterol, triglycerides, and glucose levels like a pro.

Before I had a chance to say anything to Daddy, his mother appeared behind him.

"Jenny! How delightful to see you, dear!"

My grandmother was a tiny woman with long manicured nails and a head of big white hair that defied gravity. I was surprised to see her since I hadn't known she was visiting, too.

"Hi, Granny," I said giving her a hug. "It's great to see you, too! But, I'm Carly. Jenny's in Atlanta."

My birth certificate lists my official name as Carolyn Annabelle Stone, but I've been called Carly since I can remember. Apparently, I had a head of curly hair right out of the womb, and Daddy's nickname Curly morphed into Carly when my hair decided to straighten out at age two.

"Of course you're Carly," she said, reaching up and giving my cheek a fond pinch. It was a much stronger pinch than she looked capable of giving. I gave myself a similar pinch on the other cheek to make sure they both matched.

"Your grandmother has come to live with us," Daddy explained.

I felt my jaw drop, and when no words came out of my mouth, I closed it. Two strong-willed Southern women, with differing opinions on everything from how to make chicken bog to the proper way to prune a rosebush, were residing in the same house? It was unthinkable.

"You look beautiful as always, Jenny," Granny told me, running a spotted hand through my hair, pushing the bangs out of my eyes. "How's that darling boy of yours?"

"Your grandmother has gotten a bit forgetful," Daddy whispered into my ear.

"I'm Carly, Granny," I told her again.

Although my sister is a twin, we aren't identical twins. And I don't have any kids, whereas Jenny has already produced a clan of three.

"Well, of course you're early," Granny said. "You're not the type to run late."

"And a bit hard of hearing," Daddy added under his breath.

I shot him a questioning look. The concept of my vibrant grandmother growing forgetful or hard of hearing was difficult for me to accept. The last time I'd seen her, we had conspired to write a best-selling cookbook, taken a yoga class, and broken into an abandoned cemetery in search of what she was convinced was the location of Blackbeard's buried loot. But that was before I moved north.

From Charleston, her home in Wilmington, North Carolina, was less than a four-hour drive; it was an easy weekend trip, and I saw her often. But since I'd entered Robert's world, I realized now, I'd all but cut off my family. There had been nothing to prevent me from flying to Wilmington or Charleston for a long weekend. Nothing extraordinary stood out in my memory of events, and I wondered where my days had gone. Daddy always said that days had to be embraced, enjoyed, *used*. Otherwise, they would multiply into months and years that would mock you from afar.

I tried to decide if I had been embracing my days with Robert when a vivid picture of his sweaty body moving on top of Corin Bashley's flashed on my mental video screen. I shook my head to clear the image. I wasn't ready to think about him . . . at least not yet. It was easier to *not* think about what had happened.

As far as Granny living with my folks, there was certainly enough room for her. A historic three-story wood-frame building, Mamma and Daddy's house has a garden, an open piazza, and a large screened porch. Because nineteenth-century homeowners often conducted business on the first floor of their homes and entertained on the second, the middle level has a huge drawing room with French doors that open onto an ornate balcony and a separate entrance that leads to the street. But since everyone in my family came and went through the rear screened porch that led directly into the kitchen, the second-story entrance was never used unless Mamma was showing it to a visitor who wasn't familiar with the architecture.

My most poignant memories of growing up revolved around the sturdy wood structure. Knocking out a front tooth while twirling a baton in the backyard . . . the lopsided tree house where Jenny and I fantasized about kissing Billy Benton . . . Mamma's aromatic kitchen, which always had a treat baking in the oven, and Daddy's off-limits workshop, which produced enchanting surprises like the three-foot-tall dollhouse I'd received on my seventh birthday.

I closed my eyes to inhale the rich fragrance of a memory-laden home. When I opened them, Granny was staring at me curiously, perhaps wondering which granddaughter I was.

"Where are the cookies?" I asked to replace the thought of her mental deterioration with something more palatable. "I don't see them, but I sure do smell them!"

"Sell what, dear?" Granny asked cheerfully.

"Carly! You're here," Mamma told me, hanging up the phone. Her words stretched into more syllables than Webster's claimed they should have. She gave me a kiss on the cheek and produced a platter of still-warm cookies, seemingly all at once.

Mamma's appearance was the same as always—elegant.

Slim, smart, and determined, she epitomizes a true Southern woman. She stood tall, embraced custom, and would never be seen in public wearing something as disdainful as blue jeans or sweatpants.

"Jenny!" Granny said as if seeing me for the first time. "How delightful to see you, dear."

Her condition was worse than simply forgetful; she was confused. Without bothering to correct her, I just smiled and endured another rough squeeze on the apple of my cheek. At least if she had me mixed up with my sister, she was jovial about it. Daddy always said that there was a bright side to everything. You just have to have the right perspective to see it.

The four of us gravitated to a well-polished maple kitchen table that had been in our family for generations and had come with the house when Mamma and Daddy inherited it from her grandfather Wade, along with the hardware store.

I don't know if it was Mamma and Daddy's business sense or the influx of new residents to Charleston, but the hardware store had thrived and grown into a building-supply business that served home-owners and contractors for a one-hundred-mile radius. It was a friendly and honest place where vegetable seeds could be bought by the scoopful and lumber or brick by the truckload.

Mamma poured everyone a glass of lemonade with paper-thin slices of fresh lemons floating amongst the ice. She'd barely sat down when she jumped back up to make me a sandwich, pronouncing that I looked too thin.

"A sandwich sounds good," Granny said. "Have I eaten?"

"Yes, you did," Mamma assured her. "Barbecue with slaw, corn bread, and sweet pickles. But if you're still hungry, have a cookie."

"Robert and I are getting a divorce," I blurted, getting right to the point of my visit and drawing a collective gasp of shocked attention. Even Taffy quit slurping from her water bowl to give me a quizzical look. "He is apparently no longer happy with me. Or perhaps he just wasn't ready for marriage. I'm not sure. Anyway, I got Cheryl to handle my caseload for the next few weeks . . . so I'm just going to take some time off and relax."

Although I was a lawyer, I preferred conciliation to conflict. I was a mediator by profession, and the law degree simply added credence. The law firm I worked for had a special mediation and arbitration division. The bottom line was that if I couldn't settle a dispute on friendly terms, it would go to arbitration or end up in litigation in an actual courtroom. My job was to help those with a disagreement settle their differences out of court. In essence, I persuaded opposing sides to sit down and compromise.

I was blessed with genes that produced great skin, a perfectly straight smile, and thick hair. My eyes were an odd shade that couldn't be classified as any single color, but I'd been told they were beautiful. Although I didn't seek out attention, I drew plenty of interested glances from the opposite sex and cold shoulders from the same sex. When working a case, I found the most effective tactic was to counteract this reaction by paying an almost sexual attention to the females and a professional, detached attention to the males.

"A divorce?" Mamma said incredulously. "Lord God Almighty."

"Yes," I said to her and the Lord.

We were all quiet for a moment. I drank some lemonade. Granny took out her lower denture to remove what may have been a piece of walnut and, fortunately, remembered to reinsert it.

"Well," Daddy said thoughtfully, "he wasn't the right one for you anyway, little girl. Best to do it and get it over with. And don't let the son of a bitch take a dime of your hard-earned money or get his hands on that house you bought!"

I let out a sigh of relief, grateful for his no-questions-asked show of support. Daddy always had been a straightforward man. Make your decision and move on. No second guesses. No self-doubt. It's either black or it's white, and if it looks gray, pick a side and put it there. Find what you went into the store for, buy it, and get out.

Growing up, Jenny and I always had multiple items of the exact same article of clothing because when we found something that fit our gangly bodies, Daddy would have Mamma buy a dozen of them in different colors.

"What do you mean, he wasn't the right one for her?" Mamma said to him. "Robert is a darling young man. Successful. Polite. Handsome."

She looked at Daddy. Granny looked at them. The three of them looked at me.

"I found him in our bed with Corin Bashley. A neighbor."

"He had sex with this floozy in *your* house? The bastard!" Mamma said.

I think she was more outraged at the fact that Robert screwed his girlfriend in our house rather than the fact that he'd screwed her. Southern women had their standards. You simply did not insult a woman in her own home. And you did not cheat on your wife in her bed.

"I'll kill the son of a bitch!" Daddy said, not caring whose house Robert had been unfaithful in.

"It's okay, really," I told them with a brave front. "I guess we shouldn't have gotten married to begin with."

"Are you going to eat that sandwich, dear?" Granny asked, reaching for half of a pimiento cheese on white bread that Mamma had put in front of me. "I don't think I've eaten yet."

A genuine smile tugged at the corners of my mouth. I was feeling much better about life and my role in it, and I'd only been back in Charleston an hour.

3

On my second day in Charleston, I fell in lust, over a country-ham biscuit at Diana's. While I admit that I am occasionally prone to exaggeration, it's an inherited trait and therefore an excusable one. Mamma was the queen of embellishment, and I got the skill from her.

On the other hand, *something* about the man had put every one of my five senses on alert and made me temporarily forget about my woes with Robert. Maybe my reaction to him was an unconventional defense mechanism, my body's way of giving me some temporary pleasure, my mind's way of taking a respite from the gnawing feeling of failure and disappointment.

I wasn't sure whose idea it was, but the night before, the five of us had spread ourselves out on the back porch to look at the stars and not talk about what a loser Robert was. Me, Mamma, Granny, Daddy, and the dog. As we argued about whether or not the constellation we were looking at was the Big Dipper, and I took comfort from rubbing the underside of Taffy's neck, someone decided that a nightcap would be good. And like old buddies trying to outdo each other at a pub, Daddy and I didn't stop at one. When it's just the two of us, we're competitive like that. Mamma left us for Jay Leno and *The Tonight Show* promptly at eleven-thirty, and Granny wandered off in pursuit of some pecan pie. Even Taffy sauntered into the house, seeking the comfort of her L.L. Bean doggie bed.

But Daddy and I, well, we embraced the night. As the euphemisms stacked up and the level of bourbon in the bottle of Jack

Daniel's dropped, we cheerfully greeted midnight and persuaded it to go on without us. We pondered meaningless questions like why Taffy liked to turn in circles before lying down. We talked about Robert, Daddy's business, my job, the importance of wearing sunscreen and getting regular oil changes, and the benefits of annuities. I cried, we laughed, Daddy sang me a song, and I have a fuzzy recollection of a nearby dog howling and us joining in, the three of us harmonizing quite nicely.

When I woke up, I could barely open my eyes to search for the perpetrator who'd coated my tongue with glue. I peeled the fuzzy appendage off the roof of my mouth, piled myself into my car, and pointed it toward Diana's restaurant in the historic district. My head hurt too bad to go back to sleep, and my plan was to surprise everyone with country-ham biscuits. They weren't specifically on the menu, but homemade biscuits were and country ham was, and Diana's would happily make a take-out order if they had the ingredients. Plus, I could sit at the espresso bar and drink coffee while I waited for my food.

It was not quite seven-thirty in the morning, a time during which I should have still been in bed, sleeping off a hangover. I was not ready to face the perky server who retrieved my biscuits, much less a construction worker with the deepest blue eyes and easiest smile I'd ever seen.

Eager for anything to ease the nausea in my alcohol-saturated stomach, I'd plucked one of the crumbly biscuits from the bag and begun eating it while I sat at the counter, waiting on my change. During a struggle with a tasty, but uncooperative piece of ham, the whole biscuit fell out of my jumpy hand and hit the floor with a soft thud.

"Shit," I mumbled.

As I debated whether to get off the bar stool and pick up the mess or push it under the counter with my foot, he swooped right out of heaven to assist me. I temporarily forgot about my swollen brain and complaining stomach to appreciate the mesmerizing conglomerate of muscles, faded denim, and blazingly white teeth—all packaged in one tall, well-mannered body.

He gracefully retrieved the remains of my splattered biscuit.

"You probably don't want the rest of this one," I heard him say.

I nodded dumbly, agreeing.

"I'll just drop it in the trash." His voice was deep and smooth and self-assured.

"Thanks," I heard myself reply.

When our eyes made contact, my stomach lurched. Whether from nausea or desire I wasn't sure, but I was suddenly very conscious of the fact that my eyelids were puffy, my face was lacking makeup, and I was wearing the same pair of crumpled jeans that I'd worn yesterday driving to Charleston.

I started to say something else to the stranger but forgot what it was.

I decided against ordering a replacement biscuit, thanked the server when she returned with my change and a to-go cup for my coffee, nodded at the construction worker, and made a hasty retreat.

Minutes later, he came to my assistance again as I stood frozen in the parking lot staring at my car. It had a very flat right rear tire. I'd gone car shopping to cheer myself up upon moving to New York and ended up behind the wheel of a brand-new BMW 5-Series. It was less than a year old and wasn't supposed to have a flat anything.

"Shit," I said with disgust for the second time that morning.

"Expansive vocabulary you've got there," his voice came from behind me, and I could tell there was amusement in it. "You got a spare in the trunk?"

"I certainly hope so," I answered.

I held the hubcap and lug nuts while he went to work. Fifteen minutes later, I'd finished my coffee and he'd finished changing the tire.

"Thanks so much for helping me out," I said. "Can I pay you for your time?"

He declined my offer of cash. "It's a full-size spare, but you should still run by a station to have the flat tire fixed. It's probably just a nail hole."

We replaced the contents of my trunk. In went a plastic bag of clothes destined for charity, a box of microwave popcorn that must've fallen out of a grocery bag, an unopened emergency tool kit, and a spiky black dress shoe with a broken heel.

My gut rumbled as a cloud of queasiness engulfed me and I did my best not to burp or fart or make some other unfeminine bodily noise. The sensation rapidly progressed to a warm tingle that traveled the course of my body in every direction until I felt positively hot.

A flash of shame raced into my consciousness, hesitated, then melted into anger. I was ignorantly and happily married just two days ago. I'd been a faithful, loving wife. But like a marked heifer, I'd been cast aside by the head bull. He'd already had me and lost interest. He wanted a new cow.

To hell with him, I thought suddenly. Why shouldn't I have a sexual fantasy about another man?

And, oh, *what* a man.

Loose-fitting jeans resting low on narrow hips showed off well-muscled thighs when he moved. Muddy tan work boots anchored a confident stance. A squarish jaw covered with a fine layer of dark stubble complimented high cheekbones.

And the eyes. The ice-blue eyes that caught me openly staring at him.

I tried to focus on what he'd just said and remembered that it was something about having the flat tire fixed.

"Uh, okay, right. I'll do that," I said.

"Good." He folded his arms across his chest, studying me.

"Thanks again for your help this morning. . . . I actually shouldn't even be up yet because I drank too much last night and I'm hung over. But I just wanted to surprise my folks with breakfast and, uh, so far the day has not treated me well," I blurted. Then as an afterthought, "My name's Carly."

"Good morning, Carly," he replied with the grace of a veteran politician endearing himself to a potential voter. "I do hope that the rest of your day progresses in a manner much more to your liking."

He certainly didn't talk like a construction worker. But he had the truck to prove it. It was a big white thing with an extended cab, an impressive-looking toolbox in the bed, and double wheels in the rear.

"I'm Trent," he added, since I hadn't asked.

And that's how my second day in Charleston began. Hung over, dazzled, and feeling only slightly guilty at being outrageously aroused by a stranger named Trent.

Taffy's nose must have detected the presence of people food because when I turned in, she was waiting at the edge of the driveway, her body poised in an alert begging stance.

Inside, Granny sat at the table with a Popsicle in her mouth.

"Jenny!" she said with delight upon seeing me. "You want a Popsicle? They're orange cream."

I didn't bother to tell her that I was Carly and, with a flicker of jealousy, I wondered if my sister had always been her favorite granddaughter. "No thanks. I got us ham biscuits for breakfast."

"Breakfast?" she said. "I thought we already ate breakfast. I'm just having a Popsicle for lunch."

It was nowhere near lunchtime, and I opened my mouth to correct her but swallowed the words before they emerged. She was enjoying the Popsicle, eating it with the abandon of a child.

"Well," I told her, "breakfast . . . lunch, what's the difference? If you're hungry, then you should eat."

"Right on, girlfriend!"

I thought I heard a flash of my real Granny, the feisty one whose brain hadn't begun to exhibit signs of deterioration. I studied her closely. She returned my look, and I caught a glimpse of humor in her eyes. It quickly changed to detached contentment, and I wasn't sure if I had really seen the old her or just wished for it.

Before I had a chance to put the biscuits on a serving tray, Daddy came through the back door carrying a pastry box. The enthusiasm in his stride was forced, and I knew that he was hurting as much as I was. But like me, he would never admit it.

"Morning, everyone," he said, and the tone was overly enthusiastic, even for him. "I went out and got us some beignets from Joseph's. What do you have there, little girl?"

"Country-ham biscuits from Diana's. I woke up early and thought they'd be good for breakfast."

"Looks like we both had the same idea. What could be better than warm beignets *and* country-ham biscuits for breakfast?"

Situated in the French Quarter, Joseph's restaurant made the most amazing New Orleans–style beignets. Although I knew that some food would make me feel better, imagining a doughnut and a ham biscuit sloshing around in my stomach on top of all the coffee I'd already drunk was unsettling. I looked at him and forced a smile. "Sounds yummy."

"You feeling alright this morning?" he prodded.

"Sure. I feel great. How about you?"

"Fine, I feel fine," he said, sitting down carefully, probably trying not to agitate a pounding headache with brisk movement. "Why do you ask?"

"No reason."

My puffy eyes met with his bloodshot ones, and we burst out laughing.

"What's so funny?" Mamma asked, strolling by in a royal blue gown and matching robe. Her pedicured toes, painted bright pink, poked from beneath it with each step.

"Your daughter has a hangover," Daddy told her.

"I do not!" I lied.

We laughed some more, carefully so as not to jostle our brains too much, and Mamma just shook her head. Ignoring all of us, Granny was focused on capturing the last bit of melting Popsicle with her tongue before it slid off the wooden stick.

Daddy settled down with a cup of coffee and the newspaper while Mamma set out plates and poured everyone some juice and coffee. She stopped momentarily to rub my back in passing. It was good to be home.

"It looks like it's really going to happen," Daddy said from behind the business section of the newspaper. "Protter is going to put me under, damn it!"

"You can't stop progress, honey," Mamma said.

"Who is Protter and what progress are you talking about?" I asked.

"Protter Construction and Development," Daddy said with a mixture of admiration and disdain. "The Protter family. They buy parcels of land and put up everything from residential subdivisions to shopping malls. They just bought the sixty-two acres across from our store for a commercial development project."

"So? Won't more retail traffic help your store?" I said through a bite of a beignet. The dough was warm and puffy and had been fried just long enough to make the outside a golden brown. It was decadent, and after a few seconds of indecision, my stomach decided to accept it. An almost human feeling was rapidly replacing my hangover.

"The plans call for a Handyman's Depot building center. It will put me out of business."

"But your customers are loyal. They've been buying from you forever," I replied, licking the powdered sugar off my fingers. I noticed that he was eating a country-ham biscuit.

"Service doesn't mean all that much to people anymore. Oh, they'll complain about bad service or how they have to deal with a different person every time they go to buy supplies. But ultimately, after proximity, they go for price. And chains like Handyman's Depot buy in such quantity that I could never compete."

"What's really got your daddy all bowed up," Mamma said, "is that Paul and Mary Beth promised to sell the land to him if they ever decided to sell. That was a long time ago, before they took in Robert. They agreed to a price and shook hands and everything."

"You mean Robert's stepparents? They sold the Protters their land?"

Mamma nodded. "I hear that Paul hasn't been well lately, and I'm wondering if they're out of town. We tried calling several times to ask why they didn't let us know that the land was for sale, but they don't answer the phone."

Mary Beth and Paul were Robert's aunt and uncle. When Robert was six, both his parents were killed in an automobile accident. Although Robert never developed a close relationship with his stepparents, I genuinely liked the older couple, and Mamma and Daddy were on friendly terms with them. I couldn't imagine what would cause them to go back on their word and sell the land to a developer without first offering it to Daddy.

"An oral contract is just as binding as a written one," I said. "If you can prove that you had the standing agreement. But I don't understand why Paul dishonored your agreement to begin with. It doesn't sound like him."

"I don't know how it happened," Daddy said, "and I'd never force the issue of a handshake agreement in court. But somehow Protter got to them, and the land was sold out from under me."

"Well," I started, the mediator in me coming out, "if this Protter company didn't get the land across from your store, chances are they would've put up the Handyman's Depot anyway. Just somewhere else."

"Right," Mamma answered for Daddy. "But there's not another suitable location anywhere near our store. They'd have to put it a good distance away from us."

"You see," Daddy said, "I can compete with hardware stores and building supply centers. I *do* compete with them. Even the big boxes, because convenience and personal service count for a lot. But directly across the street? I may as well just shut down right now."

I had to wonder if Robert knew about the property sale and didn't tell me. Although they were not a close-knit family, he was a successful investment broker. Surely Paul and Mary Beth would have called Robert to ask his advice before selling the property. I felt a sour taste in my mouth that I couldn't blame on the hangover.

I also had to wonder how well Daddy would cope with this unexpected turn of events. I knew he wasn't ready to retire. He enjoyed work the way another man might enjoy golf.

Taffy barked exactly twice, and on cue the doorbell rang. I opened it to find my best friend, Lori Anne, standing there with disbelief.

"So it's true! You are in town. One of the girls at my spa said there had been a Carly Stone sighting," she said.

It felt good to hug her. Since I'd moved away, we stayed in touch with emails and an occasional phone call. But seeing her again made me realize how much I missed her company. When we let go of each other her smile faded to anger. She was pissed.

"Why didn't you call me?" she demanded, crossing her arms and ignoring Taffy's plea for some attention.

"I . . . I guess I'm trying to visit incognito. You know, keep a low profile."

"You didn't even want *me* to know you're in town? What's up with that?"

Her hair, I noticed, was a golden blond. It had a tendency to change with the seasons. Since high school, when Lori Anne's mother gave in and allowed her to start using hair color, it had been every tint on the Clairol chart from fire-engine red to jet black. That was more than fifteen years ago, and today she owned one of Charleston's hottest day spas. Her clients could get everything from a cut and color to Botox injections.

The short curls bounced around her face as she looked at me, questioning, and I knew she was hurt. Were our roles reversed, I'd have been mad, too.

"You always look good as a blonde," I said, motioning her in-side.

"That's your answer to my question? Flattery?" She suddenly froze in place and studied my face. Her anger melted. "Carly, what's going on?"

"Nothing, really. I just needed to get away for a few days, and it's been a while since I've seen Mamma and Daddy."

I headed into the kitchen.

"Bullshit," she said, following. "I know you better than that. And I like your hair, too. The highlights look great. But you look like hell."

Lori Anne got a round of hugs from my family and a few licks on the hand from Taffy, and we all settled around the table. Mamma set a plate in front of her while Daddy handed over the remaining country-ham biscuit and the box of beignets.

"You people know how to do a good breakfast," Lori Anne said.

"Thank you," Daddy and I said together.

"So," she opened the box and selected a beignet, "tell me what's going on. If you don't, I'll just ask your mamma. She'll tell me."

"What's the big secret?" Granny said. "Carly's husband did the nasty with a neighbor."

Lori Anne froze in midbite, questioning me with raised eyebrows at the same time I questioned Granny with an identical expression. I hadn't realized she was cognizant of my situation.

"If your granddaddy ever did me that way, I'd be inclined to get me a pair of pruning shears," she made an exaggerated cutting motion, "and chop the little sucker off! He wouldn't be a puttin' his peg in the wrong hole no more."

Daddy cringed and Mamma laughed.

"Oh, Carly, I'm really sorry for you," Lori Anne said. "But I still wish you would have called me. You know we can tell each other anything."

She was right. After all, when she was twenty-six, Lori Anne married a beautiful man who later admitted he was gay. He thought Lori Anne would turn him into a happy straight man but quickly decided otherwise. The marriage was annulled before they celebrated their one-month anniversary, and Lori Anne had been pretty hard on herself for not recognizing the obvious before they got married.

I nodded. "You're right and I apologize. It's just that I didn't want to have to explain. . . . I didn't want to be crying on anyone's shoulder."

"You're not going to be crying on my shoulder," she countered, tugging at the collar of her blouse. "This is a Fendi."

I had to laugh and mentally reprimand myself for thinking she wouldn't understand.

"She found Robert having sex with one of their neighbors," Mamma's voice lowered to a whisper. "In her own bed."

"The bastard!"

Mamma nodded.

We ate the rest of our breakfast in emotional silence, catching up on Lori Anne's business and purposely avoiding any talk of Protter Construction, the store, or Robert. There would be plenty of time for us to talk later, after Lori Anne had a chance to digest the news.

4

For only being back in Charleston less than a week, I'd acclimated to living in my old room quite nicely. New York was already beginning to seem like a hazy part of my distant past.

After completing law school when I was twenty-five, I'd returned to Charleston and severed the financial umbilical cord by renting a townhouse rather than taking Mamma up on her offer to move back into the family home. But I knew my old room would always be there if I needed it. The knowledge was empowering then and it was still empowering now.

Like a dieter fighting the urge to guzzle a milkshake, I tried not to think about moving back to Charleston, tempting as it was. Something nagged at my consciousness, telling me I shouldn't quit Robert even though he was quitting me. Plus, he hadn't yet signed the preliminary divorce papers, and I wondered if he was reconsidering. His cause for wanting the divorce was that I refused to have children, which wasn't entirely true. I just didn't want to have children so soon.

It was nearing lunchtime, and the Charleston day was breezy, warm, and inviting. Granny and I were sharing a porch swing and a plate of sugar cookies, munching, watching the squirrels dart around. Swinging with her, I realized that even though Granny's mind had retreated to some happy place I couldn't conceptualize, she was entombed by the Stone family bond. Just like I did, she had a place to go where she was welcomed unconditionally. Families just took care of each other.

"Carly, you're such a beautiful young woman. I'm real proud of what you do," Granny told me. "People are too sue-happy nowadays.

You keep them out of court, so the courts can be used for the stuff that matters."

"Thanks, Granny," I replied automatically before realizing she hadn't called me Jenny. And she had spoken knowingly about my job. I looked at her more closely, wondering what was going on inside her head.

"You married last year, right? Robert, is it?" She was back in the present and she was lucid. Mamma told me it happened once in a while, but until now I hadn't witnessed it firsthand. "I'm real sorry I didn't make it to the wedding. I had a plane ticket, but got the dates all tangled up!"

"That's okay," I told her, mentally crossing my fingers in hopes she'd stick around for a while.

"He's the one messin' around on you, and you came back home to figure it all out?"

I nodded. "That, and because I just really miss Charleston. Maybe I should move back. If Robert goes through with the divorce, there won't really be anything keeping me in New York."

"He's divorcing you? You're the one who oughtta be divorcing him!"

"As angry as I am, I was kind of thinking that neither one of us should be wanting to divorce the other one. Marriage is supposed to be forever! But regardless of what happens between us, I really do miss living here."

"Well, Charleston is wonderful. As much as I enjoyed living in Wilmington, I'm happy here, too. But, in your case, moving North had to be a wake-up call."

"I know. I guess it took moving away to make me realize I could live here forever. I can be a professional mediator anywhere. That's the good thing about what I do. No matter where you go, people always have disagreements!"

Sharing a conversation with Granny suddenly meant so much more than it had in the past. I wanted to keep talking for hours. I wanted to tell her so many things, ask her so many questions.

"You know Carly," she began, then hesitated to figure out how to phrase her thoughts. "I know my mind is going. I know that, at any second, I'll go back to that place where I live now. And the worst of it is, I probably won't remember this talk with you. But I want you to know I love you, very much."

My throat got tight, and it was difficult to make the next words come out.

"You may not remember it, Granny, but I will. It means a lot to me. And I love you, too."

"I just don't want to be a burden to your mamma and daddy. I hate being helpless . . ." Her words trailed off. "I have money, you know. Your granddaddy made some good investments before he died. I could afford to go into one of those—what do you call them? Assisted living places?" She let out a thoughtful laugh. "I guess it's done gotten pretty bad when you need assistance just to live."

I took her hand. "Mamma and Daddy would never allow you to live anywhere but here. And you're not helpless. You just can't remember things. There's a big difference."

"You think so?"

"Absolutely. Besides," I said trying to think of how to phrase what I wanted to say. "You're . . . happy. You're always smiling. You're cheerful. All the time. Even when you can't remember a damn thing!" I smiled at her.

"I am? I don't get mean or ugly like those books on Alzheimer's say that some people do?"

"Never. You're always in a good mood, and Mamma and Daddy are glad to have you here. They wouldn't have it any other way."

I looked into her eyes, willing her to understand, to remember our conversation. She hugged me tightly for several long seconds. I didn't want our time to end and was about to ask her if she wanted to go out clothes shopping when she spoke first.

"Jenny! How's that darling boy of yours?"

"Fine, just fine," I answered, grateful for the five precious minutes we'd shared.

5

"Well, this week is just turning out to be a family reunion!" Mamma declared, raising her wineglass into the air. "Your granny, both my girls, and all my little darlings here at the same time!"

An hour before, my twin had shown up piloting a Lincoln Navigator loaded with a plethora of luggage and toys, her twin seven-year-old girls, her two-and-a-half-year-old son, and a white toy poodle with the disposition of a junkyard rottweiler. It snarled at everything within a five-yard radius of its quivering, fluffed-up body. The pink bow attached to the top of its head by a brave dog groomer didn't make it any more approachable. Like the rest of us, Taffy just ignored it. Granny declared that it needed a Valium. Either that, or a good "ass-whuppin."

"I'm leaving the bastard!" my sister told us through a mouthful of Mamma's pecan pie. It was a declaration that didn't mean much, since Jenny threatened to leave Stephen or quit the show every few months. It was simply her way of getting attention.

"Watch your language around the kids, honey," Mamma scolded gently. "Now tell us what happened."

Jenny studied the ceiling, perhaps trying to remember why she had loaded up the Navigator and driven from Atlanta to Charleston. She was my size, with dark brown eyes and shoulder-length hair lightened to a near-white color. Despite the bleached look, she was a beautiful woman. That was, when anger hadn't twisted her features into the expression of a venomous snake.

We had just finished eating supper when Jenny and her clan arrived, unannounced. After a thorough round of hugs, Mamma immediately set to the task of feeding them.

Every Southern household always had plenty of food for anyone who happened to stop by, whether for a quick dose of gossip or a lengthy stay. I think other families called them leftovers, but in our house, the remains of Mamma's efforts in the kitchen were edible treasures.

The twins happily accepted fried chicken, mashed potatoes, and butter beans while the toddler, Hunter, refused everything except a pile of whipped cream that my sister had scraped off the top of her pie. She was watching her weight.

"He told me I was getting fat," she finally answered, biting into a forkful of pie. "He said the owners aren't going to renew my contract if I don't lose some weight. And my new haircut makes my cheeks look pudgy. And viewing audiences want youth, youth, youth, so I'd better not let myself go!" A heavy tear popped out and dropped onto the kitchen table.

Jenny was the host of *In Home Now*, a hugely popular Atlanta-based television show that aired in regional cable television markets across the country. A cross between a shopping show and a morning talk show, it specialized in the new, the trendy, and the upscale. She and her on-air partner peddled everything from cosmetics to lawn equipment to cruise packages, while entertaining the viewers with witty banter and surprise guests. Her husband, Stephen, produced the show.

Jenny hiccupped, then sneezed. Other people sneezed from pollen or freshly ground pepper; my sister sneezed from tears. I often wondered if she got her way with Stephen not because he couldn't stand to see her cry, but because he couldn't deal with the sneezing attack that would follow.

"The bastard!" Mamma said with genuine sympathy. She and Jenny always had appreciated each other's ability to exaggerate.

The twins, Sherry and Stacy, giggled at what they knew to be an off-limits word.

"What is it about my girls that attracts bastards?" Daddy asked the dogs. Taffy cocked her head and wagged her tail. Jenny's dog picked itself up from Mamma's tile floor and aimed a short growl of an answer at Daddy.

"Basta, basta, basta!" Hunter said happily from his perch atop a booster seat that had come out of the Navigator, along with half of Jenny's household. From the looks of what she'd brought with her, it was apparent she was planning to stay a few days. I wondered what excuse she offered to the teachers for pulling the twins out of school. Because she was a television celebrity, Jenny could usually get away with things other people couldn't.

"Bast-ard. It's bastard," Stacy corrected her brother's pronunciation.

"Basta!"

"Now let's everybody just quit saying that bad word," Mamma interjected. "Nobody is a bastard."

"But you just said my daddy is a bastard," Sherry, who was emerging to be the more logical of the twins, said.

"Basta!" Hunter repeated.

"Lord have mercy," Mamma said before shooting a "do-something" look at Daddy, who was busy squeezing a lemon wedge into his iced tea. Obliging her, he set to distracting the kids with talk of going to Folly Beach and searching for shark's teeth.

Jenny polished off the last bite of her pecan pie with an angry flair and was distractedly chewing it when she suddenly stopped and gave me a long, questioning look.

"What are you doing here?"

"It's nice to see you too, sis."

"Oh, come on. You know I didn't mean it that way." She plucked a stray pecan from the plate and nibbled it. "I'm just a little stressed. You would be too if you'd just driven from Georgia with a dog that growled at every passing car. And with a son who was trying to fart because he thinks the sound is funny. And with twins who fought over air space!"

"She was breathing my oxygen," Stacy pointed out.

"I was not," Sherry said. "You were moving onto my side!"

"I was not! I was trying to get away from his stinky farts!" Stacy threw the accusation at Hunter.

"Basta!"

Mamma just shook her head and excused herself from the table to feed the dogs. Taffy, always appreciative of a good meal, ran to stand by her food bowl. The poodle growled.

"That dog needs a Valium," Granny repeated.

"What is its name, anyway?" I asked Jenny.

"Her name is Precious. She was a gift from Cam, for the kids."

"Uh huh," I said, wondering if there could possibly be a more ill-fitting name. Cam, Jenny's cohost on *In Home Now*, must have given her the dog after one of their frequent spats. Though they were perfect on the air together, their off-air disputes were common knowledge among everyone on the staff. Jenny probably thought the dog was his way of apologizing, and Cam was probably still laughing.

"So what *are* you doing here?" she asked me again. "And where is Robert?"

"I'm visiting. And he's probably rolling around naked somewhere with Corin Bashley."

"Who's Corin Bashley?"

"His girlfriend," I snarled.

"You mean he's cheating on you?"

Not wanting to elaborate any more on Robert's unfaithful nature, I just nodded gloomily.

"But you haven't even been married a year!" Jenny reminded me, temporarily forgetting about her own problems by deciding that mine were much more interesting.

"He wanted a new cow," I explained.

She cocked her head and frowned, not understanding. Apparently my sister didn't watch the animal channel with her kids, or she would have known that a bull never mated with the same cow twice. His goal was to impregnate the entire herd.

Surprising me, Granny chuckled. She got it.

"Carly caught him fooling around with this woman in her own bed," Mamma added in a stage whisper, having returned to the table after feeding the dogs.

"The bastard!" Jenny dropped her fork.

"Basta! Basta!" Hunter said happily.

"Well, at least he didn't tell me I was getting fat," I said, but the sarcasm was wasted on my sister.

"Tell me about it. Stephen is a pig," she said with disgust.

"Basta pig!"

"Lord have mercy," Mamma said.

The cordless phone rang, and Precious growled at it.

"I'm gonna draw a bead on that dog," Granny told us.

I was closest to the phone and answered it.

"Jenny, thank God you're there," Stephen's voice rushed across the line, and it was a mixture of anger and relief. "I've been calling everywhere. You're not answering your mobile, and I didn't know where you went! You shouldn't have left like that. . . . I love you, baby. You're beautiful, and you're the best host *In Home Now* has ever had. Why didn't you just tell me you were going to your parents' house?"

If everyone kept confusing me with Jenny, I was going to get a complex.

"Hi, Stephen," I said and got right to the task of sorting out their problem. "She said you said she was getting fat."

"Carly? Is that you? What are you doing there?"

"Your wife asked me the same thing. After she said you said she was getting fat."

"I never said that! All I did was get us a health club membership. I thought she'd enjoy it," he said, exasperated.

"Hold on," I told him and held the receiver against my stomach. "Stephen says he never called you fat. He simply got you a health club membership," I told Jenny, who was attempting to look disinterested even though she was obviously pleased that her husband had tracked her down.

"Well, it's practically the same thing," she said after a pregnant pause.

Daddy and Hunter had occupied themselves on the back screened porch, attempting to free a small lizard that had gotten itself trapped inside. Granny had busied herself at the kitchen counter clearing dishes. But the twins were still at the kitchen table, and their small ears were soaking up the conversation.

I pressed the phone back to my ear. "She says it's the same thing. The club membership suggested you thought she was getting fat."

"But she's the one who wanted us to join! It was her idea!" He muttered something unintelligible. "Let me talk to her."

I offered the phone to Jenny, who made a show of declining to accept it.

"You can just tell him to forget it!" she said to me, but the volume of her voice indicated the message was meant for him. "I don't want to talk to him. Let him go find some *skinny* woman to host his stupid show!"

A bright green lizard skirted across the kitchen floor and found refuge beneath the pantry door. Hunter ran in after it.

"Dadda basta!" he said, pausing to point to the phone before flushing out the lizard and chasing it back onto the porch.

"Oh, good grief. Let me talk to him," Mamma said. She took the phone and disappeared to the back porch to join Daddy, Hunter, and the elusive lizard.

After a silent debate as to which conversation was going to be more interesting—mine with my sister or Mamma's with Stephen—the twins followed Mamma. The information they gathered from her end of the conversation would weigh heavily, like water that needed to be squeezed from a sponge, until they shared it with us. After all, they did have the Stone family genes in them. All the Stone women, beginning with the ancestors we'd tracked down as far back as the late 1700s, had enjoyed the pleasure of good gossip. My family history was rich with scandal, and I, with a little help from Robert, was apparently going to carry on the tradition. But my sister could instigate trouble all by herself.

"I'm tired of him taking me for granted," Jenny told me.

I nodded. Except for Granny and the dogs, we were alone in the kitchen.

"He has no idea what it takes to be in front of the camera, day after day after day."

I nodded again.

"It can be exhausting. You have to pay attention to every little detail. My hair stylist practically lives at the studio, and I have to get a manicure every three days! And God forbid if I should let something slip on camera that could be construed as politically incorrect. We don't want to turn off any potential shoppers," she paused for a breath to add a disclaimer. "Of course, we don't do live shoots all that often, unless we're promoting a travel destination. So they can usually edit something out when they want to. But still. It's a demanding job. All the people staring at you and asking for autographs every time you go somewhere. They want to know which food processor is really in my kitchen and if the Sensual Sack Pak herbal pills really work. There's no privacy. None."

I kept nodding.

"And I have to act like I really believe in all the stuff I sell. You know, like it's such a good deal that the viewers are nuts if they don't pick up the phone or go online right then and order? Of course, most everything we sell is a wonderful product. But, still, it gets tiring because I have to be *so* enthusiastic about *everything*."

I nodded some more.

"Do you think I look fat?"

I almost nodded again before I realized what she had asked.

"Of course not. And, even if you were, the American public would still love you. They want to buy stuff from a real person, not some anorexic pixie doll."

"So you do think I'm looking fat!" she accused.

I tried a different tack. "How much do you weigh?"

"One-nineteen," she said without hesitation.

"And you are five feet, nine inches tall, which means you could actually weigh a hundred and forty-five pounds and not be fat. In fact, you're way too thin."

"You think so?"

"Sure. You really could stand to gain a few pounds."

The twins burst into the kitchen to tell us the news.

"Daddy's flying here in his plane tomorrow," Stacy said.

"To talk some sense into Mama," Sherry finished.

As the producer of *In Home Now*, Stephen had access to several of the studio's assets, including a Bombardier Learjet. My guess was that he would drive his wife, their kids, and their stuff back to Atlanta and let his pilot fly the plane back. Or, if Jenny really wanted to teach him a lesson about inadvertently calling her fat, she'd fly back and leave Stephen to deal with the growling dog, farting toddler, and fighting twins.

After absorbing the news about her husband, my sister harrumphed. Granny kissed us all good night on her way to the bedroom but forgot she was going to bed and ended up dozing on the sofa. Precious rolled onto her side and started snoring, loudly. The lizard skirted across the kitchen floor, mere inches from the oblivious poodle's nose, and was followed by Taffy, Hunter, and Daddy—in that order. Mamma placed the cordless phone on its charger, looked around at her family, shook her head, and smiled. It was a smile laden with contentment.

6

"Who's been messing with the thermostat?" Daddy asked the household.

In what must have been a latent automatic response from childhood, Jenny and I answered in unison, "Not me!"

"Well, I haven't touched it," Mamma added.

"Me, either," Lori Anne said. She'd stopped by for a dose of Mamma's cooking on her way to the salon. "I don't even know where it is."

"Yes, you do," I told her. "You practically grew up in this house."

"Oh, right. Well, anyway, I haven't touched it either."

That left Granny. We all looked at her, awaiting a denial. But she was engrossed in a reality television show and unconcerned by the thermostat issue.

"Those firemen boys have tight butts, don't you think? I wonder if they wear them thongs?"

Daddy did some hemming and hawing while he carefully adjusted the thermostat back to its proper position.

"It's so nice out this time of year, the air conditioner shouldn't even be on," he mumbled. "Besides, the windows are open."

Waste bothered him, whether it was energy, food, or a person's abilities. He was thrifty and believed in taking good care of what you owned. Growing up, Jenny and I had learned to use a marchlike walk inside the house and had developed the ability to speed-view the array of goodies that rested inside the refrigerator. We'd been brainwashed to believe dragging our feet would wear a path clean through the carpet and to envision dollar bills dissipating along with the cold air each time the refrigerator door was opened.

Some of the prudence must have stuck, because I found myself doing things like shopping for gasoline prices before filling up my tank and turning off the faucet while I brushed my teeth.

Enjoying a leisurely morning, my family was in the kitchen, drinking coffee and nibbling at the remains of Mamma's homemade sausage biscuits and cheese grits. Precious sat at the back door, intermittently growling at something in the backyard. The twins played with a large conch shell, taking turns holding it against their ears to hear the ocean. Hunter was busy stuffing a piece of biscuit into his nostril, and Taffy lay beneath the booster seat, hoping to catch any dropped morsels. Jenny, chatting on her mobile phone, was unconcerned about everything transpiring around her.

"That dog's not right," Granny said, forgetting about her television show long enough to give the poodle a strong look. Precious must have known the comment was directed at her, because she shot a growled response at Granny.

"I think it needs to be medicated," Lori Anne said.

The dog did a roundhouse growl, covering everyone who was looking at it.

"Do poodle-dog farms have horses and cattle, too? Maybe it got itself kicked in the head by a bull and got brain-damaged," Granny said.

The dog took a long, sucking breath before shooting another growl at her. Doggie spittle began foaming up at the edges of its little mouth.

"I swear, I'm gonna draw a bead on that thing," Granny threatened.

I looked at Daddy, wondering if any of his shotguns were within easy reach. Granny had always been a strong-willed woman, and usually when she said she was going to do something, she followed through. Lucky for the poodle, Granny had probably forgotten the threat shortly after uttering it.

Daddy dismissed my concern about the guns with a wave of his hand from behind the business section of *The Post and Courier*. "They're all locked up in the gun safe."

"All of them?" I asked, thinking about shooting the dog myself. Lori Anne and I were helping Mamma clean up the kitchen, and I was about to take the trash out when Mamma stopped me.

"The new trash can has this tricky handle lock," Mamma warned me, "and be sure to strap the bungee cords back on when you're done."

"Bungee cords?"

"Your father has declared war," she told me in a hushed voice. "With the coons."

"Coons?"

"There's a whole mess of raccoons toying with him. . . . It's been going on for a couple of months now. They keep getting into the garbage and strewing it all over the yard. He tried trapping them, but they were too smart for that. All he caught was a squirrel and a possum."

"What happened to them?"

"Oh, he turned them loose. Anyway, he's tried stacking bricks on top of the trash-can lid, booby-trapping it with a string of jingle bells, squirting ammonia around it, and he even put out one of those battery-operated pest deterrent things that emits a high-pitched sound. But all to no avail."

"What happened to the noisemaker thing? I thought they're supposed to work pretty well."

"It disappeared," Mamma whispered, shaking her head. "Your father says one of the coons carried it off."

As I went out, Precious growled at either me or the bag of trash I toted. Maybe both of us. I thought briefly about putting her outside, with hopes the raccoons would carry her off and stash her with the stolen battery-operated pest deterrent.

What should have been an easy chore turned into a ten-minute ordeal. Daddy had built a three-foot-high enclosure around the heavy-duty rubber trash can, and my first obstacle was getting through the safety latch on the short fence's miniature gate. Bricks lay beneath each of the two wheels, apparently to keep the garbage can from being pushed or rolled by mischievous raccoons. More bricks rested on top of the lid. I chipped a nail getting into the tricky handle lock Mamma warned me about. And one of the bungee cords popped me on the shoulder when I unhooked it.

Back inside, I asked Daddy if he'd given names to his new pets.

"Not you, too!" he said. "Your mamma already teases me enough about those crazy raccoons!"

"Don't you have some kind of impenetrable high-tech garbage can at your store? There's got to be something that would be better than bells, bricks, and bungee cords!"

"They're smart, the little buggers are. And their paws are like little hands. They can get into anything."

Our conversation turned to new products that were hot sellers in his store, and I brought up the Protter Development project. His mood changed instantly.

"It's a done deal, little girl. It's going to happen, and there's not a damn thing I can do about it."

"So what's your plan?" I asked. "What are you going to do?"

"I suppose we'll have a grand going-out-of-business party," he joked, but I heard defeat in his words.

Deciding she didn't need to get to work right away, Lori Anne talked me into going for a drive, just to spend some time together. Because the weather was so nice, we found a parking place on Queen Street and went for a walk. Window shoppers and sightseers filled the sidewalks, soaking up Charleston's ambiance.

We found ourselves at the Smith Killian Gallery and meandered inside to browse. One of my favorite art galleries, it was in a beautiful old building that had previously been a residence.

Colorful Charleston scenes and black-and-white photographs covered the walls. Lori Anne stopped to study an oil painting of a fishing boat, and I could tell something was on her mind.

"What?" I asked her.

"What, what?" she said.

"Oh, c'mon," I said, walking to the next display. "You've got that wrinkle thing going on between your eyebrows. It only happens when you need to get something off your chest."

She sighed. "It's about Robert. Since you've come back to Charleston, I've been thinking maybe I should have told you how I felt about him before you got married."

We stopped in front of a bronze sculpture collection, but I was no longer admiring the artwork.

"What didn't you tell me?" I asked, feeling a sudden chill and not really wanting to know the answer.

She lowered her voice. "It's nothing specific, really. I thought you were crazy to leave Charleston, for starters. I mean, if Robert loved you, he should have moved here. Plus, I just never felt good about you getting married to him."

"Why not?"

Robert had always been a flirt in high school, she said.

"So were half the other guys," I said, wanting something more definitive.

"Right, but the two of you were sweethearts, you know? So why did he flirt with everybody?"

"Because he was good looking and could get away with it," I answered. "Besides, everyone knew he was a flirt. I used to tease him about it."

"There was also the time after that football game got cancelled because the lights wouldn't come on?" Lori Anne said.

I remembered the night, but nothing unusual stood out. All the students had ended up partying in the parking lot. And that was before Robert and I were even dating steady.

Lori Anne told me that, before school administrators broke up the party and sent everyone home, she overheard some of the guys playing a game. The object was to say which girl they'd ask out if there were no chance of rejection. Robert had pointed at me and said something about my hips.

"What about them?" To my knowledge, there was nothing extraordinary about my hips.

"He said they were wide, perfect for carrying a baby," she told me. "And he'd pick you because you had nice skin and good teeth."

"Wide hips, nice skin, and good teeth? That sounds like he was shopping for a farm animal or something!" I said in a tone too loud for an art gallery.

Lori Anne waved her thanks to an employee and ushered me out.

"So the other boys were simply thinking of who would be a fun date," I said outside. "But Robert was looking for a good *baby maker*?"

We headed up State Street, and Lori Anne nodded. "I thought it was a really odd thing for your boyfriend to say. But then I forgot about it. Besides, you guys went your separate ways in college. I never guessed you'd get back together all those years later."

I thought about Robert and the responsibilities of parenthood and my wide hips.

"He flushed my birth control pills down the toilet a few months after we got married," I confessed. "I wasn't ready to get pregnant yet, but he argued that it was unnatural to be on the pill and flushed them."

"What did you do?" she wanted to know.

"Got a refill and hid them inside a box of tampons."

Deciding we needed a drink, Lori Anne guided me into A. W. Shuck's. Although I wasn't thirsty or hungry, she ordered a glass of wine for each of us and convinced me to split an appetizer of blue crab dip with crackers.

"I'm no shrink," she said as we situated ourselves at the bar, "but maybe his goal early on was to create the childhood he never had by making the perfect family. I mean, losing his parents really screwed him up, right? And it was no secret that he hated living with his aunt and uncle."

"He felt cheated," I said. "He always thought they were country hicks. Even though they're wonderful people, Robert never bonded with them."

"Look, Carly," Lori Anne said when our wine arrived. "The guy just gives me bad vibes. All of a sudden your life completely revolved around Robert. You moved to New York, for God's sake, and you weren't even married! Then you bought that house, which you told me was way too big. And instead of coming back home to visit, you spent your weekends going to conferences with him or throwing parties for his clients."

The crab dip arrived, and it looked delicious. But neither of us ate any.

"Maybe I'm jealous because he took my best friend away," she finally said.

"Well," I said, "even if you would've told me how you felt, it wouldn't have made a difference. I just thought he was so wonderful, and moving to New York was a sacrifice I could live with, since it was what he wanted."

She spread some dip on a cracker and handed it to me.

"I'm not hungry."

"You need to eat, or your wide hips could shrink."

We burst out laughing and ate some crab dip and drank our wine. It was nearing one o'clock and A. W. Shuck's quickly filled with a lunch crowd. A popular spot for fresh oysters and steamed shrimp, Shuck's was in a structure that had originally been built as a warehouse for Nabisco some eighty years ago.

In fact, the former warehouse district had been through many transitions, but about twelve years ago, it started attracting locally owned restaurants. The area has since become a restaurant row. Charlestonians love to eat well, and food critics love Charleston.

Lori Anne asked if I was mad at her, and I asked if she was mad at me, and we both agreed it would be silly for either of us to be mad. Then she predicted Robert would come to his senses, beg forgiveness, and want me back in New York, adding that I'd be a crazy fool to go.

"So would you go back to him?" she asked.

I thought about it. He'd acted reprehensibly, and his hang-ups about losing his parents were becoming more obvious. But nobody ever said marriage was easy. And despite everything that happened, I still loved him.

I honestly didn't know what I'd do, I told her. I'd always believed when I got married, it would be forever. We paid the bartender and walked back to her car, talking with much relief about her current boyfriend instead of my estranged husband.

"Daddy's here," the twins announced in high-pitched unison.

Stephen and his pilot, Mike, were welcomed with much fanfare. The twins, Hunter, and Taffy fought for their attention while Mamma and Daddy politely waited for handshakes and hugs. Precious paced between the two men, growling at the ankles of each.

"Oh, Christ, she brought the dog, too?" Stephen said, looking like he wanted to kick it.

"It's really not all that bad," Mamma told him. "It just doesn't seem to like people all that much."

"Or anything else," Daddy muttered.

"I thought it was unusually quiet around the house. It was the absence of growling. Damn."

Even in jeans and a knit golf shirt, Stephen looked like a successful executive. He complimented my sister perfectly, both in looks and temperament.

"I've got a right mind to shoot that poodle-dog," Granny told him, standing on her toes to give him a hug and a pinch on the cheek.

"I'll get the gun."

"You're married to one of the girls, right?" she asked him. Stephen didn't look surprised at the question, so he must have known about Granny's condition. Which meant Jenny must have been on the phone with Mamma a lot more than I had been lately. I felt another stab of guilt as I realized how right Lori Anne had been when she said I'd been consumed with Robert for the last year.

"This is Jenny's husband, Stephen," Mamma told her.

"I'm gonna shoot that poodle-dog," Granny told him again.

"I'll get the gun," he repeated, winking at Mamma.

I genuinely liked Stephen, and although I loved my sister, I sometimes didn't really *like* her. How the two of them made their relationship work was a mystery to me. But they did, and they doted on each other. And despite Jenny's often irrational behavior, she was still together and in love with her husband. Which was more than I could say about myself.

"So is she still mad about the fat thing?" Stephen asked me.

"Well, what do you think?" Jenny said, making a perfectly timed late entrance. "Of course I'm still mad. I'm not even talking to you, I'm so mad."

Stephen's mouth twitched in what may have been a grin, but he wisely kept it shut.

"You don't have to deal with the pressures of being a television personality! I work hard at my appearance, and then you go and tell me I'm fat!"

"Honey, I love you. You're not fat."

"Well, sure, you're going to say that now. But, you do! You do think I'm fat," all one hundred and nineteen pounds of her emphasized the last sentence.

"You know what, Baby? I really bought the gym membership for me, because I wanted to start lifting some weights again. I just got the family plan in case you wanted to join me sometime. Or play in one of those social tennis tournaments or something."

"Really? You didn't buy it for me?"

I could see that Mamma and Daddy were as intrigued by Jenny's logic as I was. Mesmerized, we eagerly waited for the next act of the play to unfold. Accustomed to such exchanges between their parents, however, the twins only half-listened. And Mike's face was politely blank. It was just another day at work for him.

Sensing that Jenny was softening, Stephen knew he was on to something. "Of course I didn't buy it for you. I bought it for me."

She rushed to hug him. "I knew you didn't *really* think I was fat!"

Since the show was over, we headed to the kitchen for lunch, some of us still rolling our eyes. Mamma served her famous chicken salad, and it was delicious. She always made it with fresh dill, crumbled walnuts, and tangy seedless grapes. Even though I had the recipe, mine never tasted as good as hers.

Jenny decided that, since her family was already at Mamma and Daddy's house, they should stay for a few days. Stephen made the necessary phone calls to rearrange his work schedule, and Mike decided to head back to Atlanta. Another crisis averted.

"Oh, and Mike?" Stephen said as Mike headed out. "Don't forget the dog. Just let the housekeeper know we won't be back for a few days when you drop the thing off."

"*I'm* taking the dog back? I don't think it likes to fly. It growls at passing clouds. And remember the last time? It got sick. Then it growled at its own puke. What if it starts throwing up?"

Stephen raised an eyebrow at him. "You'll figure something out."

"Son of a bitch," he mumbled, looking around for his four-legged cargo. "You do owe me one."

Jenny's getting-ready-for-bed routine was amazing to witness firsthand. It was like a bad car wreck: I didn't want to stop and look, but I couldn't help myself. There were fifty strokes with the ionic hairbrush, a vitamin C peel-off facial mask, vitamin E and cucumber concentrate eye cream, twenty minutes of a press-on teeth-whitening strip, and facial exercises with some type of spring-loaded contraption that fit in her mouth. That was just the beginning.

She produced something that resembled a weight-lifting belt and strapped it around her waist, beneath a silk nightgown.

"What is that?" I asked.

"It's a magnetic weight-loss and chi belt," she answered, as though everyone owned two or three.

"Of course."

"The magnetic fields improve your circulation and keep your chi flowing, and that helps to keep the fat cells from forming while you sleep. This thing is a top seller on the show. The manufacturer can hardly keep up with orders."

"Wow."

"You want one? I've still got two or three left, brand new in the box. They were samples."

"Sure . . . why not? It's important to keep the chi flowing," I said, humoring her. She didn't catch the sarcasm in my voice.

"I'll have my assistant send you one when I get back."

"Thanks."

She attached a few other contraptions to her body, including high-tech battery-operated footies to moisturize her feet and an armband that was supposed to cure carpal tunnel syndrome. Jenny didn't have carpal tunnel syndrome, but she always tested every product she hawked on *In Home Now*.

"Do you, um, sleep like this every night? I mean, do you always *test* all your products?" I tried to imagine how Stephen could get turned on by a woman wearing a chi belt, footies, and twelve differently scented products ranging from citrus to menthol.

"Sure I do," she said. "Well, unless it's a lovemaking night. Then, I'll put on my pheromone lotion, gold-glow moisture face cream, and some skimpy lingerie. Oh, and tune the nature sound machine to breaking ocean waves or something romantic like that."

Smothering an impulse to guffaw, I asked, "How do you know when it's a lovemaking night?"

"If I'm in the mood, then it's a lovemaking night. He's always in the mood, so that's never a problem." She thought for a moment.

"And if it's a Saturday. Always on Saturdays, because he takes me out every Saturday night, and then we sleep in on Sunday."

It was more information than I needed to know about my sister's sex life, but then, I had asked. I had no one to blame but myself.

It dawned on me that it was Saturday and should have been a lovemaking night according to her system. I guessed that, even though he'd flown several hundred miles to retrieve her, it didn't count since he hadn't taken her out. I heard Stephen coming down the hall, so I decided to leave my product-savvy sister in his capable hands.

I found Daddy deep in contemplation on the back porch. Cherry tobacco smoke made lazy curls from the pipe he held to his mouth. I'd poured myself a glass of chardonnay and brought him an icy mug of beer. He had a spread of papers in front of him, and I knew he was thinking about the business.

"So tell me what's going on," I demanded. "What did you decide to do?"

"Go out of business, before I'm forced out. I'll just liquidate the inventory and put the building on the market."

"You're giving up that easily?" I asked, not wanting to believe the words I'd just heard. He loved the hardware and building supply business. "Maybe there's something you can do. Maybe I can help."

"You can't negotiate our way out of this one, little girl. There's nothing to talk about. That's just the way business works sometimes: big fish eating little fish."

I took a long, slow sip of wine, shaking my head in disagreement. "There's always something to negotiate. We just have to figure out an angle."

"No, there's no angle. Nobody's done anything illegal. It just is what it is. It's time to fold my hand and get out of the game." He looked up from a plat map and smiled at me. "Protter has won."

"But are you ready to quit the business?" Daddy just giving up on something didn't happen. "I mean, would it be your choice to retire right now?"

"Who said anything about retiring? I can go be a greeter at Wal-Mart or something."

I just gave him the look. The Stone family reprimanding look.

"Really, Carly. I know you just want to help. But there've been too many small businesses that out of pride or stubbornness tried to hang on and compete with the big boys. It never works." He drank some beer. "I've even talked to Protter to see if the Handyman's Depot is definite. It is. It's a done deal. They don't have to anchor the center with a building supply business, but this area is ripe for one. It'll work and it'll go over big. Handyman's has been looking at the demographics and the competition in this area for some time now. They did their research, and they wanted that spot. Protter simply took the highest bidder." He shrugged his shoulders. "We're not the first family that Handyman's or Protter has put out of business, and we won't be the last."

Taffy had joined us, and Daddy was absentmindedly scratching the top of her head.

"We've had a good run," he said with a sigh, setting his pipe down. "I'm just glad Wade's not here to see what's going to happen to the business. He started it from scratch . . . it was his life's work. And it's been our livelihood."

So that was what was really bothering him. Mamma's grandfather had passed the family business along to Mamma and Daddy, along with all the sweat and time and energy he'd put into it. And now, Daddy felt like he was dishonoring my great-grandpa.

"You're not out of business yet," I told him. "There's always a way."

"Not in this case, little girl. Not in this case."

7

He was as gorgeous as the first time I'd stumbled across the man. Only this time, the construction worker was wearing a pair of yellow and white swim trunks. I was stretched out in a lounge chair, nestled among healthy palm trees and piped-in music, drinking an icy margarita, watching, enjoying. The swimming pool was endless, and I noticed his abdominal muscles constrict as he effortlessly pushed himself up out of the water and jumped out.

"Aunt Carly!" I felt a tug on my foot. "Aunt Carly, it's for you! Wake up. The telephone's for you!"

"Huh?"

One of the twins, Sherry, shoved a cordless phone at me. I looked at the bedside clock and realized it was already past nine in the morning. I rubbed a hand over my eyes, and thought about trying to go back to sleep to recapture my erotic dream. But curiosity got the better of me and I pressed the phone to my head.

"Hello?"

"Hello, Carly. How are you doing?" It was a man's voice.

"What?"

"I just called to see how you're doing. I'm worried about you," he said.

"Robert?" I sat up in bed.

"Look, Carly, we need to talk. I treated you badly and I'm sorry. Come home and let's talk."

"Come home?"

"Yes, come home and let's talk."

Lori Anne's prediction that Robert would change his mind and want me back had proven right. But he'd caught me off guard, and I didn't know what to say. The first rule of mediation was to always be prepared for what either side might throw on the table, but I'd just been blindsided.

Hearing his voice had induced a microsecond of pleasure, in the moments while my sleepy brain was relaxed and unencumbered by bad memories. But almost immediately a vision of him screwing Corin in my bed brought back a flood of hurt. And red hot anger at the fact that *he* wanted to divorce *me* after I'd caught him at it. The more time I'd had to think about it, the more I'd realized he should have been groveling for forgiveness. Not doing the filing.

Had the twins not been listening, I might have told him to go screw himself. Had they not been watching, I might have given in to my urge to throw the telephone against the wall. Instead, I took a deep breath and told myself to stay calm.

"It took a week to decide this?"

"I wanted to give you some time to calm down."

I couldn't believe what I was hearing. "What happened to Corin?"

"Well, nothing's *happened* to her," he said and drank some coffee. The long sip traveled through the phone line, and I envisioned him sitting at my kitchen table, the one I'd bought right after college, for my first apartment in Charleston. He'd have the newspaper on the table in front of him, the sports section on top, spread out beside a saucer of buttered wheat toast and exactly half of a banana. He wouldn't have the coffee cup on a saucer, as many new stains would attest. "We're not together, if that's what you mean."

"But I thought you *loved* her."

Silence.

"Well, you certainly told her so, when I stumbled upon the two of you. 'I *love* you. I *love* you. I *love* you,' you kept telling her," I said, dredging the only mud I could think up on such short notice. But at least it was really dirty mud.

"Look, Carly," another sip. "It was just sex. It's like, you were so busy at work and all, I turned to her for companionship. I enjoyed her company. But I was never after her. I mean, she's the one who seduced me, and, well, I did let it happen. But I know it was a huge mistake. I'm sorry, and I want you to come home. Please. Come home."

He wanted me back. And even though I wasn't sure I wanted him, a small thrill of victory rushed through my abdomen, diluting the anger. I knew I'd played my hand correctly. I'd been patient. I hadn't begged him to choose me over her. I hadn't shown any weakness, and I wasn't going to start now. The ball was back in my court, and I wanted to keep it there for a while.

"I'll be coming back in a few days, Robert," I told him, and the steadiness in my voice surprised me. "But not because of you. I've got to get back to work before my firm fires me. So I was planning on returning to New York anyway, whether you were in or out of the picture."

He sighed. "Carly, I never left the picture."

"So the divorce lawyer thing was all just for fun?" I shooed the twins away, but instead of allowing me some privacy, they climbed into the bed to hear better.

"I wasn't thinking right," Robert said. "Marriage is for better or for worse, and we'll get through this. You're the best thing that's ever happened to me, and I love you. And I know you'll make a wonderful mother. I want us to start a family. I don't want a divorce, Carly. I told my lawyer to tear up the papers. Please come home."

"Did you know about Mary Beth and Paul selling their land?" I demanded, changing the subject. "The land across from Daddy's store?"

He hesitated. "They had mentioned something about it, but I don't really know anything. You know I don't keep up with their affairs. And I don't want to talk about them. I called to talk about us."

"Is Paul sick? Mamma said she heard that he hasn't been well. But they don't answer the phone."

"Last I heard, he'd come down with some form of cancer and he was getting treatment at the medical university in Charleston. But I don't want to talk about them. I called to talk about us."

I was genuinely shocked at his aloofness. "How can you be so indifferent about the people who raised you! They're the only parents you'll ever have."

Sherry and Stacy gave each other a look, silently debating about the outcome of my phone call.

"My parents are dead, Carly. I was raised by a foster family. They did their good deed, and I've repaid them. And that's that." His voice was flat.

"Repaid them? How? You never even visit them."

"I gave them money because they were too stupid to plan ahead and buy supplemental health insurance. Medicare coverage of certain treatments is quite limited. In any case, it's really not your business."

This impatient, callous man did not sound like the same one I had married, and I wondered if I knew him as well as I thought. On the other hand, being raised by people other than his natural parents had been difficult for Robert, and perhaps he had done the best he could by offering money rather than emotional support. At least it was something. It proved he wasn't totally heartless.

"Look, I'm sorry to sound crass," he said, softening. "It's just that I don't want to talk about Mary Beth and Paul. They are not my family. I don't have a family until I make one with you, Carly."

His plea sounded genuine, and I knew he was sorry for what he'd done. People were not perfect, and if nothing else Robert had learned a valuable lesson: the cheap thrill of adulterous sex was not worth ruining a marriage. He would never screw around on me again, especially if he was serious about starting a family.

On the other hand, I was still shell-shocked and hurt. It would be difficult to go back and face the man who betrayed my trust. Confused, I took another deep breath and tried to calm the activity in my gut.

"Look, Robert. I can appreciate that you realize you made a terrible mistake. But I'm not going to commit to anything right now just because you've suddenly changed your mind and want me back. So I'll see you in a few days, and we'll talk then."

The twins disappeared to tell Mamma the news.

"Good," Robert said, and I heard what might have been a sigh of relief. "But don't wait too long, or I may have to come after you," he threatened, only half-joking.

We disconnected and, tired as I suddenly was, sleep evaded me. I lay in bed, not wanting to get up but unable to doze, until the fertile aroma of Mamma's freshly ground coffee nudged me into to action. I thought about my husband and his character and fixing our damaged marriage as I stood beneath the rejuvenating spray of a steamy shower.

Stephen's mood at breakfast was jovial, and I surmised it had turned out to be a lovemaking night for Jenny after all. The house was pleasantly free of growling. The kids were behaving, Granny and Daddy played a game of gin rummy, and Mamma fed everyone a feast of grits, peeled sliced tomatoes, homemade biscuits, ham, and scrambled eggs. It felt good to be pampered, but if I kept eating Mamma's cooking and didn't start exercising, I'd be the twin who needed to worry about getting fat.

"Robert called this morning," I announced. "He says he wants me to come home. That he doesn't really want a divorce. He had his lawyer tear up the papers."

"The nerve of him!"

"No!"

"Who does he think he is?"

"What are you going to do?"

Everyone spoke at once, and I wasn't even sure who said what. But the collective look on their faces told me the twins had already spread the news.

"Wasn't there another dog wanderin' around here?" Granny asked.

"Yes, there was another dog," I told her, "but it went home. Like I'm going to do soon. I guess I've got to go back to figure things out."

Even as I spoke the words, something nagged at my will. It was the sense of belonging and contentment. It was, perhaps, the feeling I already was home.

8

The knowledge that I would soon be returning to New York made my remaining time in Charleston that much sweeter. I didn't know exactly what awaited me up North, and I didn't want to think about it.

In a delightful state of emotional suspension, I witnessed the days come and go. There were no plans, no expectations, no deadlines or clients, and, perhaps most important, no husband to face. I went to bed when my body told me it was time to sleep, and, although I'd brought an alarm clock, I hadn't bothered to set it. Mornings in the Stone family household were my own, and I gluttonously slept until probing rays of sunlight found their way through the sheer curtains covering my bedroom windows.

I spent my afternoons playing with Taffy, rummaging through downtown thrift shops and catching up on the local gossip with Lori Anne, playing gin rummy with Granny on the porch, gardening with Mamma, surprising Daddy with lunch at the hardware store, and lying on the beach, relishing my shaded chunk of earth, where I'd stretch out beneath a colorful umbrella and watch the goings-on around me between chapters of a seductive paperback.

Late afternoons brought the traditional cocktail hour on the piazza with whoever happened to drop by, and evenings revolved around cooking supper. Each chunk of my days and nights blended fabulously with the next like the ingredients in one of Mamma's famous fresh coconut cakes.

Jenny and Stephen happily relinquished their parental duties when Mamma or I offered, and in a decidedly maternal way I found myself enjoying Hunter's fascination with the five-foot radius of world surrounding him. Mamma observed me with amusement as I successfully fished a bead from the depths of his ear canal, bribed him into eating a spoonful of collard greens, and taught him how to make sounds come out of Daddy's harmonica.

Although I was cognizant of what day it was, I was gloriously unaware of the calendar date. Robert had called twice more, but I hadn't been home and hadn't returned his calls. My boss's secretary had also called, inquiring as to when I'd be back in the office. Being as ambiguous as possible so as not to tell an outright lie, I said something about a family emergency and bought myself another few days. I knew my real life, the one with a good job, a not-so-good neighbor, and an apologetic husband, was waiting to be reclaimed. But for now, I wasn't in a hurry to do so.

It was a misty Monday morning, and the earthy smell of rain merged with that of Mamma's cinnamon buns. The house was unusually quiet because Stephen had joined Daddy for the day at the store and Jenny had taken Mamma, Granny, and the kids shopping.

My family had been thoughtful enough to leave me a cinnamon bun—just one—but it was still warm and the icing was gooey. Half-heartedly flipping through the paper, I was relishing each bite when a bold headline commanded my attention: Council Approves Zoning Request; Protter Releases Blueprints.

My cinnamon bun lost its flavor. Daddy had already read the same headline, blameless black ink pressed onto newsprint that affirmed his fears. *The Post and Courier* article simply reinforced what he already knew: the shopping center was going to happen, and it would include a Handyman's Depot.

Next to the brief article was an artist's rendering, and sardonically it looked like a first-class project. The buildings were all going to have brick exteriors, and the entire complex would be spacious and beautifully landscaped.

With a heavy sigh, I threw the offensive newspaper away and dropped my remaining bite of cinnamon bun on top of it. Taffy eyed the morsel as it disappeared into the belly of the trash can and shot me a disappointed look.

As I rubbed the top of her head, reality descended upon me like lingering day-old barroom smoke, and it made my stomach turn.

Everyone in the family and all the employees who'd worked at the store year after year had put a piece of themselves into it. And, next to Mamma, me, and Jenny, the business was Daddy's love.

Although I couldn't control what was happening with the store, reading the newspaper article made me realize I could control what was happening with my life. Things changed and sometimes life was sad, but good marriages endured. The store might close down, but Mamma and Daddy would still be together. They loved each other. And his phone call asking me to come home told me Robert loved me.

The storm had passed, and it was time for me to sort through an aftermath of battered emotions. It was time to reconcile. It was time to return to New York, fix my marriage, and get back to the business of earning a living. And in the process, I would see if my love for Robert was strong enough to repair all the damage that he had done to our relationship.

But before I hit the road, I decided I needed to find out exactly who this Protter was. The negotiator in me wondered if there was something Daddy had missed. A chip to bargain with. A way to keep the family business alive. I knew I was avoiding big issues of my own by keeping myself preoccupied, but it wouldn't feel right to leave town with this unresolved.

I called Lori Anne to see if she wanted to accompany me to the Protters' place, and luckily she was free for a few hours. I needed the moral support.

Protter Construction and Development turned out to be an unassuming two-story building with a friendly entrance in the front and a large warehouse surrounded by a security fence in the rear. When we walked into the lobby, Lori Anne acted like she owned the place. But I felt like an intruder scouting the enemy's camp. When the unseen receptionist asked how she could help us, I jumped.

"Sorry to startle you," she said. "Did you have an appointment with someone?"

"No," I told her, "but I'd like to see Mister Protter."

"Which one?"

"Whichever one is in charge."

"Well, that's debatable, hon," she said with smiling eyes. "The elder Mister Protter has a say in everything that goes on and is certainly far from retired even though we threw a retirement party for him last year. Two hundred people, live band, farewell wishes, the works. But he still comes to the office every day. So I suppose he might be the one you want. But his son manages the daily operations of the business, although he's hard to catch in. Or you might should just talk to one of the project managers, if it's about a specific development. What is it you need, sugar?"

Before I had a chance to answer, the front door swung open and *he* walked in. Him. Trent. The construction worker. The one with the mesmeric blue eyes. Wearing the same muddy work boots. And the loose-fitting, faded denim jeans that stirred my imagination like a long wooden spoon lifting up all the goodies at the bottom of a pot of homemade soup.

"Morning, Sophie," he said, without looking up from the plat map he appeared to be studying. "Tell the boss that the architect has come down with the flu, would you? He can't meet with the inspectors until next week."

"Poor thing," she said. "I'll have to send him a get-well card."

He looked up and did a double take when he saw me.

"Well, hello," he said, and the floor beneath me moved. "It's Carly, right?"

"Good memory," were the only words my brain sent to my mouth after the initial shock at seeing him. My fantasy man worked for Protter Construction and Development. So much for him playing the lead role in any more of my erotic dreams.

"You two know each other, hon?" Sophie asked.

"He was kind enough to change a flat tire for me," I answered, unable to take my eyes off him.

"Really?" Lori Anne said, looking back and forth between the two of us with raised eyebrows.

"Nail hole," he explained, staring right back.

"They're here to see Mister Protter," Sophie told him.

"Well, he's in his office. I'm sure he's got a few minutes," Trent said.

He nodded in our direction and was gone as quickly as he'd appeared.

"Wow," Lori Anne said under her breath. "Who was that?"

"Obviously someone who has absolutely no ethics and would work for anybody, including developers who like to put families out of business."

She harrumphed. "I don't know about his ethics, but he's got a damn fine body."

Less than five minutes later, I'd been served a cup of coffee, Lori Anne was sipping herbal tea, and we were both seated across from Mister Protter. About seventy, he had the look of someone who'd spent time in the military. His white hair was thick, short, and precisely cut. Although his office was that of an executive, roomy with lots of wood and leather, he wore casual slacks and a golf shirt.

Without telling him who we were, I got right to the point of asking if it was Protter Construction and Development's policy to put a family business out of business.

"What's your name, dear? I like to know who I'm talking to." It was a reasonable request.

"Carly Stone," I told him, suddenly glad I'd kept my maiden name instead of taking my husband's. "Carly Ellis" just wouldn't have worked.

During a genealogy course in high school, Jenny and I made a bond to never change our name since Mamma and Daddy didn't have any sons to carry on the family name. My sister had gotten married almost immediately after graduating from college, and true to her word she'd kept her own name. I was proud of being a third-generation Charlestonian from the Stone family and followed suit.

"And I'm Mizz Stone's personal assistant," Lori Anne said, trying to lighten my mood by needling the man. "You folks here at Protter serve up a wonderful green tea. I'll have to come back again sometime."

"Thank you," he said, not sure whether or not she was being serious.

"Stone Hardware and Home Supply is spitting distance to where your new complex will be going up," I told him. "The one with a Handyman's Depot."

"I see," he said in a distinctly Southern accent, leaning back in his chair to evaluate me. He was not a man to rush things. "You must be one of the daughters. I've already spoken with your father on a few occasions."

"You have?"

"He wanted to find out what the plans were," he said, speaking so slowly that I wanted to reach in his mouth and pull the words out. I wanted him to spit the words at me, rudely, so I could unleash my fury in return. But his face was kind when he continued.

"And more specifically, what, if anything, he could do to stop the Handyman's Depot. Your father is an impressive man. In different circumstances, we'd probably enjoy a day of fishing and a night of poker together."

"And?"

"While I appreciate your visit, I can only tell you what I already told him. The Handyman's Depot deal is already finalized, contingent only upon zoning approval. And, we just got that." He took a long pull from a coffee cup, studying me over the rim as he did so. "My company is just doing what it does. We develop land. Stone Hardware and Home Supply sits across from a piece of property that's ideal for development. Development brings competition. That's the nature of the beast."

He had a point, and I didn't have an argument. Not a logical one, anyway. I wasn't even really sure what I'd hoped to gain from my visit to Protter, other than to be able to tell myself that I'd tried. I had done what I could. Which amounted to exactly nothing so far.

"I've just been wondering how you got Paul and Mary Beth to sell you their land. My daddy had a gentleman's agreement with them, that they would give him the first opportunity to buy as soon as they were ready to sell. It's been a standing oral agreement for years and years. A legally binding agreement."

"You know how those things are. If it's not on paper, then it's not enforceable." He shrugged his shoulders apologetically. "Besides, we bought the land from an individual investor, who bought it from the original owners."

"So you didn't buy directly from Paul and Mary Beth? Then who did you buy it from?"

He smiled, but it was friendly, not condescending. "As I understand it, the man was just some investor with local ties. I couldn't give you a name without digging out the paperwork. You see, land acquisition is my son's specialty. He does all that. I just put the development package together once the land is secured."

"Of course."

Knowing I had absolutely no ability to change anything, I felt inadequate and foolish. Making it worse, Mister Protter remained quiet and in no hurry to get rid of us. He just sat, patiently, studying me with an open expression.

"What would it take for Handyman's to choose an alternate site? They've obviously set their sights on Charleston, but how attached are they to our little corner of the city?"

"Once again, you sound like your father. On his behalf, I contacted them to see if they would consider an alternate location because we could put another anchor in their space. An audio/video superstore. A department store. Any number of businesses would do very well there. But they're not interested in another location. They've done their demographic research, and they like this dirt."

So it was just like Daddy said. "It's a done deal, then?"

He nodded, up and down. "The contract is signed. I'm sorry."

For lack of anything better to do, I plucked a business card from a carved wooden hand sitting on his desk and pocketed it. "I just wanted to meet the person who's responsible for demolishing a thriving family business and putting thirty people out of work." I knew it wasn't really his fault, but I needed to vent some frustration.

"You make me sound like a villain, when you put it that way," he said. "But I'm confident those thirty people can easily find work in the new complex. In fact, Handyman's Depot has very good benefits. Health insurance, paid vacation, all that."

As we pulled out of Protter's parking lot in the same car that would soon be taking me back to New York, my emotions ping-ponged between sadness at the realization that Daddy's business couldn't be saved, determination to salvage my marriage, excitement at running into the man who'd invaded my dreams, and guilt over my body's response to him.

Sensing my bittersweet mood, Lori Anne decided we needed a

drink and wanted to show me the new wine bar at McCrady's restaurant. A national historic landmark, the building was more than two hundred years old and said to be the very first tavern in Charleston. But the wine bar was recently added, and I hadn't yet been there.

Exposed brick walls, dark wood tables, fresh flowers, and warm lighting created a sexy atmosphere, and my first thought was that it would be an awesome place for a romantic cocktail with someone. While the proper side of my brain filled in the blank with Robert, the other side of my brain conjured up an image of Trent. I chalked it up to being nervous about my impending reunion with my husband and busied my brain by studying the artwork on the walls.

Although there were nearly a thousand choices of wines by the bottle and twenty or more by the glass, Lori Anne and I ordered dry martinis with extra olives and toasted to happiness.

We planned a weekend for her to visit me in New York and see a Broadway show; she decided I needed some champagne-colored highlights around my face, which she'd apply on my next visit to Charleston; and we agreed to call or exchange emails every week.

After another hour of trying to catch up on all we'd missed during the last year and a half of each other's lives, I dropped Lori Anne at her day spa, and we said a teary good-bye. She wished me luck in working everything out and promised to kick Robert's ass if things didn't work out. I threatened to kick her ass if she told anyone about my marital woes and promised to visit during the Fourth of July weekend, if not sooner.

9.

I'd awakened early in preparation for a long day of driving, packed my suitcase, and gone to fill my tank with gas. When I got back just twenty minutes later, chaos was erupting in the backyard. Three men were at the center of it, and one of them was Robert. I pulled into the driveway just in time to see him taking a swing at . . . Trent.

The construction worker, with an indiscernible step sideways, smoothly evaded my husband's balled fist. Robert swung again with the other hand. An uppercut. It failed to make contact with Trent's jaw. Another swing. Another miss. Trent wasn't returning any punches, but he wasn't turning his back on my husband, either. Were Robert not my husband, I'd have found the scene comical.

Stephen, strategically positioned behind Robert, was trying to immobilize him. And Taffy, thinking it a new game, ran circles around the trio.

Trying not to be noticed, I eased past them to the back porch, where Granny, Jenny, Mamma, and the kids watched the commotion like spectators at a NASCAR event. Jenny shouted encouraging remarks to Stephen about keeping his hands up to protect his face, even though he wasn't in the line of balled-fist fire. Mamma and Granny each held a cup of coffee and commented on Robert's lack of boxing skills. The twins, sharing a porch step and a banana, divided their interest between keeping an eye on their daddy and seeing who could make the funniest face by squishing mashed fruit between their teeth. Southern women know how to enjoy a good brawl.

"What is Robert doing here?" I asked anybody. "And, why is he trying to fight with Trent?"

A swing. A miss. Still, Trent was not fighting back.

"Whoever Trent is, I wish he'd punch the bastard," Mamma said under her breath. She hadn't yet forgiven Robert for screwing around on me.

"He may be the boy that called a lookin' for Carly yesterday," Granny speculated, clucking her dentures with the effort of retrieving something from her short-term memory.

"What boy?" I demanded.

A stream of expletives drifted up from the yard, and we couldn't tell exactly which man they came from.

"I wonder if breakfast is ready," Granny said, losing interest in the morning's entertainment.

"What boy called, Granny?"

"No, scrambled are fine. I don't like hard-boiled eggs before noon."

"*Boy*, Granny!" I said loudly. "What boy called on the telephone?"

"Oh . . . the boy. Yesterday, I had a nice chat with a darling young man who called a lookin' for Carly. I told him how she and that fella of hers was all twisted up and intertwined like fertile grapevines. I saw them kissing like they do on that *General Hospital*, with the tongues just a goin'!"

I didn't know whether to laugh or be mad. Once again, she had confused me with my sister. Robert, not knowing about Granny's condition, jumped to the conclusion that I was having a fling with some man in Charleston and then had stumbled across the construction worker in the backyard.

What was Trent doing here anyway?

Mamma laughed out loud. "This is better than that time in high school when your two boyfriends got into it and your father had to break it up!" she said to me and my sister.

"They were both Jenny's boyfriends," I pointed out.

Stephen had finally managed to get Robert's arms pinned safely behind his back, but Trent wasn't letting his guard down.

"Where is Daddy?" I asked, realizing he was missing the entertainment.

"At the store. He left early this morning," Jenny said, then shouted in her best cheerleader voice, "way to keep his arms pinned, honey!"

Tired out but still struggling, Robert stepped backward against Taffy, lost his balance and awkwardly fell to the ground. Taffy zeroed in on him to lick his face. *Game over*, she was thinking. *Can we play again?*

Leaving him sprawled in the yard, Trent and Stephen walked toward the house.

"Lord have Mercy," Mamma said. "There hasn't been this much action around here since the two of you still lived at home."

"My God," Jenny said, blatantly checking out Trent as she got a better look at him. "What an incredible body! He could model our new line of outdoor wear on *In Home Now*. Who is he?"

They reached the porch. I made the introductions. Mamma, Jenny—Trent. Trent—my mamma and sister, Jenny. And your ringside assistant—Stephen. Jenny's husband.

Mamma offered Trent coffee and asked if he'd eaten breakfast yet. Realizing he'd made an ass of himself, Robert stood in the yard, making a show of pushing Taffy away from him. Probably waiting for me to rush to his side to fawn over him and check for nonexistent injuries. I forced myself not to go.

Realizing the humans weren't going to play the new game again, Taffy found us on the porch. After briefly sniffing Trent's shoes and legs, she got to the business of licking his hand. I couldn't help but focus on the same hand, and as Trent's fingers began rubbing the long fur behind her ears, I could almost feel his callused skin massaging the muscles at the back of my neck.

Stop it, I told myself. *You have a husband in the backyard. Who's come to apologize. Who wants to keep you.*

"Who is that fellow and why was he trying to hit me?"

"That's Carly's husband," Jenny was quick to answer.

"He put his weenie in the wrong bun!" Granny told him.

"You're married?" Trent asked me, glancing at my naked hand. I hadn't worn my rings since I'd found Robert naked on top of Corin, and he said he no longer wanted to be married to me.

"Not really," came out of my mouth, but a split second later I regained my senses. "Well, yes, but we're separated."

"So you live here then?"

"I live in Dutchess County, New York. I'm just visiting for a while. I'd love to make it a permanent stay, but I've got to get back to my job soon. I'm sure the case files are piling up."

I realized I was blathering and shut up. Not only had Robert made an ass of himself in front of this man, but now I was sounding like an idiot.

"Case files?" Trent said, standing there calmly. Looking like he got in fistfights in people's backyards every day. Calm and criminally handsome. And pissing me off, just by association of who he worked for.

"I'm a professional mediator."

Taking charge, Mamma told the twins and Hunter to go wash up for breakfast and herded everyone inside.

"So what can we do for you?" Mamma asked Trent after we were all seated around the kitchen table. She'd put a bowl of grapefruit sections and a platter of toasted English muffins in front of us.

"I came by looking for Mister Stone. I went by your store, but they said he hadn't been in yet. That I could probably catch him here. I just wanted to drop off the information he asked for."

"I thought Daddy was at the store," I said.

"I thought so, too," Jenny said, shrugging her shoulders.

Although we heard Robert come in, nobody acknowledged him for a few long seconds. He stood there looking like the family pet who'd just peed on the kitchen floor—ashamed. Finally Mamma told him to go clean up and join us for breakfast. I studied him over the rim of my coffee cup, but he walked into the hallway without making eye contact.

"Did Mister Protter send you?" I said, letting the name roll off my tongue with distaste. "What, he couldn't just send a courier? I mean, shouldn't you be out . . . hammering a nail or hauling some rebar or something?"

"Carly!" Mamma scolded in a whisper. One thing she won't tolerate in her house is rudeness to a guest. But then, she didn't yet know who he was.

"Meet one of the men that works for the company who's putting you and Daddy out of business, Mamma."

The twins quit eating, and everyone held their breath to see what Mamma would do. The situation was suddenly as juicy as the sweet grapefruit we were eating.

"Basta!" Hunter said, pointing at Trent. Even though he was entirely too young to understand the situation and it had to be a coincidence, I silently praised his uncanny timing.

The twins giggled, and Mamma told Hunter to hush.

"Like you, your son is delightful despite his vocabulary," Trent told me, grinning through a bite of muffin slathered with enough strawberry jam to cover ten muffin halves.

Trent thought I was delightful?

"First, I'm inclined to agree with him," I said. "Second, he's not my son. They're all my sister's kids."

"And, anyway," Jenny said sweetly. "Hunter knows his daddy isn't really a bastard. I just called him that because he said I was fat. He's really very sweet, aren't you, honey?"

"Of course, baby," Stephen said and gave her a kiss on the mouth. "I'm always sweet to you."

I rolled my eyes. Jenny batted hers at Stephen. Ignoring us, Mamma looked at Trent. "You work for Protter Construction and Development?"

"Guilty as charged, ma'am. But I didn't come here looking for a fight. I just wanted to drop off this report Mister Stone asked for. It's the construction time line. And I brought the information he needed on the commercial real estate folks. I believe he's going to put your building on the market."

Mamma chewed slowly on a piece of grapefruit while she digested the information.

Trent took a swallow of coffee. I noticed he drank it black. I followed the path of his gaze as it traveled slowly across the kitchen, absorbing the décor and framed photographs, before settling on me.

"So, Carly," he said, and my name sounded like velvet. "Why was your husband trying to punch me out? Over this development project?"

"No, of course not. He doesn't even know anything about the Handyman's Depot. He thinks you and I are having an affair."

Trent's eyebrows arched up, seeking elaboration. I owed him that, anyway.

"Robert has been in New York. I've been visiting Mamma and Daddy. He called, and Granny told him we were kissing like they do on *General Hospital*—the French kind, with tongues."

"That *General Hospital* show is some good TV," Granny said. "They don't need none a them Niagra pills, let me tell ya."

The twins giggled, Jenny gave Stephen's leg a squeeze under the table, and Trent's look grew more bewildered.

I couldn't help but grin.

"But Granny was talking about me and Stephen," Jenny told Trent, blinking mascara-coated lashes more times than she needed to. "She gets Carly and me mixed up sometimes. And you just happened to show up at the wrong time."

"You're Jenny Stone," he said, recognizing her. "I've seen you on that shopping talk show. What's it called?"

"*In Home Now*," Jenny said, appeased he'd identified her without having to be told who she was. "Stephen is the producer."

"Thanks for your help out there," Trent told Stephen.

"No problem."

Explaining the misunderstanding to our visitor made me realize that my husband was not only an adulterer but also a hypocrite. He could bang somebody while we were happily married, but couldn't stand the thought of me kissing another man after he wanted to divorce me? What right did he have to be jealous, even if I had deep-kissed Trent? Not that I would lock lips with my adversary, no matter how good looking the man was. He worked for a Protter. And I was still married.

The twins scrunched up their faces and eyed a spot over my shoulder. Robert had emerged from the bathroom. He looked sheepish. He'd been eavesdropping.

"It was a mistake anyone could have made," he said in defense of his actions and, after a few seconds of expectant silence, apologized to our visitor. "I heard you telling Steve how quickly it had all happened and what a beauty she was. After her grandmother told me Carly had a boyfriend here, I just assumed . . . well, you know."

There wasn't an unoccupied chair beside me so he took one at the far end of the table. Trent studied him briefly.

"I don't recognize you, but your voice sounds familiar for some reason. Have we met?"

Robert, still embarrassed, drank some coffee with a trembling hand. "No."

Trent shrugged his shoulders. "Anyway, I was talking about the new center we're developing. It did come together quickly, and it is a beauty of a deal," Trent said.

His comment hung thickly in the air, reminding everybody that he was, in fact, the enemy.

"So do you enjoy working for people who are in the business of putting other people out of business?"

"That's not what Protter Construction and Development is all about, Carly."

I shrugged my shoulders and stabbed a chunk of grapefruit with my fork.

"The company buys land and develops it. Growth in any area brings competition in business, and the competitors of Stone Hardware and Home Supply would be knocking on your door sooner or later, whether or not they were one of the anchor stores in our development," Trent said.

"Are you one of the supervisors, Trent?" Mamma asked. "You seem to know a lot about the business."

I was thinking the same thing. Were it not for the truck he drove and the telltale boots he wore, I never would have guessed the man to be a construction worker.

"Something like that," he answered, before helping himself to another half of English muffin. "Thank you for your hospitality, Mrs. Stone, but I've got to run. Would you please give this to your husband?"

He'd finished eating and pulled an envelope from his back

pocket. It was a smooth motion, confident, comfortable. I realized I was staring and looked away a split second after he realized it, too. He left with another apology from Robert and halfhearted good-to-meet-you's from Mamma, Stephen, and Jenny.

Our mood was reflective of the bad news inside the envelope Mamma held as we watched him leave. Daddy was going to quit; liquidate the inventory, and sell the building and property. We felt as though a member of the family had been diagnosed with a terminal illness. Now, it was just a matter of time.

As we finished breakfast and I thought about what awaited me in New York, Stephen told Mamma they were heading home, too. He'd already loaded their stuff in the Navigator, and they would go by the store on their way out of town to say good-bye to Daddy.

Mamma's eyes got misty. Her house had been full of kids and noise and energy and love and conflicts and . . . family. Soon things would return to normal, or at least as normal as they could get with Granny around.

I turned my attention to my husband. "What are you doing here, Robert?"

"I came to bring you home, since your visit was turning into an extended stay. Besides, I thought it'd be nice for both of us to visit with your family for a day or two," he added.

"Well, I was just getting ready to hit the road," I said. "You didn't have to come fetch me."

Robert shrugged and shot me a boyish smile.

Mamma's face showed mixed emotions. She'd be thrilled at having me around for a few more days, but she wasn't sure about playing host to the man who'd cheated on her daughter. As for Robert, his demeanor was appropriately regretful. His handsome face appeared apologetic, yet confident. Hopeful. He wanted to make it work. And he'd come after me, the same way Stephen had come after Jenny. I had to give him credit for that.

A ringing phone interrupted my reverie, and I watched Jenny's face go ashen beneath all the artistically applied makeup as she listened to the caller.

"Daddy's in the hospital," she told us.

Daddy, engulfed by the mechanical bed and surrounded by stainless handrails, looked vulnerable. He'd been larger than life as I'd grown up and had remained invincible since. Now, for the first time ever, I saw him as a mortal, and a wave of nausea rose in my stomach at the thought of his death. The room swirled around me. Sensing my condition, a nurse guided me to the visitor's chair and told me to lean forward, head down. I forced my lungs to fill with the metallic-smelling air several times, and after a minute, the room righted itself.

"Your daddy's never been in a hospital before," Mamma said quietly. "Not as a patient, anyway."

A bedside cardiac monitor was attached to his chest in several places beneath the blue hospital gown, and an intravenous line ran from his arm. His eyes opened when Mamma gave him a kiss and he took us all in. Mamma, me, Robert, Jenny, Stephen, Granny and the kids, all crowded around the huge bed in the tiny room. His expression said that while he was glad to see his family, he hated everyone looking at him like he was a zoo exhibit.

"All of you quit your staring, for crying out loud, and somebody get me some damn clothes so I can get out of here!"

"Well, you must be feeling better," Mamma said, adjusting the pillows behind his head.

"We're not staring at you," I told him. "We just want to make sure you're okay."

"The doctor said I'm fine. But they want to keep me overnight for observation, which is ridiculous. Your mother can observe me at home. Taffy can observe me. We all can observe me. Hell, I can observe my own self," Daddy said. And then he giggled. "Observe my own self," he said again and laughed some more.

A nurse had entered the room and I raised my eyebrows at her. Daddy didn't normally giggle.

"It's the morphine," she whispered. "We often give morphine to patients with chest pain because it causes the heart to need less oxygen."

"Well, I'm glad you're feeling better," I told Daddy. "But staying overnight is a good idea."

"I need to get out of here so I can observe me," he argued.

"Staying here is a better idea," Jenny said. "A night of doing nothing will be good for you. You need to relax. Look, there's even a VCR and TV on the wall. I'll bring you a copy of the *In Home Now* Yard and Garden Special. We just taped it a few weeks ago. You can be one of the very first to preview it!"

Daddy rolled his eyes so far back that I saw the bloodshot whites. Mamma refilled his water glass from a bedside pitcher. Granny found the bed's remote control and Daddy's feet and head began rising simultaneously.

"She keeps doing that," he said as his body got near to forming a V shape, "and I'll be previewing my own asshole."

"I could use me one a these," Granny said, before Mamma took the remote away from her.

Mamma and I left Daddy under the watchful eye of my sister and went to find his doctor. We caught up with the fellow, who appeared young enough to be roaming the halls of a high school instead of a hospital, at the nurse's station. He led us into a nearby office.

"To answer your first question, ladies, I am indeed a cardiac surgeon, and I'm thirty-three years old. Despite the baby face, I'm one of the best in the Southeast."

His smile was charming, and Mamma visibly relaxed. "Well, Doctor, you do look awfully young. So what's going on with my husband? Is it his heart? He's never had any problems before . . ."

"His heart appears to be okay, but he had all the classic symptoms of a myocardial infarction when he came in."

"An ambulance brought him?"

"I'm told he drove himself. Walked right into the emergency entrance and announced that he didn't feel right." The doctor smiled. "He was having trouble breathing, his pulse was erratic and racing, his blood pressure was off the charts, and he was experiencing chest pain."

Mamma's worry frown returned.

"But the cardiac enzymes are normal; the EKG doesn't show any cardiac muscle damage at this time. We're going to give him a chest

X-ray to make sure his lungs are clear and also an echocardiogram to take a closer look at the heart muscle. But I'd have to say, he's probably one of the healthier sixty-year-olds I've ever examined."

"So then it wasn't a heart attack?" Mamma asked.

"I can't say positively until we finish all the tests. But right now, all indications are that there was no myocardial infarction or pulmonary embolism."

"So if his heart is fine, what is the problem?" I am a bottom-line kind of person.

"The signs and symptoms point to a panic attack, which is a condition typically brought on by extreme anxiety. It may sound crazy, but the process of eliminating other possibilities leads me to believe that's what it was. Has anything like this ever happened before?"

"No," Mamma said. "He's the most stable, happy, and healthy person I know."

"Well, we're keeping him tonight so we can monitor his cardiac enzymes, just to be on the safe side. And, as I mentioned, there are a few test results I'm waiting for. But I believe he's going to be just fine."

"A *panic attack*? Daddy? No way," I argued, wanting to hear something more concrete.

"These attacks can hit anybody and hit suddenly." He closed a chart on the desk and leaned back in his chair. "The causes might be intangible, but the physical effects of stress and anxiety on the body are very real. Believe it or not, stress can cause everything from ulcers and simple skin irritations to panic attacks to something as odd as temporary blindness. I would guess Mister Stone is stressed over something, and in this case, the stress may have been the cause of his severe chest pain and shortness of breath."

Mamma and I looked at each other, thinking the same thing: It was the store. Losing the hardware business that had been in the family for nearly one hundred years. The business that had grown into something big enough to employ thirty people, support his family, and send his girls to college.

"Look, let's just get this out of the way. We need to have this conversation sooner or later. I'm sorry for my indiscretion," Robert told me from the driver's seat of my car, managing to make the single word that meant "screwing our neighbor" sound almost distinguished. "I shouldn't have waited so long to apologize to you, but I wanted to do it in person. It will never happen again. Okay, Carly?"

Since the medical university was keeping Daddy overnight, everyone decided to stay in Charleston another day. And since Stephen had volunteered to chauffer Mamma and the rest of the clan home, my husband and I sat alone in my car. I watched with irritation as Robert changed the settings on my stereo and adjusted the driver's seat lumbar support. I didn't like him driving my Beemer, but he always insisted on being behind the wheel whenever we went somewhere together. I used to find it endearing, like he was treating me as precious cargo. But now it was just plain irksome, even if he had rushed to open the car door for me.

"Okay, Carly?" he repeated.

I was a captive audience to his rehearsed apology and didn't have a rehearsed reply. I had planned to use my drive time back to New York as a kind of meditation. Clear my emotionally drained mind and figure out what to say to Robert. And I liked the radio stations set just the way I had them.

"Look," he persisted. "I know you're angry and don't want to talk to me. But we have to talk about it. It was really stupid to have gotten involved with her, and I'm so sorry that I hurt you. She came on to me once at the house, and, well, one thing led to another. But she's the one who started it. I mean, it's not like I was out there looking for something to happen, you know? I just didn't have enough sense to stop it. It was a Saturday when I'd been watching a hockey game and I'd had a few too many beers."

"How long?"

He gave me a sideways glance, keeping most of his attention focused on the road.

"How long what?"

"How long has it been going on?" I didn't really want to hear the details, but I needed to know.

"I don't know. A few months maybe? She said that she needed me, and I felt sorry for her. I was just being, you know, a friend. Just being there for her, because she was so distraught about her divorce. Things got out of hand."

I'm not sure what answer I was expecting, but "a few months" wasn't it. A week, maybe. Or a one-night stand. A one-night stand with the woman who'd gone shopping with me to buy Robert a birthday present not too long ago.

Or even long term. An ongoing affair with the same woman who had brought the salad and dessert when we'd broiled steaks. Perhaps Robert had dated Corin before we were married and it was simply sex for old time's sake. But *a few months*? *A few months* indicated intimacy. *A few months* indicated urgency. Fresh desire that was invasive, powerful, and demanding of attention. Had they called each other in the middle of the day just to say "hello"? Or sat up late in the evenings instant-messaging each other on the computer? Or selected their clothing for the day based on pleasing the other during a late-afternoon lunch rendezvous?

I felt dizzy and closed my eyes for a minute to mentally regroup as Charleston sped by. I wasn't sure I still wanted to go back to New York with him. I didn't even want to look at him. *A few months* with Corin also meant he'd only been faithful to me for a few months.

"Robert, we haven't even celebrated our one-year anniversary."

"Carly, I'm sorry. So very sorry."

"Plus, you said you *loved* her. It was very clear, the 'I love you' thing. I don't know about Corin, but you certainly had me convinced."

Using the tuning buttons, I changed the radio back to my favorite Charleston station. "I think you were happy at having been discovered, because it gave you the opening you were looking for to divorce me."

"You're wrong, honey," he said immediately. "The whole divorce thing was really . . . me feeling guilty. I never wanted to hurt you. I felt so awful and horrible about what I'd done to you, that I punished myself by breaking us up. I knew I didn't deserve you. But when you left, it made me realize I can't live without you. I need you, Carly. I want to make a family with you. I know you said you were coming home soon anyway, but I couldn't wait anymore. I had to come and get you."

I studied his profile as he expertly wove in and out of traffic. Self-assured movements, the relaxed fit of quality clothes, the sincere expression on his clean-shaven face. Looking at the manicured fingers resting on the bottom of the steering wheel, I remembered why I'd fallen in love with him to begin with: he was handsome and charming. The adorable puppy dog that people wanted to pick up and hug despite the fact that he just chewed up their favorite pair of Italian leather slides.

"Please forgive me," he said, coming to a red light and taking the opportunity to look at me. "Let's just put this behind us and make it work."

Exhaustion hit me like a sudden downpour of rain. I didn't want to contemplate anything anymore, and I didn't want to argue with Robert. During the past week, I'd already made my decision to reconcile. Whether he'd been with Corin for two nights or two months, I was going to have to forgive and forget. Move forward and get past the bad parts.

"Okay, Robert. I forgive you."

There was a time-stand-still pause before he grabbed my hand with a squeeze.

"Really? You forgive me?"

A horn behind us beeped. The light had turned green.

"Yes."

Somewhere deep inside, I'd known all along that I wanted to keep my marriage together if Robert wanted to. I wanted to celebrate a tenth wedding anniversary . . . and a twentieth and a fiftieth. I wanted to have children in the years to come. I wanted to build a loving, stable relationship with someone—the same kind of relationship Mamma had with Daddy. I had to believe our short-term separation would somehow make the marriage better and felt powerless to do anything other than take my husband back.

Robert told me he loved me and, relieved, turned up the volume as Edwin McCain belted out "Far From Over."

We drove the remaining ten miles to Mamma and Daddy's house

in silence, Robert bobbing his head to the beat of the music and me wondering if the bowling ball of mixed emotions stirring in my gut was what forty- and fifty-year veterans of marriage meant when they attributed their longevity to compromise.

10

"Maybe we should just have some soup and crackers since it's so late," Mamma said after we'd gotten home. We'd spent the day at the hospital and, other than vending-machine fare, nobody had eaten. It was nearing eight o'clock, well beyond both the cocktail hour and the cooking hour in the Stone household.

"Oh, I know!" Jenny said. "I brought you a Speedy Cooker. It's a new item we're selling on the show and they're terrific. Do you have any meat we could cook?"

"There's a pork loin," Mamma said reluctantly.

In the past, whenever Jenny insisted on demonstrating a new *In Home Now* product, odd things happened. Most memorable was the time she gummed up the jets in Mamma's whirlpool tub and transformed it into a cascading fountain.

"A pork loin is perfect!" My product-savvy sister declared. "With the convection-bake feature on your new oven and the Speedy Cooker, the meat will be ready in twenty minutes! Then we'll just slice it for sandwiches. We can even add some flavor. The Speedy Cooker comes with a free Flavor Fuser feature; you can infuse the meat with something like port wine or bourbon for a really incredible taste."

Jenny's arms gracefully extended in the practiced manner of a *Price Is Right* model awaiting a chorus of *ooohs* and *aaahhs*.

Mamma was skeptical. "This thing goes inside the oven?"

"Of course. See, heat from the oven cooks your meat from the outside in. But the Speedy Cooker cooks from the inside out. Put the two together and voilà! You've cut your cooking time by two-thirds, and the faster cooking time seals in the meat's natural juices."

Mamma looked at me for an opinion. I shrugged my shoulders. It was her oven.

"Okay," she relented. "But let's forget about the infusion thing. I think that right now I'd rather just drink the bourbon. Can someone make me an old-fashioned?"

"I'd be happy to," Robert offered. He was trying to score points with Mamma. She isn't as quick to forgive as I am.

Like a curious kid, Granny stayed in the kitchen to help Jenny with the pork loin. Those of us who knew better settled in to read the newspaper or watch some television. Mamma called Daddy's hospital room to check up on him one more time for the night and, after a conversation loaded with I-love-yous and me-toos, reported that he was feeling fine and watching an old John Wayne movie.

"You sound like a teenager," I mumbled, not without jealousy.

"Your daddy and I still love each other like we did way back then. We knew we were going to get married before we graduated high school." Mamma smiled. "Even our families got along well, except for that one feud my granddaddy Wade had with your daddy's grandpa over the used truck that was supposedly a lemon. But the day we got married, they shook hands and split the repair bill!"

Instead of pulling her long hair up into a twist like she usually did, it was gathered into a ponytail at the back of her slim neck. She was wearing a pair of black cotton slacks that were as near to jeans as she'd allow herself to get, and they fit her snugly. The years had treated her very well, and from a distance she could have been easily mistaken for a teenager. I studied her proudly, hoping I would look as good when I was her age. And hoping my marriage would see just a fraction of the intimacy that she knew with Daddy.

Robert served Mamma her drink, brought me a glass of wine, and found some bottled beers for himself and Stephen. Taffy sat patiently on the screened porch, watching the darkened driveway, waiting for Daddy to come home.

"That newfangled cooker reminds me of a spit," Granny said, plopping down beside me on the sofa. "We used to cook meat on a spit atop a fire when I was a young'n. Best rabbit or squirrel you'd ever eat."

"After we taste Jenny's pork, we might be wishing for some rabbit or squirrel," I said.

"I used to be a pretty good shot with my twenty gauge, you know," Granny said, remembering her childhood. "I was somethin' to be reckoned with."

Out of seven children, she'd been the only girl.

"Pappa wouldn't let me have more'n three shells at a time, and if I didn't come home with something, it was awful embarrassing. Especially if one of my brothers had done gotten himself a rabbit or two."

Although her short-term memory was almost nonexistent, her long-term memory could be quite vivid, and something about cooking with Jenny had turned it back seventy years. I told her I was glad I didn't have to eat rabbit, and we talked about gross stuff like skinning rattlesnakes until I realized my wineglass was empty and went to retrieve some more.

I walked into the kitchen just in time to hear Jenny scold quietly, "Robert!" and to see his hand drop from her upper arm.

"Oh, hey, honey," he said a bit too quickly. "Your sister was just telling me about Body Buddy—the new workout drink—and how great it is at toning muscle."

My ears grew hot, and I could feel the blood rushing to the surface of my skin. First my husband screws my neighbor. Then he feels up my sister. I wanted to punch him.

"Oh. So I suppose you were just checking out her biceps? Jesus Christ, Robert! You just got through telling me how much you miss me. How much you want me to come home. That you *love* me. What in the hell is wrong with you?"

"Oh, c'mon, Carly. It was just a playful squeeze on her arm. I know my infidelity was horrible for you, and I am so sorry. But it's made you oversensitive."

He pulled me into a one-arm hug against his side, and in the aftermath of my verbal outburst, I wondered if I was overreacting. I was too close to the situation to tell. I looked at my sister. Jenny shook her head, and I could see an apology in her eyes. She flirts with all men; it's just her nature. But she hadn't expected Robert to reciprocate by putting his hands on her.

"What's that I smell?" she said, wrinkling her petite nose and seizing the opportunity to change the subject.

Pushing Robert away, I turned my attention to sniffing the air.

Something was definitely burning, and it smelled like a mixture of broiling meat and melting plastic, with a tinge of something unidentifiable that may have been metal.

It only took a few seconds to discover that the source of the poignant odor was originating inside Mamma's new oven.

"I can't get the door open. The handle's locked!" Jenny said, trying to decide whether or not the situation warranted a full-blown panic.

A paper-thin stream of acrid smoke emanated from the top of the oven door and spiraled upward before snaking along the ceiling. Hearing the commotion, or perhaps smelling the odor, Mamma and the twins appeared.

"How can it be locked?" I moved in to get a better look at the oven door.

"Oh, Lord! It's been turned to the Self-clean setting," Mamma said. "The door locks automatically."

"The Self-clean mode reaches six hundred and fifty degrees, and the door locks as a safety measure," Jenny-the-product-spokesperson explained. "It's actually a very nice feature on this make of oven."

"Since we can't get the door open, let's just turn it off," I told Mamma.

"Of course!" she said and reached for the knob. But, panicked, she turned the knob so hard that it broke off in her hand.

The oven was still on and still trying to clean itself at six hundred and fifty degrees.

"We don't like pork loin anyway," the twins said happily with visions of Wendy's cheeseburgers or Arby's roast beef sandwiches dancing in their young heads.

"Especially one that's been speedy-cooked," Stacy said.

"The meat's hard to chew," Sherry explained.

Insulted, Jenny started to argue with her six-year-olds but stopped beneath the glare of Mamma's look. Something was on fire inside her new oven, and if anyone should be angry, she should.

"Did someone say we're having stew?" Granny asked, joining the party.

"No, we're having pork," I told her. "But the oven door is locked shut, and the Speedy Cooker appears to be melting."

"Well, I didn't lock it," Granny said. "I just turned the dial, like Carly told me to do."

"You mean Jenny," I clarified, for the record.

"I told you to turn it to Convection-Bake," my sister cried. "Not Self-clean!"

Taffy trotted up to sniff the air around the oven. After a quick assessment, she began to wag her tail. Any time there was a calamity in the kitchen, it usually meant extra food in her bowl. And burnt people food was better than dry dog food any day.

"This never would've happened using a good old-fashioned spit," Granny declared, with a click of her dentures, and walked out of the kitchen. "Best rabbit you'll ever eat. And we didn't have to do none of that amusing, neither."

"Infusing," Jenny shouted to her retreating back, taking the situation personally. "The free infusion feature is what sells the product!"

"Maybe the infuser is really just a miniature fire extinguisher, of sorts," I said. "You just add the water to the meat up front, before the fire begins."

Jenny glared at me.

A pool of menacing smoke was gathering above our heads, and Stephen, toting Hunter on his shoulders, came to investigate. Accustomed to Jenny's product trials in their home, he evaluated the crisis calmly. After putting his son down a safe distance away, he tried the oven door and realized it was locked. Then he looked at the space where the control knob should be. A smile tugged at the corners of his mouth.

"Oh, good Lord," Mamma said. "What would your daddy do in this situation?"

"He would turn the power off at the circuit breaker," Stephen answered. "And then he would call for pizza delivery."

"Yay, pizza!" Sherry and Stacy chimed in unison.

"It would appear you've had to do this before," I said to Stephen.

His smile was a combination of patience and humor and love for my sister. "Let's just say I could locate the individual circuit breaker that supplied any electrical outlet in our house, in the dark, with my eyes shut."

Mamma led Stephen to the breaker box, Robert tagged along for something to do, my sister and I opened windows, and Taffy sat in front of the oven to wait, tail moving slowly back and forth like wiper blades set on Intermittent.

"Well, I'd give the Speedy Cooker high marks," I told Jenny after I'd ordered three large pizzas from Sharkey's.

"Oh shut up. And anyway, it wasn't the Speedy Cooker's fault."

"I wonder if that burnt plastic smell will linger?"

"Well what do you expect at six hundred and fifty degrees? The Speedy Cooker is designed to work in an oven set at three hundred and fifty degrees."

"Well, if I were you, I'd warn your viewing audience not to try and speed up their Speedy Cooker by using a higher temperature."

When our food arrived, we unceremoniously ate it from paper plates, sprawled in front of the television in the living room. Daddy's absence was discomforting and the house retained a twinge of smoky odor, but Mamma's spirit was bright. Her oven had survived, a catastrophe had been averted, and Daddy would be back at home with her tomorrow.

11

"Are you sure you didn't do something to your hair? You just look different somehow," Cheryl, a good friend and fellow mediator, told me for the third time in as many days. We had been hired at the same time and had gone through orientation together.

I was back at work, in bustling Manhattan, sitting at my desk while trying to assimilate nearly three weeks' worth of absence into one half-hour update. I'd been back for several days but had been assigned to help one of the attorneys with a high-profile court case and was just now getting a chance to look at my own workload.

After Daddy came home from the hospital clutching a pamphlet on stress and a prescription for an antianxiety medication, Jenny and her clan headed west while Robert and I headed north. Jobs and yards and social commitments screamed for our attention, and the time had come for all of us to return to our everyday lives.

Armed with a Thermos of Mamma's coffee and enough food for five picnic lunches, I'd taken the lead, with Robert following closely behind in his red Mercedes two-seater. While his presence behind me was comforting in a possessive sort of way, I had felt somewhat trapped, like a sheep being mindlessly herded back to the reality ranch. The sensation lasted two or three hundred miles, until I convinced myself it was just remaining anger. I decided that, if the marriage was going to work, I needed to get over it. I needed to erase the image of the two of them screwing on my yellow cotton sheets. I needed to quit thinking about how much I was going to miss Charleston. Quit fantasizing about the man I knew only as Trent. And quit wondering how long it would take for me to immerse myself in the local New York culture. I was determined to make the best of my decision to stay with Robert and become a Northerner.

Pawling was a small town in the hills of Dutchess County, about seventy miles north of my office in Manhattan. Most homes in Pawling were situated on several acres, and many would be considered mini estates. It was beautiful country with mountainous views and trendy restaurants. Although commuting distance for those of us who work in the city is two hours, my neighbors happily make the workday trek, grateful for their ability to live away from the inner city.

In the upwardly mobile hills of Pawling, old money got along well with new money, and the pretenses of pursuing the good life were seen as the only way to live. The New York lifestyle centered around business twenty-four hours a day, and people planned their social schedules solely on networking potential. On Monday mornings, coworkers didn't ask, "How was the cocktail party?" but rather, "Who was at the cocktail party, and what did they bring to the table?" The lifestyle suited Robert perfectly but occasionally struck the same nerve in me that became inflamed when someone ran a long fingernail across a chalkboard.

While the views from both my house and office were fabulous, the New York air was disturbingly different from that which surrounded Charleston. It carried a distinctive odor that reeked of near-stifling wealth, damp woods, and an unidentifiable spice that was entirely unlike the comforting salty marsh scents that mixed sweetly with South Carolina's warmer temperatures.

Although it had only been a week since I'd left Mamma and Daddy's house, I was already homesick and ready for another visit. I even missed the ever-present humidity, an admission most Southerners would scoff at.

"Relaxed, maybe?" Cheryl prodded, seeking some details to explain my unplanned vacation, perplexed as to why I hadn't yet filled her in. "You seem calm, or something. Your mother's cooking must agree with you."

I just nodded, not wanting to disclose the real reason why I'd left on such short notice. Especially now that Robert and I were husband

and wife again. What Cheryl had picked up on was probably my resolution to make it all work. My marriage, my job, and living in New York.

I currently had six active mediation cases, four of which were carryovers from before I'd left to visit Mamma and Daddy. Six manila folders, each containing the details surrounding an isolated chunk of people's lives. Various conflicts resulting from disharmoniously crossed paths, some merely business and others fueled by emotion or greed. Six instances of discord; six opportunities to smooth things over and make everyone happy without going to court. I shuffled through the folders, hoping Cheryl would let me get back to work.

"Well, you know where to find me if you need me," she said, realizing I wasn't in a talkative mood. "Let's do lunch tomorrow, okay?"

"Sure. And, Cheryl, thanks for all your help. I don't mean to be moody . . . it's just that I've got a lot on my mind. But you've been great, and I owe you for taking over my caseload while I was gone."

"No problem. Besides, I needed the overtime. It worked out well for both of us."

Alone with a pile of unopened mail, unread memos, and an awesome view of the city below, I sipped coffee from a Styrofoam cup and decided that my time in Charleston had gone by much too quickly. Although nearly a month had passed since I'd walked in on my husband having sex with Corin, the shock was still as fresh as though it had only been yesterday. Whereas in Charleston I'd been able to keep the memory repressed, my normal routine had brought it to the surface.

Get over it.

I took a deep breath to clear my thoughts and forced my uncooperative brain to focus on the work in front of me. I opened the Jackson/Ledlon Technologies folder, my newest acquisition, and began poring through the statements. On the surface, it appeared that a disgruntled ex-employee wanted to sue over an unfulfilled three-year contract. But the same contract that promised the scientist ninety-four thousand dollars a year also mandated either mediation or arbitration in the event of a dispute. The scientist wanted damages in addition to his remaining two years' salary, while Ledlon Technologies claimed the employee revealed trade secrets, thus violating the contract. The company didn't want to pay the alleged traitor anything and was threatening to press criminal charges. The case would require hiring an independent investigator and could potentially drag on for several months. The partners loved this type of case because of its billing potential, and there was a good chance I'd have to pass the file along to arbitration because tempers and pride would surely get in the way of reaching an amicable agreement.

Another cup of coffee and an hour later, just as I was about to pick up my telephone to make some calls, it rang.

"Your Daddy's back in the hospital," Mamma told me. "This time his heart rate was so out of sync, they had to give him a teeny shock. But he's okay now, other than complaining about the soreness and bruising on his chest."

"What? Back in the hospital?"

"I don't want to worry you, but then I figured you'd get mad if I didn't let you know about it. He's going to have to take this drug that will help to regulate his heart rate until these panic-attack things stop."

"What room is he in? I want to give him a call."

"Oh, no, don't do that," Mamma said in her melodic drawl, as close to admonishment as she could get. "He'd be madder at me for telling you than you'd be at me for not telling you!"

She insisted that I didn't need to come home and that Daddy was okay and that I needed to focus on my job since I'd been gone so long and that she and Granny were taking good care of him. His young cardiac doctor was going to keep him overnight, like before, but Daddy would be home tomorrow.

I replaced the handset and silently cursed Protter Construction and Development. A headache danced at the base of my skull, threatening to become a full-blown migraine. The ability to concentrate on work eluded me, and I decided to head home. Even though I'd planned on working late, I had no pending appointments and everything could wait until tomorrow.

Upon our return to New York, Robert had made a declaration that he was not going to take me for granted anymore and that he would do something positive for "the marriage" every day. His good deed for today consisted of grilling steaks for dinner, and a meal I didn't have to prepare was gaining appeal by the minute, especially since I'd skipped lunch.

I decided to leave work early so I could shower and relax before sitting down with Robert to eat. To eat, share a bottle of wine and talk. Not rehash old news but just talk. Catch up. Try to gain back a little intimacy.

Just as I was turning off the light in my office, the phone rang again. It was Robert, calling to let me know that I should stop by the grocery store before I headed home. We were having a dinner party for a group of his clients, and I was the unsuspecting host. Throwing a dinner bash for twelve to fifteen people was the last thing I wanted to do.

"Tomorrow night?" I massaged my temples with my free hand. "Couldn't you have mentioned this to me before now?"

"It was an impromptu thing," he said. "I know how you love get-togethers, and I was sure you wouldn't mind."

I loved get-togethers with friends. I hated get-togethers with Robert's clients. Especially at our house.

"Why don't we all just meet at a restaurant?"

"No can do, hon. I've already invited everyone. I can't call back now and change the plan. How would that look?"

The muscles in the back of my neck cinched up tight, and I could feel the soon-to-be migraine snaking its way up to the top half of my head.

"Did you also already tell everyone what I'd be serving?" I said. The sarcasm in my voice eluded him.

"Nope. Anything you make will be great!"

I didn't want to do the dinner, but I also didn't want a fight. "Sure. Okay. Maybe I'll do chili or something like that."

"You know," he said thoughtfully, "those steak fajitas you make are awesome. The ones with the red and yellow peppers?"

"Whatever. I'll see you later, Robert."

"Don't work too awfully late tonight," he said.

Instead of telling him I was through with work for the day, I slammed the phone down. "Goddammit!"

Cursing Robert, I looked up to see Cheryl standing in my doorway again.

"What's up? Anything I can do?"

"You know any affordable caterers?" I said and told her what had just transpired.

She came in and plopped in a chair. "Just tell him no. You know the word, Carly. It means the opposite of yes? You don't have any trouble using it around here!"

"I can't do that." I felt my body folding into my chair as the energy drained out of me. The tension in my neck exploded into a throbbing headache. "He's already invited everyone."

"So tell him to un-invite them."

She looked at me with raised eyebrows and nodded at the phone. I made a "yeah, right" face at her. We both knew that, rather than upset Robert, I would cook the damn dinner and act the perfect hostess.

"Carly, I swear to God, if Jason ever did that to me I'd kill him. You just get back to town and he has you throwing a party for fifteen people? Without even asking you first?"

"You don't know the half of it," I muttered without elaborating. "Oh, and I just found out that Daddy's back in the hospital, too."

"Carly, this is ridiculous!" She pulled herself out of the chair. "You know, you're one of the best mediators we've got. For that matter, you ought to make the move into litigation. You take the toughest cases and just kick butt. But when it comes to your personal life, you suck at it. Negotiating, that is."

I knew she was right. I just didn't know what to do about it. "You shouldn't have to negotiate your marriage."

"Maybe not," she said. "But you sure as shit shouldn't let your husband walk all over you, either."

"It's just a stupid dinner party," I snapped, searching the contents of my desk drawer for aspirin.

"It's not about the party. It's about respect," Cheryl said softly. She patted me on the arm and removed herself from my office without waiting for another lame response.

Angry and drained, I skipped the gym workout and the grocery store, leaving both for tomorrow. When I arrived home, Robert's car was in the garage, but the house was quiet. He often finished up at his office in the early afternoon and would monitor the market closings from home.

He wasn't in front of his computer checking quotes, and he wasn't outside, prepping the grill for the steaks I'd put in the refrigerator last night to marinate.

Two foil-wrapped baking potatoes sat on the kitchen counter next to a bottle of merlot and the makings for a Caesar salad. So he hadn't forgotten about dinner. But where was he? If one of his poker buddies had picked him up, he'd've left a note even though it was not quite four-thirty, and he wasn't expecting me until after eight since I had a lot of catching up to do at work. And it was doubtful he was out for a late-afternoon stroll, because Robert hated to walk anywhere. He preferred to get his aerobic workouts on a treadmill.

I hadn't eaten anything since half a banana for breakfast, but my appetite was suddenly lost. A feeling of apprehension hit, and something made me pick up the cordless phone that sat next to the potatoes. I stared at it for long seconds before pressing the redial button. A stream of electronic beeps sounded. The line rang once, twice. No answer. It rang again. Feeling foolish, I was about to hang up when I heard the click of an answering machine and Corin Bashley's voice told me to leave a message.

So he'd been washing potatoes and talking to . . . her.

I got to Corin's house ten minutes later, still trying persuade myself that the ball of lead in my stomach was an overreaction. I trod up the quarter-mile long driveway, rang the doorbell, waited. I rang it a second time and waited some more, but she didn't answer. I pushed through a layer of overgrown shrubbery and headed to the back of her house, mindless of the cold gusts of air that penetrated my inadequate sweater.

The rear of her house was surrounded by a wooden privacy fence that enclosed a garden, greenhouse, and bricked courtyard. I found the gate, and when my hand gripped the ornate metal handle, I knew. Although I couldn't see beyond the wood, I saw clearly. I *heard.*

Muffled sounds, carried by a cool breeze. Hushed words and

laughter, mingled with the high-pitched hum of a Jacuzzi motor. Bubbling water. And music. Not a radio station, but music from a compact disc flowing through the outdoor speakers that Robert had installed beneath Corin's covered patio overhang several weeks ago. She was going to hire a contractor to do the work, but Robert insisted it was no trouble.

I pushed through the gate and witnessed the scene already running through my head, instantaneously realizing I'd been a complete idiot. I'd been had. Even though I had a knack for accurately assessing other people's situations, I'd been unable to see my own. I'd been so gullible. There the two of them were, alone in the hot tub.

"I think I'll take the filet mignons," I said to Robert, not even wasting the effort to acknowledge Corin, "with me to Charleston. Plenty of room in the cooler. So you might want to grab something to eat here, before you head back to the house. In fact, I think you should just stay here period. So I don't have to look at you while I pack."

Both pieces of a skimpy black bikini hung over the side of the round hot tub and a thick terrycloth robe hung next to it. Corin slid low into the foamy water until it reached her chin.

"Oh, and you can take your little impromptu dinner party and shove it up your cheating ass," I said, and it came out sounding like a snarl.

A glance at the patio furniture revealed Robert's boxers and wristwatch lying beside a robe that was identical to Corin's. So they even had a set of matching robes. How cute. If I had something in my hand other than a set of car keys, I probably would have thrown it at them.

Robert started to climb out, but I put a hand up to stop him.

"Don't bother getting out for me," I said, seething. "In fact, you'd best just stay here. Or get a hotel room. I don't want to see you in my house again. Ever."

"Carly, this isn't what it looks like. Do you think I'd've taken time off work and driven all the way to South Carolina to talk some sense into you if I hadn't wanted to make it work between us? Corin was just having a little cocktail party, and we all ended up in the spa because everyone was complaining about how cold it was, wishing the weather would warm up. But they all left a little while ago. In fact, I was just getting ready to go myself, to start our dinner."

It was a lame thing to say. There had been no cocktail party. I didn't even have to look around a second time to check for signs of other people. The scene, every detail, was emblazoned in my head. Knowing I would be divorcing Robert as soon as I could and fast-forwarding through a list of possible scenarios, my mind kicked into lawyer mode.

I cocked my head, as if in thought, and tried to look ashamed. "Really?"

"Really," he said. "You're overreacting, but it's my fault. I shouldn't have stayed behind after everyone else left the party."

"Jeez. You know, you're probably right," I said with a shrug. "I guess I'm too quick to draw conclusions because of the way you two hurt me before."

I paused, pretending contemplation. "You really messed with my head, you know? But you're right, Robert. Corin having a cocktail party is no big deal. In fact, to show there're no hard feelings, I should join you."

The two of them looked more shocked than when I'd first burst in on them.

"You know what? I *will* join you! Don't go anywhere. Let me run to the house for a swimsuit and I'll be right back."

I double-timed it to my car and started the engine, just in case they were listening. Then I retrieved a digital camera from the glove compartment. On a particularly volatile case that involved property or material damages, I often took photographs. People's memories tended to skew with time, but digital photos remained exactly the same as the day you took them.

When I got back to the hot tub, I was pleasantly surprised to find they hadn't yet bolted for cover in Corin's house. Mistakenly believing they had a little time to come up with a game plan, they were just about to climb out.

Messing with the tub's control panel, Corin was bending over, showing me her bare ass. Robert stood in thigh-deep water, exposing a weight-conditioned, foam-covered, naked body. Before he could react, I took a picture. The camera flashed and beeped. Corin spun around, and I took another one, this time capturing both of them full frontal.

They immediately dropped into the water, even though the jets had been turned off. I took a third picture of their stunned faces, just for good measure, and forced myself to concentrate on the issue at hand rather than the indescribable emotions threatening to make me throw up.

"Carly, what the hell are you doing?" my husband said, managing to sound indignant.

I took a picture of his neatly folded clothes, another of their empty drink glasses, and still another of Corin's bikini hanging on the side of the tub.

"The divorce thing?" I said. "I'll be getting the lawyer. And *I'll* be doing the filing, in South Carolina, where I'll soon be residing."

"Carl—"

"We'll divorce on my terms. Not yours."

"You don't mean that. You don't know what you're doing."

"For the first time in quite a while, I know *exactly* what I'm doing. I'm getting rid of you."

His face paled a shade beneath the steam that rose in front of it. He had never seen this side of me. I wasn't sure *I'd* ever seen this side of myself.

"Let's go home and talk this over."

"I don't think so."

"Well, I need to at least come and pack a few things if you're kicking me out for the night. It's my house, too. You can't just lock me out."

"Robert, you shallow piece of scum. Yes, I *can* lock you out."

Although he was down for the count, he didn't give up. "You're not thinking straight right now. And, you love me, Carly. I know you do. You really don't mean what you're saying," he said with an amazing amount of confidence, considering he was sharing hot tub foam with his mistress.

"Yeah, I do. Trust me on this. And don't try to screw with me, Robert. I may not practice law but I have a lot of lawyer friends that can twist your balls until you'll think they're in a vise. And even more important than all that . . ." I let my voice trail off.

His eyebrows rose in question. *Yes?*

"I've got an angry daddy with a shotgun. You really *don't* want to screw with me."

12

Through stinging tears I punched Cheryl's number into the phone.

"Can you come over tonight?" I asked without bothering to say hello first.

"Carly?"

"Jason has a truck, right? Have him come, too, and bring the truck."

She explained that Jason had just put the boys to bed and they were about to relax with a glass of wine and a pay-per-view movie on cable.

"Bring the kids and the wine," I told her. "They can watch television in the spare bedroom until they fall back asleep. And you guys can watch your pay-per-view movie tomorrow."

"You want us to come over to your house right now and drive the truck? Are you okay? Carly, what's going on?"

I didn't want to talk about it over the phone, I said, and convinced her to load up her family and head my way.

My next phone call was to a locksmith who advertised twenty-four-hour emergency service. I could tell from the number of rings that the call had been forwarded from the business office to someone's home and when that someone answered, he didn't sound happy about going on a service call after he'd just gotten home from work.

"You're not locked out, then?"

"No."

"You just need a house rekeyed?"

"Yes."

"No problem. Someone can be there at seven in the morning. What's the address?"

The tears had dried up, leaving behind a runny nose. Not caring about social etiquette, I grabbed a tissue and blew loudly. "It must be done now. Tonight."

The line was silent.

"There's an extra hundred in it for you. Cash."

He agreed. I gave him the address, and he promised to be at my door in forty-five minutes or less.

Next I called a neighbor whose church was having its annual rummage sale in two weeks.

"Remember when you called looking for donations for your church bazaar?" I said. "It turns out I do have a donation for you, after all. A bunch of stuff that should bring in at least a few thousand dollars for your mission work. But it's a one-time offer, and it has to be picked up tonight."

Unfazed by such a demand, she said she'd get the church van and be at my house within the hour.

While waiting on everyone to arrive, I busied myself throwing armfuls of my clothes and toiletries into suitcases and boxes. I hauled loads of stuff to my car and tried not to chastise myself for making such a rotten decision in getting back together with Robert. At the same time, I allowed myself to accept the fact that I wasn't cut out to be a New Yorker. I was an outsider who didn't want to get in. I couldn't fully appreciate the sophisticated Northern way of life or the dynamics of a twenty-four-hour metropolis. I could work anywhere, and I wanted to be in South Carolina with my family. My real family, who loved me. I was going home.

I'd just made the last trip to my car when Cheryl, Jason, and their two young boys arrived. After we got the kids situated in front of the Nickelodeon channel in the spare room, I told them everything that had happened, including why I'd taken off to Charleston just weeks earlier. I would miss them, I explained, but I was going back to my hometown for good.

They'd brought their bottle of wine with them, and while Jason opened it, Cheryl agreed to act as my power of attorney and take care of any matters regarding the sale of my house. I was so grateful that I couldn't do anything but give her a hug.

The locksmith pulled in shortly after and, apparently happy with his one-hundred-dollar tip, got right to the task of rekeying my locks without asking questions.

"I guess this means Robert's little dinner party is off, huh?" Cheryl said.

When my friend arrived in the church van, I handed over plastic lawn bags stuffed with the contents of Robert's closet: suits, button-down shirts, silk ties, a variety of expensive shoes and belts, three full-length wool coats.

Although Jason disagreed with my act of benevolence on Robert's unwitting behalf, Cheryl was eager to pitch in. We helped load up two sets of golf clubs, enough shoes to fill two trash bags, a Bose stereo system, and a pair of water skis. Three wristwatches, several pairs of cufflinks, a Sony camcorder, and an MP3 player.

When we sat down to take a break, Jason refilled our wineglasses, and Cheryl had a sudden thought.

"Why did you tell us to drive the truck?"

"Oh, that was so you can take my new wide-screen plasma TV with you. I even have a tarp you can tie around it, just in case it starts raining before you get back. The Weather Channel says there's a chance of showers tonight."

"We're taking your new plasma TV?" she said.

"It's my gift to you," I said. "Consider it your fee for being my power of attorney and getting this house listed for sale."

"Awesome! The kids are going to love it!" she said brightly.

"I'm going to love it, too," Jason said. "But I really don't think this is a good idea, Carly. Despite what the man has done to you, you shouldn't give away everything he owns."

"I bought the television before we got married, so don't feel bad about taking it," I told him. "And as far as Robert's stuff, it was either give it away for a good cause . . . or burn it all in a backyard bonfire. I figured the socially responsible thing to do was the former."

Jason shook his head, still disagreeing with what I was doing.

"He came on to me once," Cheryl stated matter-of-factly. "At our company Christmas party."

I was beyond the shock threshold, but her comment caught Jason's attention.

"What do you mean?" he said. "I was with you at that party."

"Right, but you took that call from the sitter, remember? One of the boys had eaten dog food, and she was freaking out. You had to talk her down. And then you spoke with both boys, one by one, and explained that there was to be no more eating of dog food that night."

Remembering, Jason laughed before his expression suddenly hardened.

"He hit on you while I was in the lobby on my cell phone talking to the kids?"

Cheryl nodded. "I'm sorry, Carly. I didn't say anything to you because I just wrote it off as Robert being drunk. I mean, damn. You guys were practically still newlyweds! And, before that night at the party, he was always polite and charming."

"It's okay," I said, standing up to get back to work. "It wasn't your fault. He's just a prick."

"I was getting some hors d'oeuvres—those little bacon-wrapped scallop pastry things—when he came up and—"

"Cheryl," I cut her off. "Stop. It really doesn't matter now."

"Yeah, it does," Jason overruled me. "What did he do?"

"He, uh . . . propositioned me, I guess you'd call it. Made some reference to the fact that my husband was off playing 'mommy' and asked if I'd like to find out what it was like to be with a 'real' man. He said we should get together for a happy hour the next time Carly was working late. That I'd never had it as good as he could give it."

I sat down hard, the queasy feeling returning. I had no idea that Robert could be so forward, so blunt. There was no misunderstanding what Cheryl told us.

Jason's look was fiery. "Did he touch you?"

"Of course not," Cheryl said. "If he had, I would have told you right then. But I honestly thought he was just being an obnoxious drunk."

Motivated by the disclosure, Jason jumped up, ready to help. "Come on. Let's get a move on! What else goes in the van?"

We finished giving away Robert's belongings at the same time the locksmith finished rekeying my doors. I thanked my friend for tackling the last-minute pickup and she assured me the money from the sale of it would be put to very good use. But before the locksmith left, I had one more job for him. I wanted him and Jason to move Robert's pool table into the front yard. It would involve removing the massive wooden legs to get it through the door. But I knew he had the tools to do it. There was a stocked toolbox by his feet.

"But it's going to rain tonight," the locksmith argued. "The table will be ruined."

"Exactly," Jason, Cheryl, and I said in unison.

By the time I tackled the stretch of asphalt between Pawling and Charleston just a week after making the same trip in reverse, I experienced an odd calm, as though my anger had been redirected into something useful. I was heading home—to my real home, and I was never going to let someone walk all over me again.

In record time, I'd loaded up my car, given away Robert's stuff, and hit the road. Cheryl had my power-of-attorney paperwork, a new key to my house, and the security alarm code. In my absence she could hire movers to ship my furniture to Charleston and list my house for sale.

I also took ten minutes to write a letter of resignation to my firm expressing my gratitude for the opportunity and support they had given me. But due to personal circumstances, I was relocating immediately. Cheryl promised to deliver it the next day.

With everyone's help, I'd done it all and put myself on the highway in less than four hours, despite flashes of reservation about throwing away a good job and a rapidly developing thunderstorm that threatened to make driving difficult. I probably should have waited until the next morning to get on the road, but the thought of spending another night in the same bed that Robert had used for sex with Corin was intolerable. I would have given it away, too, if the church van had been bigger.

It felt good to be doing something other than sitting at home, and once I reached Interstate ninety-five and was speeding away from Robert and New York at seventy miles an hour, I knew I'd made the right decision.

The drive was an opportunity to plan, to dream, to plot, to think about everything imaginable. And after I'd done that and the rain had stopped, I meditated and thought of nothing at all except keeping my car between the lines. I played the stereo loud, stopped often for stretch breaks, and wondered what the future held for me.

Somewhere in Virginia, as it neared two o'clock in the morning, an attack of self-pity blindsided me. Anger and frustration battled for a dominant position in my thoughts, and new tears pushed at the back of my eyeballs. I cried for twenty or thirty miles until one of Daddy's life lessons filled my head. It was something he'd told me and Jenny over and over again growing up. *Think about what you have, not what you don't.*

I had enough savings to get by for a while without worrying about a job, even factoring in the mortgage payments I'd have to make until the house sold. I had Cheryl, a good friend I could count on to take care of things for me in Pawling. Although I wanted children someday, not having any in my current situation was definitely a positive. I had the freedom to go anywhere and do anything I wanted to do. I had a family that loved me. And I had some major attitude. I wasn't going to put up with any shit from anybody, anymore. Certainly not from Robert. And not from Protter Construction and Development, either.

As it approached three o'clock in the morning, I found a Hampton Inn in Petersburg, and when I awoke at nine, a plan was brewing in my head. By the time the Charleston city limits reached out to greet me eight hours later, I knew how I was going to help Daddy. The knowledge was exhilarating.

13

When I pulled into Mamma and Daddy's driveway, I felt a delightful sense of connection, as though I hadn't really moved away and my married days were just a bad dream. Instead of walking down the aisle of the small church on that fateful Saturday, I'd actually encountered a mysterious vortex. I'd been sucked through a door to another dimension in another place and been dropped into another life. But I'd come to my senses and found my way back through the vortex, to the place where I belonged. I knew there was still plenty to do, like file for divorce and get rid of Robert as fast as possible. But it just felt damn good to be home.

A peculiar odor reached my nose at the back screened porch, and it grew more potent when I walked in the house. It seemed to be a mixture of sandalwood and lavender with some orange and eucalyptus mixed in. Scents that individually would have been pleasant but entwined struck a chord of dissonance.

Mamma was at the sink, washing fresh collard greens. She dropped them when she saw me.

"Carly! What are you doing here? I told you that you didn't need to come; your daddy is fine. And your boss can't be too happy about you taking off again."

Her hug was welcoming and warm and not at all admonishing like her words.

"Did you fly in and rent a car? Is Robert with you? I could've picked ya'll up at the airport."

"I drove, Mamma. I left yesterday and stopped overnight in Virginia. Robert's not with me."

Her face was a tangle of emotion. "I'm so happy to have you back home for a while. But something's wrong. What happened?"

"I'm divorcing Robert. It's for good this time. He's a shallow, self-serving, immature man, and I made a really bad decision in marrying him. I've resigned from the firm, quit my job. I'm going to put the house on the market. I'm moving back to Charleston."

"You quit your job?" Mamma said, more shocked by my career path than my split with Robert. I guess she'd cleared the divorce hurdle earlier in the month. "You're moving back?"

I nodded.

I mixed us each a Beefeater and tonic and told her everything that happened since I'd returned to Pawling with Robert.

She hugged me and asked if I wanted a crab cake sandwich leftover from yesterday. Southerners throw food at everything; it's just what we do. A full stomach makes happy times even better and makes rough times a bit more bearable.

"I'll just wait for supper. I haven't had collard greens in forever," I said. "But I have to know, what is that weird smell?" I asked.

"Oh, that's an Aroma-magic Ionizer and Environment Enhancer," Mamma said with a dismissing wave of her hand, sounding very much like my sister. "It's in the living room."

She wore a long black cotton skirt with heeled sandals and a white sleeveless sweater. Only Mamma could cook in a lily-white top, sans apron, and emerge from the kitchen unscathed by stains.

"Jenny overnighted it. They're going to start selling them on the show, and she says no house should be without one. Aromatherapy is supposed to cure whatever ails you," Mamma explained.

She was only halfway through her first gin, but my glass was empty and I mixed myself another.

"Uh huh. So what's ailing you?"

"She sent it for your daddy, to relax him."

I searched for the odor-producing machine. It was sitting on an end table in the next room and resembled a humidifier on steroids.

"It comes with an assortment of oil mixtures that you add to the reservoir, like Energy, Love, and Concentration. What you're smelling right now is Calm. Jenny sent an entire case of Calm."

"My God, she's brainwashed you," I said, returning to the kitchen.

"I figure she went to the trouble to send it, we ought to at least try it out."

"So how's it working?"

"Your daddy says it was a waste of postage and that burning some fu-fu oil isn't going to relax him. Although he is thinking about plugging it in outside, by the trash can, to see if it'll keep the coons away. They're supposed to have a pretty good sense of smell, almost like dogs. He's thinking that a bottle of Calm might chill them out enough to keep them from getting into the garbage cans."

"Speaking of dogs, where is Taffy?"

Besides the smell, something had been bothering me since I'd come in, and I just figured out what it was. I hadn't received the usual enthusiastic canine greeting.

"Probably in the living room watching television. She seems to enjoy ESPN."

"Taffy watches television?"

"She does since your granny gave her a tranquilizer."

"Did Granny confuse her with Precious?"

It made perfect sense to medicate Jenny's growling excuse for a family pet, to keep from strangling it. But not Taffy. Taffy was a great dog.

"No, your granny found the prescription for anxiety that I picked up for your daddy, and she thought they were vitamins. She took one, too."

As if on cue, Granny pirouetted—literally—into the kitchen, before flopping down in a kitchen chair next to me.

"Jenny!" she exclaimed, calling me by my sister's name yet again.

At least that much was normal.

"Hi, Granny."

"Where've you been?" she asked, before pulling her dentures out of her mouth. "You're almosth lathe for sthupper."

She studied the teeth for a moment before arranging them on the kitchen table in front of her. After rotating them a few times, she started playing with them, her spotted hands carrying them in a chomping motion as though they were eating an imaginary hot dog.

"I think she may have taken two pills," Mamma explained, shaking the collards to drain the water off. "The prescription was for thirty. And now there are twenty-seven. So either the dog got two or she got two."

We watched Granny for a moment.

"Probably she took two," we said together.

Hearing our conversation, Taffy ambled in to investigate. When she saw me, her tail wagged lazily, twice. Then she sneezed and plopped down by my feet. She explored my ankles for a few seconds with a cold nose before rolling onto her back to study the underside of my chair with great interest.

"So you're cooking supper, Granny and Taffy are stoned, and everyone is calmed by the wonders of the Aroma-magic machine."

Mamma laughed. "Welcome home."

"How's Daddy? Where is Daddy?"

"At the store, stubborn fool. We got home from the hospital a couple hours ago, and he went straight to work."

Granny's teeth finished eating their invisible hot dog and began munching their way around the perimeter of a rectangular placemat.

"Should he be driving on this medication?"

"He hasn't taken pill one out of that bottle."

"Oh, right," I remembered. "Granny and Taffy are the only ones into the 'vitamins' so far!"

Mamma laughed. "He says he doesn't need any drugs for anxiety, that he's not stressed out. You know how he is with pills. I had to force him to take the other prescription, the one to regulate his heartbeat."

Daddy had issues with the pharmaceutical industry and thought that America was an overmedicated nation.

"I think I need another vithamin," Granny said through bare gums. "They're prethy good thuff." Her teeth were now sitting in Mamma's vase of white daffodils, smiling at me.

"The vitamins are all gone," Mamma told her.

"Damn."

"But if you put your teeth back in your mouth, you can have some supper soon."

I watched with amazement as Granny's teeth munched their way up an invisible pole and levitated in front of her mouth for a moment before she slid them back in place and smiled brightly at us.

"You're supposed to take a vitamin every day," she said matter-of-factly.

Mamma and I were still laughing when Daddy walked in.

"Little girl! I saw your car in the driveway and wondered what you're doing here. Is Robert with you?"

I shook my head as we hugged. "No, he's in New York."

Daddy was carrying a briefcase full of paperwork and, despite a smile of surprise at seeing me, he looked haggard. His chin held three or four days' worth of growth, and he'd aged ten years in the seven days since I'd last seen him. Although he'd worn a mustache forever, I couldn't recall the last time I'd seen him go more than a day without shaving.

"Your mamma told you I was in the hospital, didn't she?" Daddy said, setting his briefcase on the table to give me a hug. "And I'll bet that she exaggerated and you jumped in your car and drove straight here with visions of the preacher saying a prayer over my deathbed. I'm not believing this! Don't get me wrong, it's great to have you at home, but you shouldn't have come on my account. Other than this little glitch with my pulse, I'm perfectly healthy."

He dropped into a kitchen chair.

Daddy wasn't accustomed to dealing with medical issues and having been admitted to the hospital twice in one week had unnerved him. He hated being the center of attention. And he was the last person to ever want sympathy, especially from one of his daughters.

"That's not why I'm here, really."

"Your mamma didn't call you?"

"Of course I called the girls," she told him. "But I also told them you were fine and that it was just an overnight stay in the hospital, like before."

Mamma waited for me to tell Daddy why I was home. The explanation was made more difficult by the fact that he had always been so proud of me. Impressed by my level-headedness and thrilled at the ease with which I'd earned my law degree and passed the bar.

Like Sherry, who was straightforward and turning out to be the logical half of Jenny's twin girls, I had always been expected to make the right decisions and do the smart thing.

Daddy wouldn't blink twice if Jenny abruptly declared that she had quit a high-paying job, was divorcing her husband, selling her house, and moving back to Charleston. He would know that it was just melodramatic exaggeration and that she'd change her mind soon.

But such a declaration from me would be totally out of character. I'd always been the methodical one. The twin who carefully thought things through. The good judge of character.

Daddy fixed me with a look that demanded explanation. It was a skill he must've acquired by watching Mamma do it over the years.

"Robert's in New York with his mistress," I said, then repeated everything I'd told Mamma earlier.

"Well, like I said before, it's best to just do it and get the split over with, especially now that you're one-hundred-percent positive," he said and gave me another hug to comfort me. "And I'm really proud of you for being strong and standing up to him."

Mamma nodded her agreement.

"Let's just make sure the son of a bitch doesn't get anything in the settlement," Daddy continued. "Not a dime. Not even a dish."

I told them about giving Robert's stuff away to the church for their rummage sale.

Daddy let out a belly laugh. "That's my girl!"

"I think I will take a whirl!" Granny said. She stood, pirouetted to the antique butcher's block that stood against the wall, retrieved a banana from a fruit bowl, and returned to the table.

"What's wrong with my mother?"

"She got into your prescription bottle, thinking they were vitamins. I called the doctor, and he said she'll be fine. It'll wear off in a few more hours. She should sleep very well tonight."

Taffy yawned loudly, ambled over to Daddy, rolled over on her back, and stayed that way. Spread eagle, with all four limbs sticking out and the flap of her snout hanging away from her teeth, she resembled fresh roadkill. Although it didn't look very comfortable, it must have worked for her because she immediately started snoring.

"The dog, too?" Daddy asked, leaning over to get a better look.

"Yes," Mamma said. "But Taffy only got one pill. I think your mother took two."

"For crying out loud."

"You're thuppose tho thake vithamins every day," Granny told Daddy through sunken-in lips. Her teeth were back in the daffodils, giving the tabletop centerpiece an amused appearance, as though it were laughing at the Stone family.

Daddy just shook his head and rubbed his eyes as though washing away a long day. Mamma rolled the thick collard leaves, expertly sliced them into strips and dropped them into a large skillet. She added two strips of bacon, freshly ground pepper, a cup of water, and a capful of apple cider vinegar before turning on the burner.

Granny plucked a flower from the vase and stuck it behind her ear.

"Are you sure she just took two pills?" Daddy asked.

"Pretty sure."

"Are your dentures bothering you?" Daddy asked Granny, trying to understand her logic. "Is that why you keep taking them out?"

"Nope. I love my theeth. They're weally gweat theeth."

She popped them back inside her mouth and ran her tongue over their surface.

"It's good to have teeth," she said. "Life would be hard without teeth."

"Maybe I should try one of those pills after all," Daddy mumbled, heading for the small refrigerator on the back porch that held a supply of Palmetto Pale Ale, his favorite local microbrew from the Palmetto Brewing Company.

When he returned, we toasted to me being back in Charleston and starting a new life. Once again, it was good to be home. The feeling was made sweeter by the fact that I was staying this time.

The effects of the pills on Granny and Taffy had mostly worn off by suppertime. Granny's dentures chewed actual food inside her mouth instead of imaginary food on the tabletop, and Taffy had resumed her customary position at the base of the table, poised to receive any offerings that came her way.

We got to talking about the job market in Charleston, and Daddy wanted to know if my firm would give me a good recommendation, even though I'd quit after such a short time period.

"I seriously doubt it. But I'll worry about that when I start looking for a job. I'm not even sure that I want to keep doing mediation."

Mamma reached across the table and patted my hand. "Whatever you decide to do, I'm sure you'll be wonderful at it. And it's great to have you back home."

"Speaking of home," I said, "there's something else. I want to know if I can live here until the house in Pawling sells and I can buy a place in Charleston."

I knew I could have moved back home after I finished school and it wouldn't have been a big deal. But that was a lot of years ago and things were different now. I was in my thirties, for Pete's sake. I was supposed to be a self-sufficient adult. They'd paid for my schooling to ensure that.

"You don't ever need to ask if you can stay here," Daddy said.

"Of course you'll stay here," Mamma said.

Feeling silly for thinking they might be disappointed in me, I was reminded once again that the Stone blood bond was unconditional.

"Hot water runs out right quick," Granny said as though critiquing one of the area's bed-and-breakfasts. "But the food's mighty good."

She snatched another daffodil from the centerpiece and stuck it behind her other ear.

"Besides," Daddy said. "It'll be good to have you around. You can help to keep your grandmother out of the damn vitamins, for crying out loud."

14

"This stupid humidifier has got to go," Mamma said. "It's giving me a headache."

We had washed all the dirty clothes I'd haphazardly packed in Pawling and were folding them in the living room.

"I thought you said it's an Aroma-magic Ionizer and Environment Enhancer," I teased her.

"Well, that was before it gave me a headache. Now, it's a stupid humidifier. And besides, it's starting to smell funny. Fishy or something."

"The air-maker gizmo oughtta be fine," Granny said. "I just fed it some more oil."

Mamma and I stopped folding and looked at each other with apprehension, wondering what she put in the machine.

"Taffy sure likes it," Granny continued. "I figured it'd be good for the air-maker, too."

"What does Taffy like?"

"South Carolina has a turnpike?"

Unlike most people with a hearing loss, Granny wouldn't ask for something to be repeated if it didn't come through clearly. She just made do with whatever she got.

"Show me what you put in the machine, Granny," I said loudly.

"What's all the fuss about? It's over yonder, right next to Taffy's food."

We followed her into the kitchen. With a flourish, she produced a bottle of cod liver oil.

"Oh, good grief," Mamma said.

She always put some of the fish oil on Taffy's food to keep her fur coat healthy.

"No wonder I was smelling something stinky. Let's get that thing out of here!"

"What did it do wrong?" Granny asked, as though it were a family pet that had gotten in trouble.

"Nothing," Mamma told her. "We're just going to let it enhance the environment somewhere else for now."

Granny shrugged her shoulders and harrumphed, either accepting Mamma's explanation or forgetting what she'd asked.

Careful to keep it level, Mamma and I unplugged and carried the Aroma-magic out of the kitchen and stuck it on the piazza until someone could come up with a better idea of what to do with it.

When we returned to the living room, Granny had arranged her tiny frame inside a big chair and was watching the cooking channel. Taffy was stretched lazily across her feet.

My mind wandered to the future, and I felt a sense of excitement. The type of rush that a boxer might feel before a fight. For the first time in my life, I was going to instigate something that would create conflict.

Yesterday, I'd walked the land across from Daddy's store, assisted by Lori Anne and three individuals who were experts in their respective fields. During the short trek, I'd gained some empowering knowledge. Even without all the spurring on from Lori Anne, I was ready to annoy the hell out of someone. I was ready to get some attention.

In the three days I'd been back, I'd also learned quite a bit about Protter Construction and Development and Handyman's Depot.

Protter was a family-owned real-estate development company that had been in business for more than forty years. They had their own crew of supervisors and owned their own heavy equipment but contracted out most of the labor.

They had done a few residential subdivisions but preferred commercial projects. In some instances they bought the land, erected an office building or strip mall, and then turned the property for a profit. In other cases, like the development across from Mamma and Daddy's store, they retained ownership, hired a management company, and leased the space to retail tenants.

Handyman's Depot was slated to be one of three anchor stores and had signed a twelve-year lease with an extension option. The organization had more than one hundred and ten stores, all company owned. A well-run, well-managed organization with steady growth, their claim to fame was innovative tools and home improvement products sold exclusively at Handyman's. Some stock-market analysts were watching the company, as they anticipated it would go public in the near future.

The bottom line was that anything I could do to slow or stop the construction progress would cost the both the Protter family and Handyman's Depot money. In real-estate development, time was money. Having crews and heavy equipment on standby, unable to proceed with their jobs, cost money. Not finishing the strip mall on time cost money. Not being able to occupy your building and open as scheduled cost money.

It was time to have a talk with Daddy and get his feedback.

Although he put up a jovial front around Mamma and me, he couldn't hide that he looked tired. The laugh lines surrounding his bright eyes had become taut and revealed more worry than character. Planning to shut down the business was wearing him out.

Mamma had told me Daddy was definitely closing Stone Hardware and Home Supply before the grand opening of the Handyman's Depot. The two of them had discussed opening another business in the same building, one that wouldn't face direct competition across the street, but quickly decided against that option. Their hearts just weren't in anything else.

Yes, it was definitely time to talk to Daddy and convince him not to close the store. At least not yet.

"A penny for your thoughts," Mamma said, stacking my neatly folded clothes in piles to carry upstairs.

"I was just thinking about . . . the future."

I was saved from having to elaborate further because Daddy walked in.

"What's Jenny's machine doing on the porch?"

"Your mother put cod liver oil in the reservoir and it started stinking up the house," Mamma answered.

Daddy, accustomed to strange happenings around the house since his mother's arrival, simply nodded.

"Well, I wasn't kidding about trying it on the raccoons. They got into the trash again last night, for crying out loud. Garbage was all over the place."

Mamma shrugged. "Why not? It won't bother me if you try some aromatherapy on them."

"But wouldn't cod liver oil attract them?" I asked. "You know, make them hungry? Then they'd be more aggressive about getting into the garbage."

"What if he dumps out the fish oil," Mamma asked, "and then puts in something that would keep them away? Something they wouldn't like . . . but what doesn't a raccoon like?"

"I know," I said. "Let's pour in a few bottles of Calm to relax them. Then they'll be too lazy to break through all your garbage can barriers."

"What if it rains?" Mamma asked Daddy. "Is the machine water-proof?"

"I guess we'll find out soon enough."

A man on a mission, he retrieved the Aroma-magic and headed outside with Taffy on his heels. He reappeared moments later to retrieve the case of Calm and disappeared again.

Twenty minutes later he happily reported that he'd put a recipe of Calm, citronella oil, and mothballs in the machine. Strategically placed between the two handle-locked, bungee-corded, brick-topped industrial-strength garbage cans, the electrical cord was just long enough to reach the outlet on the outside wall of his workshop. It was meant to be. Daddy felt good about his latest strategy in the battle with the raccoons.

"You put mothballs in there? I hope the fumes won't be danger-ous," Mamma said. "I'd hate for something to happen to them."

Daddy just shook his head.

Mamma had begun making a banana rum cake but realized she was out of spiced rum, so Daddy and I offered to take a drive to the package store. Other people called them liquor stores, but South Carolinians had nice names for things. Fat people were "big-boned," bless their hearts; hurricanes were "windstorms"; and roaches were "palmetto bugs."

We hopped into his company truck, and I used the drive as an opportunity to talk to him about the store.

"Hypothetically," I began, "if there were a way that you and Mamma could keep the store and operate at the same or higher volume than you do now, would you want to?"

He didn't even have to think about it.

"Of course. If I was ready to retire, maybe it would be different. But I'm not ready to quit working. Not even close. And the store . . . well, you know what it means to me. What it means to your mamma. What it means to all the people who work there."

He paused to change lanes and formulate his thoughts into words.

"I love everything about the store, from the smell of sawdust in the lumberyard to teaching the home improvement seminars to hearing a customer thank one of the staff for their help. Running the store isn't work. It's pure pleasure."

"I thought so."

"But I'm also a realist, Carly. I've explored all the options, and the only choice I have is to shut it down. All the full-time employees will get a severance package, and I'm going to talk to the personnel manager for Handyman's in case anyone wants to go work for them."

Daddy let out a sigh that was heavy with resignation.

"I don't think you have to."

"Talk to their manager?"

"I don't think you have to shut down the store. At least, not without a fight."

"But there's no point to fighting a battle when you already know the outcome."

"We can change the outcome."

I told him about the research I'd done and revealed my plan.

By the time we got home after buying Mamma's spiced rum, Daddy was grinning.

"What the hell," he said. "It might just work."

15

Mother Nature smiled down on us as Lori Anne and I walked the plot of dirt across from Mamma and Daddy's store again. The day was a page right out of a fairy-tale book: sunny, mercury flirting with the low seventies, endless clear blue sky. I wore sandals, a sleeveless T-shirt, and a flowing cotton skirt that invited the refreshing breeze to caress my bare legs. Lori Anne was in her usual daytime attire of skintight jeans, high-heeled sandals, and a flamboyant cotton top. Being able to dress however she wanted was one of the perks of owning her own business. For that matter, she could go to the salon in a burlap sack and get away with it because people would chalk it up to her being a "creative" type.

"You want to do a happy hour tonight?" she asked me. "We can dress up. Maybe find someplace with live jazz? I'll get Britt to bring one of his friends."

Lori Anne's current boyfriend, Britt, had been taking her out for nearly two months, which meant he wouldn't be around much longer. She went through them at the same rate she changed her hair color. And ever since her one attempt at matrimony failed in a few short weeks, she was my only friend who thought of marriage as an ancient ritual serving no present-day purpose.

"No. I told you I want to hang low for a while, and if we go to a happy hour, we're bound to run into somebody I know."

"So?"

"So, I'll let everyone know I'm back in town . . . soon. After I get things worked out. But not right now. And besides, I'm not up for a double-date kind of thing."

"It'll get your mind off Robert," she said. "And anyway, you're separated, woman! It's time to put yourself out there."

I gave her a look. "It's time? I've been back less than a week."

Easy to navigate, the land was a beautiful piece of earth with flat terrain, plenty of mature pines, and just enough live oaks to give it character. Construction was progressing quickly, and the property had changed in just the few days since we'd visited last. Seven or eight acres of timber had already been cleared, and piles of miscellaneous infrastructure materials, like conduit and culverts, were stacked in neat rows. A construction trailer sat near the perimeter of the property with several trucks and cars parked haphazardly around it.

I felt good, and not even the rumbling tractor creating construction access roads dampened my enthusiasm.

"By the way," I told Lori Anne, "thanks for turning me on to Chief Hatcher. He's a very cool guy."

I'd given my best friend a condensed version of my strategy to stall the Protter development, the same one that Daddy agreed just might work. She'd enthusiastically supported the plan, and even added an idea of her own. Chief Hatcher was an expert in his field, and he owed Lori Anne a favor.

"No problem," she said. "Now let's go kick some ass."

As we neared the wooden steps leading up to the trailer, *he* walked out. Trent. In a faded black T-shirt that couldn't conceal the muscled chest beneath it. Wearing the scuffed-up leather work boots and the loose-fitting denim jeans that pushed my imagination into overdrive. Moving quickly, confidently, his eyes studying something on a clipboard as he nearly walked past me.

"My, oh, my," Lori Anne whispered, giving me an elbow in the side. "Look who's here. He is freakin' hot!"

Although I agreed with her assessment, I forced myself to forget about how good-looking he was and remember how much I loathed everything he stood for: crushing a small business in the name of progress.

"Good morning," I said, startling him.

Seeing me, his face revealed a rapid flip chart of emotions before it settled into a cordial expression.

"Carly Stone," he said slowly. "I didn't realize you were still in town."

"I left, but now I'm back."

He nodded. "Who's your friend?"

Lori Anne stuck out her hip along with her hand. "I'm Lori Anne. We sort of met at your office a few weeks' back. When Carly was there to speak with Mister Protter."

"I'm Trent." He shook her hand.

"Yes, you certainly are."

He returned his attention to me. "Welcome back. How's your father?"

"He's fine. He'll be even better if he can manage to stay out of the hospital."

"He's been in the hospital?"

"Twice, in the past week. But it's nothing I care to discuss with a stranger."

His eyes clouded for an instant, and I wondered if my verbal barb stung. Whether it did or didn't, I was ready to hit him with something more tangible than nasty words.

"So what brings you here?" he said. "Is there something I can do for you?"

"Yeah," I said with some attitude. "You can tell all your boys out here to go on home."

"Come again?"

Before I could elaborate, Mister Protter walked out of the trailer. He looked the same as when I'd met him in his office. Powerful, confident, casually dressed.

"Well, hello, Miss Stone," he said. "I see you've already met my son."

Blood drained from my face and pooled somewhere near my heart, refusing to move. I couldn't think.

"Your son?"

"Yes, my son Trent," Mister Protter said. "Are you feeling okay? You look pale."

"You son of a bitch," I spat at Trent. "You let me believe you were just a hired hand. Why didn't you tell me you were a . . . a *Protter?*"

He smiled. "Most of the time, I am just a hired hand."

"Right."

"What's going on, Trent? I take it you've met Miss Stone before?"

"We've crossed paths a few times. And I don't know what's going on, Pop. Carly was just fixing to tell me why she and her friend stopped by."

Father and son, their physical resemblance blaring now that I was looking at them side by side, waited for an explanation.

"The wall," I told them, regaining my composure.

"What?" Trent said.

"There's what may very well be a piece of the original city wall on this property."

They looked at me like I had just told them the sky was green.

"What wall are you referring to, Miss Stone?" Mister Protter asked in the manner of an elementary school teacher humoring a child.

"Charleston, back when it was called Charles Towne, was the only English walled city in America. It was the colonists' way of defending their land."

The two men continued to look at me in an uncomprehending way, so I continued to share my newly acquired historical knowledge.

"There are clues from archeological excavations and documentary sources that paint a picture of Charleston beginning as a city completely encircled by walls . . . similar in appearance to the medieval walled towns of Europe, with a lot of palisades and trenches. See, when the proprietors began forming Charles Town over three hundred years ago, it had to be a defensible town, because it was surrounded by water and quite accessible."

I paused to make sure I had my facts right. My historian friend had been enthusiastically thorough.

"During the late 1600s, border disputes were common, and much of the Carolina province was simultaneously claimed by the French, Spanish, and English. Everybody wanted to stake claim to our little piece of low-lying paradise."

Mister Protter's eyebrows arched with what may have been surprise, but Trent's tightened over blue eyes that weren't amused.

"I've read accounts about Charleston being a walled city, but I thought it was a small area near the Battery," Mister Protter said.

I nodded. "The generally accepted view is that Charleston's walls, bastions, and even some moats were in place by the year seventeen-oh-four, but all except a seawall were dismantled just thirteen years later so the town could be enlarged. It's merely a blip in the history journals. But the thing is, there's no evidence to support the notion of such a large-scale effort to remove the walls that enclosed the town. And in fact, there is evidence that demonstrates areas of wall being repaired and improved upon throughout the Revolutionary War years. So, while most of the original defensive wall structures were either torn down or the wooden stakes and palmetto logs that formed palisades rotted away, other parts were reinforced with more sturdy materials, like brick."

Trying not to grin in victory, I continued with my announcement.

"And, according to one of the leading historians in the area, the remains of a section of wall could very well be standing on your property. It appears to be a section that was connected to a small bastion, because there is a layer of oyster shells and cobblestones around the area, about a foot and a half down."

I looked around to get my bearings and pointed to an area near the center of the plat, "right over there."

The four of us looked at the crumbling wall, barely visible from our vantage point, standing insolently where it didn't belong.

"So?" Trent was agitated. "What does a pile of debris that might possibly have been a wall at one time have to do with anything now?"

"Maybe nothing. But this could be a really big find. A gold mine, so to speak, to a history buff. And historians feel strongly enough about it to keep you from tearing it down and hauling it off to the dump."

My historian friend was chomping at the bit to notify the Protters and get a group of experts to the site immediately, because she really did think that the mound of debris could have some historic value. But she'd agreed to let me be the one to deliver the news, and I was enjoying every minute of doing so.

"You've got to be kidding," Mister Stone said. "It's a splotch of old bricks and stones and mortar. It could've been anything. The history is fascinating, but how do they know it's a piece of the wall?"

"The location and the materials," Lori Anne said, enjoying the moment as much as I was. Although pushing people's buttons was a newly discovered activity for me, she had always loved to stir things up just for the hell of it.

"Many members of the society are retired and have a lot of time on their hands." I shrugged. "Studying and preserving history is what they do."

In reality, if the wall dilemma escalated to become a problem for Protter Construction and Development, all they'd have to do was agree to leave it in place and erect a barrier of some sort around it. End of story. But they didn't know that. At least not yet. And whether or not it turned out to be a historic artifact, the process of finding out would slow them down. In my best imagined scenario, it would require a modification to the master plan.

"Well, I've got a meeting to get to," Mister Protter said abruptly, deciding to let his son deal with us solo.

"See you later, Pop." Trent muttered.

"Nice to see you again, Miss Stone," Mister Protter said, to be cordial. "My son will take care of any concerns you have about the . . . er, alleged piece of wall."

He told Trent good-bye and nodded in Lori Anne's direction before climbing into a Lincoln Towncar and driving off.

Trent turned to face me full on, thick arms folded across his chest. "We will be happy to talk to the historical society to resolve the situation. Is there anything else you wanted, Carly?"

I stood close, defiantly pushing myself into his space, and had to arch my neck to see his eyes. The crystal blue eyes had darkened with irritation.

As he shifted his weight from one leg to the other, sunlight coming from just the right angle created a halo of golden red color at the edges of his short hair and briefly silhouetted a sculpted frame. He smelled of soap, sun, and leather. I nearly forgot what I was about to say. Then I remembered he was a *Protter*. I hated him.

"No," I said. "There's nothing else I wanted, other than to let you know that you won't be moving dirt in the area of the wall. Well, actually, you won't be moving any dirt anywhere on this property after tomorrow. At least not for a few weeks."

"Oh, really?" The eyes went black. "Why's that?"

"Because Chief Hatcher believes a portion of this land belonged to his ancestors and may be sacred soil. A Native American Indian burial ground, actually."

"What! You have got to be kidding. Yeah, there's a pile of rubble sitting over there, that may have been a wall at one time, but there's certainly nothing to indicate this property ever held human remains. You're reaching, Carly."

It was Lori Anne's turn to jump in. "He's a full-blooded Waccamaw Indian, not to mention a historian. And Chief Hatcher knows for a fact there were some burial grounds around Charleston. See, Native American Indians traded furs and skins and navigated the waters of the South Carolina coast until diseases like smallpox wiped a lot of them out. And then, settlers forced most of them west."

Trent looked back and forth between the two of us. "Chief *Hatcher*? You couldn't have made up a better name than that? Like, say, Chief Running Creek or Chief Rising Sun?"

"Chief Hatcher is a real man, Trent Protter," I said. "And for your information, many Native American Indians consider their tribal names a very personal thing. It's something they only share with close friends and family. And besides that, Hatcher is a common Native American Indian name in South Carolina. Just like Norris or Creel or Locklear. Do some research before you jump to the conclusion that I'm inventing Indian chiefs."

I could almost feel the heat from Trent's glare. "So what does your chief want, Carly?"

"He just wants to make sure you don't desecrate any graves. You'd feel the same way if there was a possibility your ancestors had been buried on this property."

He unfolded and refolded his arms, and his eyes narrowed even further.

"You'll be receiving an injunction to prevent you from disturbing the soil any further," I said, "until experts evaluate the area to determine if it was, in fact, a burial ground."

"And you've got some sort of evidence to back up your claim?"

"Yes, we do. Just finding a grouping of broken shards of pottery or flint, or in this case discovering a sloping mound of dirt that looks like a giant bump on otherwise flat terrain can be cause enough for an investigation. The federal government says so."

I pointed to an area on the southernmost section of the plat, where there sat just such a mound. He looked at it for several seconds before taking a step toward me, reducing the already miniscule gap between us. He opened his mouth to say something but shut it before any words came out. Then, like a caged panther pacing, he turned and walked a short distance away from us before pivoting and walking back.

"I don't think he's very happy to see you, Carly," Lori Anne said brightly.

He glared at her, clenched his fists and did another walk back and forth.

"This is private property. You trespassed when you were out here with your historian. You trespassed when you were out here with your Native American Indian chief. And the two of you are trespassing today. I'd like for you to get off my land. Right now."

"We've got an appointment for a manicure, anyway," Lori Anne said with attitude, looking at her nails. "We were just leaving."

I tried to keep from grinning as we headed back to my car.

"What is it that you really want, Miss Stone?" Trent said to our departing backs. He had quit using my first name.

We stopped and turned. "I just want to preserve history and protect sacred soil."

I could see his jaw muscles clench and unclench as he formulated words.

"I know you're angry about the Handyman's Depot situation, but your childish tactics won't work. There is nothing you can do to stop this retail center," he said. "I've overseen the development of a lot of different sites, and I've never run across any pieces of historic walls or old burial grounds."

"You've also never run across me before," I told him, still fuming that he hadn't properly identified himself. I'd been blindsided by the knowledge that my fantasy man didn't just work for the enemy; he was the enemy.

"And, sure, it may not prove to be a piece of the wall. And there may not be any Native American Indian bones beneath this dirt. But you know what? I sure as hell can have a judge slow you down while we all find out."

"Is that a threat?"

"No, it's a fact. The court orders are being prepared right now," I told him. "Did I mention I'm a lawyer?"

"No," he said flatly, running a hand through his hair. "I thought you were a mediator from New York."

"Well, now I'm lawyer from Charleston."

"Then you ought to realize trespassing is illegal. Get the hell off my land."

16

As dusk descended on the city known for its gentility, chanting crickets filled the air with a comforting cadence. Daddy and I were stretched out on the back porch, sharing a bottle of merlot and a plate of benne wafers, discussing the Protter project. He was smoking his favorite pipe, the one Mamma's grandpa had given him, and delicate swirls of cherry tobacco danced above his head.

Earlier, when I'd confronted Trent, I had been confident and gutsy. But, even with Lori Anne's moral support, I'd also felt nervous. Afterward, having begun laying the groundwork for a battle, I felt sick. As we were driving home, nausea pounded my gut, and I wanted to throw up. But I recovered quickly, and the queasiness morphed into exhilaration. A small step toward victory. I'd done it. For the first time in my life, I'd confronted someone with the intention of provoking rather than mediating, and it resulted in a natural high better than any drug could have induced.

The experience made me realize what I wanted to do for a living. It was a startling revelation, and the anticipation of my new career pursuit was delightful.

"I've decided I want to be a trial lawyer," I told Daddy.

There was a stunned pause before he smiled. "A trial lawyer? Hot damn!"

"I'm tired of mediation and tired of selling compromise. In fact, I've had a few cases where one side was overwhelmingly in the right, but I convinced them to make concessions anyway, just to avoid the courtroom. To avoid the fight."

"And now you're ready to go for the fight?"

"Absolutely," I said with gusto, meaning it.

"I wondered when this would happen," he said, as though he'd known something about me that I hadn't known about myself. "You are going to make one fine lawyer."

We talked about some of the law firms that I might want to approach and what areas I could specialize in and how proud he was of me.

The desire to litigate had been brewing ever since I became a professional mediator, I explained, but I just hadn't realized it was in me. It took getting rid of Robert and taking on Protter Construction and Development to make me believe in myself enough to make the career change. Thinking of my earlier confrontation with Trent and the discovery that he was Mister Protter's son, I felt myself growing angry all over again.

Daddy laughed when I told him what happened and how hot I'd been. "Well of course he's a Protter, little girl. He's the old man's son! Who did you think he was?"

"I thought he was just a stupid construction worker."

"What gave you that idea?"

"The way he was dressed, for one. And the truck. It's a construction worker's truck."

"Trent is obviously the type of man who doesn't mind getting his hands dirty. He'd rather be on the site, overseeing things, than sitting in an office."

"So you knew they're father and son?"

"Sure," Daddy said. "They never hid that fact. I met Trent when I went to Protter's office to see what could be done about Handyman's. They were both there and were quite pleasant as they told me what I didn't want to hear."

He paused to pack some tobacco into the bowl of the wooden pipe and refill our wineglasses.

"When did you meet Trent?" he wanted to know.

It dawned on me that when I'd been around Trent, Daddy hadn't been there. And when Trent delivered the envelope to our house, when Robert tried to punch him out, Daddy hadn't been there, either. And I'd never mentioned my Diana's restaurant encounter with the handsome construction worker. I never thought I'd see him again.

"At Diana's," I answered, with some embarrassment. "The first morning I was here, when I got country-ham biscuits for breakfast the same time you were out getting beignets from Joseph's? I had a flat tire, and he changed it for me. He looked like any other construction worker out to get some breakfast before a hard day."

Only much more clean-cut and handsome and sexy, I thought. But at the time, I didn't know he was a Protter. I suddenly wished he were troll ugly.

"Guess you should be careful with your assumptions." Daddy's eyebrows arched in amusement.

"Thanks. I'll remember that in the future," I said, curiosity about Trent momentarily outweighing my desire to crush Protter Construction and Development.

Staring into my wine, I wondered what the man was like and how his family got into land development. When I looked up, Daddy was watching me watch my wine.

"So what do you think of Trent?" he asked.

"I think he's a deceitful prick," I said. "I hate him. I don't know how his wife stands to live with him."

Daddy, accustomed to such language from me when Mamma wasn't within earshot, shook his head. "He's not married."

An unwelcome jolt of hope shot through me in response to learning Trent was single. He didn't wear a wedding band because there wasn't one to wear.

"So? Why would I care if Trent is married or not?"

Daddy raised an eyebrow. "I just mentioned it because you said you don't know how his wife can live with him. You sound defensive, little girl."

"I'm not defensive," I grumbled.

We sipped our wine and ate the legendary sesame seed cookies that as rumor has it bring good luck and listened to the crickets sing.

"You do know," he said after some thought, "the elder Mister Protter will be calling me soon. To find out what your motives are and if I'm putting you up to these stalling tactics."

He tapped his pipe on the edge of a marble ashtray to dump out some loose tobacco. He'd smoked a pipe for as long as I could remember, always outside on the screened porch or the open piazza, and I loved watching the process. The preparing, the packing, and the actual burning that created entrails of climbing smoke.

"So, let him call."

"I rather like the fellow. In different circumstances, we'd probably be good friends," Daddy confessed.

"That's exactly what Mister Protter said about you."

Not surprised, Daddy smiled. He had a way with people and usually made a good impression right off the bat.

"His son is an upstanding young man in his own right," he said. "It must be difficult for you to have such a personable adversary."

"It's not difficult at all. Besides, I have no interest in Trent or any other man right now. The divorce won't even be final for about a year. That's twelve months before I should even start thinking about thinking about dating. Plus, I'm not exactly over my lying, cheating husband who had me totally fooled."

"I don't know when it will be time for you to start dating. But I do know one thing: you didn't have real love with Robert. Love involves respect for each other. You couldn't possibly have been in love with a man who is so wrapped up in himself."

I thought about that while I munched on another benne wafer. Robert was charming, and he had been crazy about me. And I had thought I loved him. But had we had friendship or passion or intimacy? Obviously, he was not husband material. I didn't want to dwell on my bad judgment call. I changed the subject.

"How do you think of the Protters? As adversaries?"

"While I'm not happy about the entire situation, I do realize it's business," Daddy said. "It's not personal."

I was taken aback. "How can you say that? You don't take forcing your store out of business personally? We're talking almost a hundred years of operation, in the same location!"

"It's called free enterprise, little girl," Daddy said with a heavy sigh.

I started to argue, but he held up a hand. "Let's just agree to disagree on this one, okay? Even though you're in the process of becoming a litigation expert and may want the practice, I don't have the energy for a debate right now."

Daddy probably was tired because the Handyman's Depot issue was taking a toll on him. He had the prescription drugs to prove it. I dropped the issue.

"Back to Mister Protter . . . if he calls, you just tell him that I'm a grown woman, and you can't control what I do. I have a mind of my own."

"Well, that certainly wouldn't be lying, would it?"

The crickets continued making nature's music as we discussed various options for the store. Daddy told me he would hold off on listing it for sale, but he would have to notify his employees of a possible closing. If my plan didn't work, he was going to follow through with his. And he owed it to his long-standing employees, most of whom were also friends, to warn them that their jobs might be eliminated. The ones who couldn't take that chance would have a jump start to find other employment.

Talking about the employees, Daddy started acting like he couldn't get comfortable in his chair and finally leaned forward to take several deep breaths.

"What's wrong? Are you okay?"

"I'm fine," he said, but his voice was strained. "It's just the pulse thing again. I can recognize it now, before it happens. I probably need to take a pill."

I told him to stay where he was and hurried to retrieve one.

"Don't bring me one of those tranquilizers," he called out. "Just one of the other ones. And don't go alarming your mamma, either."

When I returned with a pill and glass of water, he looked a little better but took the tablet anyway. Leaning back, he continued to breathe deeply until whatever was going on inside his body subsided.

"Quit watching me, for crying out loud."

"Okay. Just tell me you're feeling better."

"I'm feeling better."

Mamma came out to announce supper was ready and to see who wanted to pick up Jenny and the kids at the airport.

"Jenny's at the airport?" Daddy and I said in stereo.

"Apparently there was a fire on the set of *In Home Now*. Jenny and Cam were demonstrating some sort of a vacuum steamer cleaner thing, and as it turns out, the cleaning solution was flammable."

Daddy started laughing so loudly he woke Taffy up from one of her fifteen or so daily naps. She sashayed sleepily out of the house to investigate.

"She says they won't be doing any taping for at least a week, so she thought she'd come check up on you."

I found her at the luggage carousel, surrounded by a pile of bright yellow baggage. A skycap was in the process of loading it all onto a cart.

The twins each toted their own wheeled bag, and Hunter lugged Jenny's matching makeup case, carefully, as though it contained diamonds instead of mascara. My twin had probably lectured him on the important job he had, being the protector of the case. She'd rather lose a garment bag full of clothes than her makeup.

"Aunt Carly!"

Through the kids' hugs and chatter, I heard a familiar sound. It was Precious, growling from within the confines of a pet carrier as she was hoisted onto the cart with the rest of the luggage.

"I'm going to wait until we get outside to take her out," Jenny explained. "I wouldn't want her to run away."

"I would."

"What?"

"I said, 'that's good.'"

"Oh."

"Where's Stephen? And why *did* you bring the dog?"

"Stephen had a meeting with some of the sponsors, so he had to stay in Atlanta. But I couldn't leave my little Precious behind, could I? The girls would miss her!"

"No we wouldn't," the twins said in unison.

"We want a horse or maybe a pot-bellied pig," Sherry said.

The dog's growl, low and steady, only paused when it had to stop for a breath. The skycap made sure to keep his fingers well out of snapping distance.

"Or even a nice doggie, like Taffy," Stacy said.

"Taffy never growls," Sherry added. "Precious growls at her own poop."

My sister rolled her eyes and pulled a ten-dollar bill out of her purse for a tip.

"What are you doing back in Charleston?" she demanded in a low voice so the kids couldn't hear.

"Later," I mumbled back, picking up Hunter and getting whacked in the hip with her makeup case for my trouble. It was even heavier than it looked.

When we got home, Daddy took over as skycap, and Jenny demanded an update. I told her I'd much rather talk about the fire and asked if the cameras had been rolling at the time, because if so, I'd love to get a copy of the video. She glared at me, but she also stopped giving me the third degree.

Everyone situated themselves around the kitchen table to eat. Mamma served sweet potato biscuits and shrimp jambalaya, Jenny complained that flying first class wasn't what it use to be, and the twins thoroughly laid out their case as to why they should have a horse with the number-one reason being that horses whinnied and didn't ever growl.

Jenny was sensitive about the fire, since she'd been the one to insist that the show peddle the flammable vacuum against the advice of the *In Home Now* buyers, so Mamma and Daddy carefully avoided any subject of conversation that made reference to heat or flames.

"You know, I wouldn't mind going to a RiverDogs game one night," I said.

The Charleston RiverDogs were a minor-league affiliate of the Tampa Bay Devil Rays, and their baseball stadium sat on the banks of the scenic Ashley River.

"They are going to be *red hot* this year," I announced. "They've won every single game so far this season. I'm telling you, they are on *fire*."

"Bite me," Jenny said under her breath.

"Bite me! Bite me! Bite me!" Hunter said, exhibiting his uncanny ability to repeat any unsavory words that entered his virginal ears.

After a dessert of bread pudding with a sweet whiskey sauce, I cleaned the dishes, and my sister graciously offered to take out the garbage. Everyone, probably even the neighbors, heard her shriek.

She was back inside the house before Daddy could get up to investigate.

"There was raccoon under the lid! It jumped out at me! *Eeee-uuuow!*"

Mamma laughed. "You probably startled it more than it startled you."

Jenny, acting like she'd just had an encounter with a twenty-foot rattlesnake, was offended.

"It could have attacked me! It could have rabies or something!"

Precious let out a high-pitched bark that turned into a growl, as if backing up her owner's complaint.

"I doubt it," Mamma said. "If any of the raccoons had rabies, they'd be acting strange and coming out during the daytime. They never get into the garbage until after dark."

Jenny realized she wasn't going to get the sympathy she was seeking and changed the subject. To us, she was simply family. Not a celebrity. We weren't starstruck and weren't up to humoring her.

"Well, I want to know what the Aroma-magic Ionizer is doing in the trash! Answer me that!"

"It's not *in* the trash. It's *by* the trash," I told her. "It was supposed to keep the raccoons away."

"Well it's *obviously* not working!"

"Damn," Daddy said.

"Damn!" Hunter repeated. "Bite me damn!"

Mamma hushed him, explaining that some words were bad to say.

"I can't believe you did that," Jenny complained to Daddy. "It was a gift for you, to use inside. It wasn't meant to be outdoors."

"Granny put cod liver oil in the reservoir and it stunk," I told her. "We had to get it out of here."

Precious had fallen asleep on the kitchen floor, by the door that led to the back screened porch, and alternately snored and growled.

"I did that?" Granny said. "Lord only knows what I was thinking. It's hell to get old. And, what on earth is wrong with that poodle-dog?"

Granny was cognizant. I smiled at her. *Welcome back.*

"There's nothing wrong with my little Precious!" Jenny said. "She's probably just jet-lagged."

"I think your poodle-dog has issues. You might want to think about putting it down before it goes and takes a bite outta someone," Granny said seriously.

"Bite me!" Hunter cried happily.

"I'd never do that, Granny! And I'm telling you, there's nothing wrong with Precious."

Jenny put on a pouty expression, long enough for us all to get a good look at it. But nobody jumped to the defense of her dog.

"So why do the raccoons keep gettin' into the trash cans, anyhow?" Granny wanted to know.

"Because they're hungry, I suppose. They're looking for something to eat," Daddy said.

"Well then, why on earth don't you just feed them?"

Daddy harrumphed. It made sense. We cleared enough table scraps from supper plates each night to keep a few raccoons happy. And, as much as Daddy had been spending on deterrent gizmos, Granny's answer to the problem was cheaper, too.

Although Daddy was a straightforward kind of man, Granny often had him beat on sensibility. She'd been a schoolteacher before retirement, and her world had always been fundamental. When anyone found out she was a retired teacher, they would inevitably ask what she taught. Her answer never changed: "I taught *children*."

"I guess some solutions can be right in front of you the whole time," Daddy said.

17

What started out as a search for hats became an afternoon adventure. The twins were going to make their first appearance on *In Home Now* to demonstrate the Beach Buddy, a wagon-looking apparatus that tripled as an umbrella, table, and insulated cooler. For their debut, Jenny decided her girls should wear bright swimsuits and big-brimmed hats, so all the women in the household journeyed to Mamma and Daddy's attic in search of beachwear. Not wanting to be left out, Hunter and Taffy came, too. Fortunately, Precious was scared of stairs and chose to growl at us from the bottom of them.

When Stacy saw the piles of haphazardly stacked boxes, knickknacks and out-of-style clothes, all begging to be explored, examined, or tried on, her young eyes lit up. She wore the expression of a pirate on a treasure hunt. Sherry, not as enthused at the prospect of digging through dusty discards and sounding very adult, declared the attic needed a thorough cleaning out.

"Oh, good heavens, no!" Mamma said. "An attic is like a well-seasoned iron skillet: it should *never* be thoroughly cleaned out."

The seven of us—eight, counting Taffy—split up and rummaged through a cornucopia of the past. There were batons, roller skates, water skis, softball equipment, and other remnants of Mamma and Daddy's attempt at raising well-rounded children.

I came across my trumpet. It hadn't been used in a very long time, except by a tiny spider who found the three valves a suitable place to spin her web. The instrument had appeared thanks to sixth-grade musical aptitude testing implemented by an administrator whose brother-in-law owned a musical instrument business.

As it turned out, the trumpet hurt my lips, and, despite instruction from the band teacher, I never quite got the hang of making the proper seal while blowing into the mouthpiece. On several occasions, I almost passed out from hyperventilating. I had, in fact, found fault with a succession of instruments during my juvenile years. In addition to the brass trumpet, I found my tambourine and set of maracas. A guitar. A pair of cymbals. A flute. A xylophone. A drum set.

Daddy was a patient man.

While the time line of my extracurricular activities could be documented in abandoned musical instruments, Jenny's teenage time line consisted of apparel. Ballet shoes, dance attire. Theater props and costumes. Drill team paraphernalia. Several cheerleading outfits complete with a set of time-flattened pom-poms.

Granny discovered a trunk loaded with Halloween costumes that, packed in reverse order, became progressively smaller as we dug through them. The twins found matching tiger costumes of mine and Jenny's and, after a quick quarrel as to who got which one, put them on. Hunter wanted to get dressed up, too, but the only costume we could find in his size, other than a fairy princess getup, was a giant padded red delicious apple.

"Well at least now he can say 'bite me' and mean it," I told Jenny.

"You shouldn't be teaching my kids that kind of language," she said, fluffing a blue and white pom-pom. "Just wait until you have a kid of your own."

"You're the one that taught him 'bite me,'" I said.

"Basta!" Hunter added.

"Oh, right, and 'bastard,' too."

Jenny threw a pom-pom at me.

Two hours after our excursion for hats commenced, Granny wore a pair of Mickey Mouse ears and a black feather boa, and gripped a Ping-Pong paddle in each hand. The twins had assembled a pile of toys; I reclaimed the trumpet that had taken my musical virginity, and Jenny discovered a pair of white patent leather boots she felt sure would come back in style.

It didn't occur to anyone that we remained hatless until we'd carried our loot down the stairs and were dusting ourselves off.

As we debated a return trip, someone knocked at the back door.

The twins, still dressed as tigers and alternately roaring, ran to see who was there.

"It's Mister Protter," Stacy called, "and another Mister Protter."

"From Protter Construction and Development," Sherry yelled.

"Can they come in?" the girls said.

"Of course they can come in," Mamma said.

Hearing that two men were entering the house, Jenny made a dash for her makeup case and a mirror.

I was suddenly self-conscious, too, and didn't like the idea of facing my adversary in bare feet, a pair of cutoff jean shorts and one of Daddy's Stone Hardware T-shirts.

Despite my telepathic message to slam the door on the Protter men, the girls led them into to the kitchen.

When Trent saw me holding my trumpet defensively, as though it were a shield to deflect incoming arrows, amusement washed across his face. In explanation of our disheveled appearance, Mamma told the Protter men that we'd been romping around in the attic. As if to prove her point, Granny emerged from the bathroom to see who our gentlemen callers were.

"Ah," Mister Protter said. "That would explain the Mickey Mouse ears and feathers."

Mamma offered them a glass of iced tea, which to my irritation, they accepted.

And since they hadn't, I got right to the point of their visit.

"As you were so quick to remind me the other day, Trent, you are now the ones who seem to be trespassing. Is it something that couldn't be handled over the phone?"

Unfazed by my rashness, Trent smiled. "A mediator, a lawyer, and now a musician. You have multiple talents, Miss Stone."

"It was the first instrument I played growing up."

"First?" he said.

"There were several," I admitted.

"You, too?" Mister Protter nodded in the direction of his son. "This one here went through enough musical instruments to create an entire marching band."

In different circumstances, Trent and I would have laughed and compared youthful war stories. In different circumstances, I'd have thrown my arms up to hug the strong neck rather than suppressed an urge to strangle it.

Stop it! I silently scolded myself. Trent was the reason Daddy had made two trips to the emergency room.

Mamma filled tumblers with ice and poured sweet tea from a glass pitcher while Granny openly studied Trent.

"Have I met you before, dear?" she asked him.

"Yes, ma'am you did. And you liked me, too."

Satisfied, Granny turned her attention to Mister Protter. She still had the black feather boa around her neck and twirled one end of it. They got into a conversation about grandchildren, and Mister Protter told her he didn't yet have any grandchildren.

"Carly and Trent would make you a beautiful young'n, don't you know."

I almost choked on an ice cube, and had I been sure Granny was cogent, I'd have been mad. Even though she was probably right.

Trent acted like he hadn't heard her comment. "We stopped by your store earlier, but your father said we should just catch you here," he told me.

"Why would Daddy tell you that?"

"I suppose he figures I ought to deal directly with you and leave him out of it. Pop feels the same way. He's only along right now because we're headed to a heavy-equipment auction from here."

Like a late-arriving bird stirring up the rest of the flock, Jenny made a show of entering the kitchen. We moved chairs to make room at the table, Mamma retrieved another glass of ice for tea, and both Protter men half-stood while my sister settled into a chair.

After I introduced Mister Protter to those in my family he hadn't yet met, Trent told me why he'd stopped by. He wanted to deliver the test results in person.

It was my turn to be surprised. Only three days had passed since I had the cease and desist orders delivered to the offices of Protter Construction and Development. I wouldn't have thought they'd have found their own experts so quickly. Forcibly sidelining tractors apparently caused other things to get moving.

He produced a report and slid it across the table, upside down from his vantage point, so I could follow along while he explained it to me. I had made the same move frequently with my clients, and it proved that he'd thoroughly read the report and was familiar enough to point out paragraphs as he spoke.

There definitely was not a burial ground on the land, but then, I hadn't thought there was. Chief Hatcher didn't think so either, even though we'd found the mound of dirt. It wasn't the right shape, he'd said, but since Native American Indians roamed freely throughout South Carolina at one time, theoretically, there could be a burial ground most anywhere. If there was any possibility at all, he thought it best to investigate.

But soil testing conclusively found no human bones in the dirt. The archeologists could only produce some broken pieces of pottery estimated to be around two hundred years old.

I flipped through the four or five pages of the report until I came to the end. The last page was an invoice for eighteen hundred and fifty dollars. I mentally smiled. It was a start.

"Well, this is good news," I said. "Chief Hatcher will be relieved."

"I'm sure," Trent said, scowling at me.

"So, is there any news on the wall, yet? You don't seem to be wasting any time."

"We try not to waste time in the land development business. And, yes, there has been some progress made on plans for the piece of wall."

"Well?"

"Why don't you stop by the site tomorrow, say around noon, and I'll go over it with you."

He took a drink of tea, and my attention was drawn to his mouth. I imagined his full, strong lips would feel as smooth as they looked if pressed against mine. He put the glass down, swallowed, smiled. I had to force myself to look away and knew he'd caught me staring.

"I wouldn't want to *trespass*. Why not just tell me now?"

"I'm still working a few things out. And since I invited you to visit, you won't be trespassing. Didn't you learn that in law school?"

I stifled the urge to shoot him the finger.

"You're welcome to visit the site anytime, Carly," Mister Protter said.

Mamma called Daddy to see if he could come home for lunch, and he told her he could. To my dismay, she invited the Protter men to join us for barbecued chicken pizza, and to my horror, Mister Protter accepted.

Trent shot his father a questioning look at the same time I gave Mamma a "what-are-you-doing" look. Happy to have some men around, Jenny shot me a "shut up" look. Mamma, demanding politeness above all else, gave both of us a "behave" look. The twins gave each other an "it's-getting-juicy" look.

An awkward twenty minutes passed before Daddy got home, and Jenny and I served the pizza. Halfway through the meal, Mamma told Trent to call her "Doris" rather than "Mrs. Stone," and, appalled, I nearly spit up a piece of sun-dried tomato. *Didn't she understand these were the men who were causing Daddy so much grief? That they were putting our store out of business? The store that both her grandfather and Daddy had put their souls into?*

But Daddy didn't look upset either. He was being as cordial as Mamma.

I managed to get the half-chewed bite of food down without making a scene and sat back to assess the situation. Hunter had gravitated to Mister Protter and was happily perched on the old man's knee, eating off his plate. Mister Protter didn't appear to mind at all and had cut pizza into pieces small enough to accommodate Hunter's little hand.

Trent had started addressing Mamma as "Miss Doris" and Daddy as "Mister Lloyd." The twins had removed their tiger costumes and now acted like perfect little ladies, trying to impress our guests with a demonstration of proper dining etiquette. Even Taffy turned traitor and sprawled out lazily between Mister Protter's leather loafers and Trent's worn work boots. Precious was the only one acting normal. She kept her distance and growled at something invisible to the rest of us.

A ringing phone interrupted my disbelief.

"Can I hand you the telephone, Miss Doris?" Trent asked Mamma, and I wanted to throw up. I think I rolled my eyes.

To be polite, Mamma left the table to talk. She returned seconds later and asked me if I wanted to speak with Robert.

"What does he want?" I snapped, annoyed to hear his name.

"The snake wants you back, Carly," Granny said, as though she'd been clearly following my dilemma all along. "I'm tellin' ya. Get you a pair a them pruning shears . . . and chop, chop!"

18

Robert had indeed wanted me back. Corin was reuniting with her ex-husband and moving to Philadelphia. He admitted he was emotionally immature and had begun seeing a shrink. He would even attend marriage counseling. He swore I was the best thing that had ever happened to him, and if I came back, he would treat me like a queen. I hung up on him.

Although the phone conversation had happened yesterday, it stuck in my head like a bad radio jingle and kept replaying against my will. I forced it out of my mind and focused my attention on the gorgeous day as I drove to meet with Trent at the construction site.

Hunter was strapped into a child safety seat in the back, and Granny rode shotgun. A commanding entourage it wasn't, but they were the only family available to go with me. Mamma, Jenny, and the girls were shopping for the wide-brimmed hats for *In Home Now*, and Daddy was working.

"Pull over," Granny shouted. "There's a bird in this car! Sounds like a wren."

My purse was chirping.

"That's the new mobile phone Jenny gave me. It has forty different bird rings."

"That's a lot of dang birds to cram into one teeny phone."

I managed to silence the annoying wren without running off the road. It was Lori Anne.

"I thought you were off somewhere frolicking with Britt," I said.

"I am. In fact, we were thinking about running by the spa and microdermabrasioning each other. But I just had an epiphany."

"Lay it on me."

"Trent Protter. You need to come on to him a little. Turn that dazzling Stone smile on him. Get him sweet on you, so you'll have an edge."

I explained that I already had an edge and that I'd rather shave my head than come on to a prick like Trent.

"Prick!" Hunter said from the backseat.

"No, I'm a tellin' ya, it was a wren," Granny said.

"Look, Robert is the one who's a prick," Lori Anne said. "Trent is an incredibly gorgeous hunk of male who just happens to be on the opposite side of an issue."

"A crucial issue," I told her. "Thanks but no thanks." I pressed a button and the phone chirped itself off.

Three men stood by the construction trailer, talking. Two of them were the Protters, and the third was Daddy. While he was staying out of my battle with the Protters, he was curious about how my plan was progressing and must've walked across the street to see what was happening with the wall. Irritation over Daddy becoming chummy with the Protter men pricked at my skin. I didn't understand how he could act so objective about the threat they posed. But then, Southerners were nothing if not polite.

Or maybe it wasn't Southern etiquette at all. Maybe Daddy had already made up his mind about shutting down the store and was just humoring me and my plan to change the outcome.

Hunter's chubby hand held Granny's spotted one as we made our way toward the men. Without any small talk, the six of us walked to the crumbling stone and mortar wall. It didn't look like much. Of uneven width, it spanned a total distance of about twenty feet. Its highest point was less than six feet off the ground, but it appeared to have been much taller at one point. Strangely, nothing stood on either side of it. No remnants of a building or a chimney or anything indicative that the wall had been a part of something else. I wondered if it really was a piece of Charleston's city wall.

"It's a piece of the wall," Trent said. "They can tell by the artifacts they found around it, among other things."

I moved closer, and just the pressure of my hand on one of the larger stones caused it to tumble to the ground. I jumped out of the way to avoid a smashed toe, tripped over a mound of dirt and stumbled backward. Trent's hands were around my waist before I had a chance to completely lose my balance and fall. I wore a skirt and cropped blouse that fell just at my hip bones, but his hands went beneath the silk material to steady me. His skin felt smooth and callused and hot and cool all at the same time. Before my nerve endings could settle down and determine which sensation they were actually receiving, I regained my footing and Trent turned me loose.

"What's the matter?" Granny demanded, putting the back of her hand against my forehead. "Are you woozy? Did you get yourself knocked up and you're havin' one a them faintin' spells?"

"Good grief, Granny. Of course not."

"Damn skippy, you oughn't to wear a corset. It could hurt the baby."

"There is no baby!"

"The two a you's would've made a fine tot together," she clacked her dentures and strutted off, shaking her head at some imagined injustice.

Mister Protter and Daddy struggled to suppress their laughter, but Trent ignored Granny's comments about our imagined copulation. Because I needed something to do with my jumpy hands, I picked up Hunter and carried him on my hip as we walked back.

The trailer that doubled as a site office was clean, functional, and distinctly masculine. I deposited Hunter on a sofa and asked Granny to keep him out of trouble. The rest of us encircled the table that held the blueprints. The master plan lay on top, and I had to admit the center would be fabulous.

"Here's what we're going to do," Trent said, using the eraser tip of a yellow pencil as a pointer. "We will reinforce what remains of the wall, so it doesn't disintegrate any further. A decorative picket fence will be erected around it to keep kids from climbing on it. An oval walkway will go around the fence along, with benches and some nice landscaping. An information stand will go here," he pointed with the pencil, "that will tell people about the history of the wall."

"It will actually be a nice little area for shoppers to sit and relax," Mister Protter said. "So your discovery has worked out for the best, Carly. Building three will have to be moved slightly from where we originally intended it to go, so the plans will have to be redrawn. But no harm done. The historical society is going to give us a good citizen award."

"An award?" I repeated without meaning to.

"Yes. Some sort of appreciation thing," Mister Protter said. "We'll probably get a write-up in *The Post and Courier*. This is actually pretty big news among history buffs."

"So you were right after all, Carly," Trent said. "We're grateful you brought this matter to our attention."

I had an urge to slap the smug look off his face but smiled instead. I had a more professional way to remove it.

The good news was that the chunk of debris had turned out to be a piece of history. But the bad news was that it hadn't slowed the Protters down much, and they were going to come out looking like saints. I could already envision the headline: Local Construction and Development Company Preserves Charleston History. It would be great public relations.

But even though my wall plan had backfired, I still had ammunition. Daddy always said timing was everything when it came to getting what you wanted. And this was going to be impeccable timing. I couldn't wait to deliver the news.

"So the tractors will start rolling soon?" I said.

Trent nodded. "Tomorrow."

I retrieved an envelope from Granny's handbag. "Well, then, I'd better give you this to keep your boys on break a little longer."

Mister Protter's eyebrows rose simultaneously with Daddy's.

Trent's eyes darkened, and his words were stiff. "Why don't you just tell me what's in there, Carly."

"I'd be happy to save you some time. Woodpeckers. You've got some."

"So?"

"Red-cockaded woodpeckers. They're an endangered species. It's illegal to disturb a nesting area. And guess what?"

"Do tell," Trent said through clenched teeth. His father looked thoughtful, almost amused. Daddy was slowly shaking his head.

"My ornithologist has located three active red-cockaded woodpecker homes," I picked up a pencil to use as a pointer and paused with enough dramatic effect that would have made even Jenny proud, "right here. Just outside the footprint of building number three, in this parking area."

"Jesus Christ."

"They just love the seventy- and eighty-year-old longleaf pines."

His nostrils flared as he inhaled through his nose, lips pressed tightly together to prevent the nasty thoughts in his brain from emerging as words. He looked at his father, who only raised an eyebrow. He looked at Daddy, who made a near-identical motion, but added a shoulder shrug.

Trent was furious. "This is a bunch of crap! Another stalling tactic. Whatever nests you've found could belong to any kind of woodpeckers."

"Crap!" Hunter said, but everyone was so engrossed in the drama that nobody bothered to hush him. "Crap!" he said, trying again.

"No they can't," I rebutted. "You see, the red-cockaded is the only woodpecker on earth that carves a home out of the trunk of a living tree, and just pecking away long enough to reach the heartwood of the pine, where they make their hole, takes *years*. And, once they've got their hole, they come back to the same tree year after year."

"Crap!" Hunter said. This time Granny hushed him by tweaking his ear.

"Besides, the ornithologist got some great pictures last week with a telephoto lens. Luckily, we're in the peak nesting season right now."

Trent looked like he wanted to hit something.

"We're familiar with the endangered bird," Mister Protter said. "But we've not encountered any so far. Don't they typically nest in undeveloped areas of a couple hundred acres or more? This plat is only sixty-two acres."

"You're right," I told him. "But since Hurricane Hugo hit in 'eighty-nine and destroyed a lot of their nesting trees, the birds have been doing unusual things, just trying to survive. And you've got three families of them."

"What does this mean?" Trent demanded. "What's the bottom line?"

He was a bottom-line kind of person, too. Like me.

"It means the trees have been marked with white circles, and you can't cut them down. In fact, you're not allowed to develop within several hundred yards of an active red-cockaded woodpecker habitat. To do so would be a state and federal offense."

"Isn't there a relocation program for the birds?" Mister Protter asked. "Where they move them to the Francis Marion National Forest?"

I explained that they did have some options, but even if their birds were eligible for relocation by the Department of Natural Resources and the Fish and Wildlife Service, it could take several months to do so. The information caused the jaw muscles in Trent's magnificent face to start working.

"You're gonna blow out a vein or something, you keep a doin' that," Granny told him. "Now at our house, we keep this oily machine running to keep everybody relaxed. Don't work on the coons, though."

I dropped the envelope on top of the master plan, kissed Daddy good-bye just for show, collected Granny and Hunter, and left. Closing the door behind me, I heard Mister Protter's confused voice.

"Oily machine?"

19

"Boy, he sure is a looker, that man," Granny said. "Just downright handsome."

We were walking along the aisles of the old City Market in the historic district, where vendors hawked goods ranging from benne wafers and dried-bean soups to handmade jewelry and artwork in their distinctly Southern, laid-back way.

I stopped to sample a praline-coated pecan and sighed. If Trent wasn't so gorgeous, it would be easier to hate him.

"That he is," I agreed.

"Polite," Granny continued. "And he wears good shoes. A good man knows how to wear good shoes."

"Good shoes?"

I hadn't seen Trent in anything other than scuffed-up work boots.

"And that head of silver hair," Granny said thoughtfully. "My fingers could get lost in that hair."

"Silver hair?" She was having a sweet moment of lucidity, and I was the confused one.

"Your granddaddy had hair like that."

It finally dawned on me that she was talking about Trent's father.

"The bad thing is, I probably won't remember who he is next time I see him," Granny said.

"Maybe," I said. "But you know what? He'll be just as handsome. And you'll get to discover him all over again."

"I hadn't thought about it that way," she said thoughtfully. "I guess there're some advantages to gettin' forgetful. Why, I can go and entertain myself for hours with a single picture album. By the time I'm back to the first page, I've forgotten that I already done saw those photographs!"

"If something makes you angry, you don't stay mad for very long," I added.

Granny laughed. "True. And I never complain about a TV show bein' a rerun."

"I love you, Granny. You're the best," I told her.

She gave my hand a squeeze. "And, speakin' of hair, what in God's name happened to mine?"

"We went to Lori Anne's spa and she gave you a color rinse."

Granny fluffed her hair. "How does it look?"

"You look beautiful as a redhead," I said.

"Did she give me these striped fingernails, too?"

I nodded. "They're all the rage."

We were shopping for a thank-you gift for Cheryl, who had proved to be a true friend. She'd handled all the details of putting my house on the market for sale and had been emailing me regular updates of both news and gossip. My boss at the firm was not at all happy that I'd quit without notice. I regretted that, but there was nothing else I could have done. Robert disappeared, but she wasn't sure where he was living. His mail was being forwarded to a post office box, and although he was furious that his clothes were gone, he hadn't raised any objections to the house being sold. I'd never changed the title to include his name after we married, so he didn't have any grounds to complain. Besides, since I was selling it so soon after buying it, I wasn't going to make any money on the deal. I'd be lucky to get back all the money I'd used as a down payment.

We came across a display of sweetgrass baskets and decided that Cheryl would love one. An art form originally brought to Charleston by slaves from West Africa some three hundred years ago, the skill had been passed down through the generations, from mothers to daughters. The grass grew wild in marshy habitats and once dried, gave off a vanillalike fragrance. I chose a beautiful oval basket that would be perfect for the kitchen, and Granny found a similar one that she bought for Mamma.

"If I forget, remind me I got this basket for your mamma."

We decided to take a tour around the historic district and

climbed into a roomy wooden replica of a classic carriage, pulled by two magnificent black percheron draft horses.

Enjoying the day with Granny, I was reminded why I loved my hometown. I loved the old-world atmosphere, the narrow streets, the people-filled sidewalks, the award-winning gardens tucked away at every turn and the multicolored historic buildings with their blooming window boxes. And I loved that, in Charleston, people didn't live by their watches and thought nothing of stopping at a street corner to chat.

The sound of hooves clopping on the road was comforting, and I let my body move with the swaying of the carriage. Now that I was back, I couldn't imagine living anywhere else. For that matter, I couldn't believe I'd ever moved to New York. A Charlestonian doesn't belong in a place where people honk their horns to vent frustration in traffic, or a place where it snows.

"You know, his boy is right handsome, too," Granny said from our perch atop the wooden bench seat. "You might should give some thought to courting him."

"Date Trent? You can't be serious. You sound like Lori Anne."

"He's from much better stock than that one you married. I can tell just by looking at his father."

"That may be, but you're forgetting that Trent is the enemy," I said, exasperated. "It's *his* company that is building the development with the Handyman's Depot! If my plan to stall them into submission doesn't work, Stone Hardware and Home Supply will be shut down!"

"Would you be angry if you saw an eagle swoop down and catch a baby rabbit?"

"No," I said, knowing where she was going. "I'd be sad for the bunny rabbit, but that's just what eagles do. They hunt to survive."

Granny eyes were bright, and I imagined it was the same expression she used to have when teaching children. "Exactly."

"It's not the same thing," I argued.

"The heck it's not. You can't blame the Protters for doing what they do to keep their business alive. Same way you oughtn't to blame the eagle for killin' the rabbit."

"So, you don't care if Daddy's store is forced to close?"

"Don't tangle up my words! Of course I don't want the store to shut down, 'cause I know how much your daddy enjoys running it. All's I'm saying is, you ought not to put down the Protters. What you should be puttin' your mind to is going after that man before he gets away. Ones like him don't come 'round all that often."

"I despise Trent Protter. Besides, I'm not even close to being divorced from Robert yet. The law dictates a mandatory waiting period."

"Psshaw. That'll work itself out."

We talked above love and valor and the virtues of a good man. Granny spoke of what Grandpa was like when they first met but forgot what she was saying and suddenly declared she was hungry.

Looking at the sweetgrass baskets we'd purchased reminded me of SNOB, because they served fresh bread to every table in a handmade sweetgrass basket. Since we were the only two in his carriage, the driver agreed to drop us there, and I tipped him well.

"Did you just call that nice man a snob?" Granny said, after we'd climbed out.

I laughed. "No, SNOB is a restaurant. Since you're hungry, I thought it would be a great place to get something to eat."

Housed on the bottom floor of what was once a cotton gin warehouse, Slightly North of Broad was one of my favorite places to eat seafood in Charleston, and I didn't need a special occasion to go there. The name was also a dare to the more well-heeled Charlestonians who normally never crossed over to the north side of Broad Street. That was reason enough in my book to visit as often as possible.

A jovial crowd greeted us, and we were seated at a table with a view of both the open kitchen and East Bay Street. Johnny Cash's "Rowboat" flowed through the speakers, which meant that Chef Frank Lee was there. A native South Carolinian with classic French training and eclectic tastes, he was a huge Johnny Cash fan. Since he was also one of the owners, he could listen to whatever he wanted to.

The server welcomed us to SNOB and took drink orders.

"Did she just call you a snob?" Granny said. "Young'ns today don't have the manners they should!"

We shared an order of barbecued tuna topped with fried oysters and talked more about the virtues of a good man. I decided that, whatever Trent's virtues were, his despicable occupation far outweighed them.

20

The glamorous woman that returned my gaze from the full-length mirror was barely recognizable, and I had to admit my sister was a fashion virtuoso. A few days earlier, we'd done some power shopping for clothes and shoes. And this morning, we'd decadently indulged ourselves at Lori Anne's spa. We looked fabulous.

My solid-black sleeveless long gown demanded attention. Its neckline plunged to a point that would have looked tacky on a shorter dress, the silky fabric had a side slit that stretched to my upper thigh, and the design was completely backless from my waist up. My hair was pulled up into a twist on top of my head and piled into loose curls that barely touched my shoulders. Jenny finished my look with sheer black stockings, high-heeled black satin pumps, and a pair of outrageously large diamond stud earrings she'd loaned me for the night.

She wore a clingy sequined floor-length gown the color of sparkling white sand. Between the two of us, some heads would definitely turn.

We were going with Mamma and Daddy to a formal ball in the grand ballroom at the Mills House Hotel, a fund-raiser for the Historic Charleston Foundation, where there would be a meal of traditional low-country cuisine, a silent auction, and live music by the Frank Duvall Jazz Trio. Even if the wall discovery hadn't slowed down the Protters much, I owed the foundation. Plus, I hadn't been to a black-tie event in years and was thoroughly enjoying playing dress-up with Jenny.

When Daddy saw the two of us, he let out a slow whistle.

"I will be the most envied man at the ball," he declared, adjusting his bow tie. "I'm escorting not just one, but three beautiful women!"

"Why, thank you, sweetheart," Mamma said, giving him a kiss.

She wore an elegant royal blue gown that fit her body snugly to the knees before flaring whimsically at the bottom. She was radiant.

"I just hope people aren't going to want autographs or come up and ask me about some silly product," Jenny said, studying the tip of a freshly painted crimson pinky fingernail. "I'm not in the mood."

"You've been in Atlanta too long," Mamma told her. "Folks around here are too polite for that. They'll respect your privacy."

"Why would folks want your autograph?" Granny asked bluntly.

"Because a lot of people watch me on television," Jenny explained.

"Not me," Granny said.

"Not me!" Hunter said gleefully.

Jenny tried to decide whether or not she should be insulted by the comments of an old woman and a toddler. I was going to help make up her mind by adding that I didn't watch her show either but was silenced by a look from Mamma.

"The babysitter's here," the twins called, somehow detecting the doorbell that even Taffy had missed.

"I hope she lets us stay up really late, if we promise not to tell," Stacy said.

"I hope she lets us eat huge bowls of strawberry ice cream!" Sherry said.

"Ten o'clock is bedtime, and you'd better both be under the covers by then," Jenny said. "And don't let Hunter use the Krazy Kids toothpaste tonight, you hear?"

Jenny was testing bubblegum-flavored toothpaste that had the consistency and sugar content of corn syrup. It was part of the Krazy Kids Clean Case, a new item designed to encourage good hygiene in children. Unfortunately, the fluoride content could become toxic in large amounts if children liked it so much that they were eating it. *In Home Now*'s health advisor advised the producers not to carry it unless the manufacturer reduced the sugar content to make it less tasty.

"Well, it does taste pretty good, Mama," Sherry said.

"I bet it would be good with peanut butter," Stacy said.

"You mean that tube of candy you keep hidin' in the bathroom?" Granny asked. "I've a right mind to try it on top of some ice cream."

"Good grief," Jenny said, sounding exactly like Mamma when she got exasperated. "Everyone knows you're supposed to spit toothpaste out, not *eat* it!"

Daddy led the babysitter into the house, and after thoroughly briefing her about bedtimes and emergency phone numbers and the growling poodle, and Granny's penchant for blurting odd commentary, we piled into Mamma's Cadillac, leaving behind an aromatic trail of perfume, cologne, and hair spray.

At Jenny's insistence, we arrived after the appointed cocktail hour had begun, and the ballroom was pleasantly filled with beautiful people engaged in animated conversations. Mamma and Daddy melted gracefully into the crowd, and observing them from the sidelines, I couldn't imagine any two people belonging together more than they did.

Because Jenny and I had grown up in Charleston, a lot of people at the fund-raiser watched *In Home Now*, and my sister was a local celebrity. As we moved about the room, handshakes and hugs greeted us, but nobody whipped out a pen and asked Jenny for her autograph.

"Daddy told them when he bought our tickets that he didn't want anyone pestering you," I lied to console her.

"I should have known," she said. "Stephen always runs interference for me, too."

"Jenny Stone!" a woman finally said with unconcealed enthusiasm. "I heard you were in town! You look absolutely stunning. Does that firming cream made from foreskin really work as well as everyone claims?"

My sister breathed a sigh of contentment, and the two of them disappeared to discuss the wonders of technology in cosmetics.

"Who would want to rub foreskin on her face?" I mumbled to myself, snatching a flute of champagne from a passing tray. "How disgusting."

"The champagne?" a voice behind me asked with amusement.

My heart did a tap dance inside my chest. The voice belonged to Trent.

I turned around to see a gloriously outfitted man: a model who had just walked off the set of a catalogue shoot in a custom-fitted black tuxedo, white pleated shirt, French cuffs with single-stud onyx cufflinks, satin bowtie, and black patent leather shoes that had replaced the muddy leather work boots. I took it in all at once—the clothes, the body, the amused, strikingly blue eyes—and tried to look disinterested.

"No, not the champagne. The foreskin stuff," I said. "They manufacture this face cream from the original foreskin cells of a circumcised baby boy. It has growth factors in it and costs around four hundred dollars a bottle."

He raised an eyebrow at me. "No kidding."

I shrugged and took a sip of champagne. "Women can't get enough of the stuff from *In Home Now*. Or so Jenny says."

Pretending to look for someone, I turned away from the captivating sight of him and forced myself not to think about his body part that, at one time, had a foreskin. I could feel his eyes taking in my fully exposed back and a shiver ran the length of my spine as though he'd physically touched me.

"Are you here with friends?" he asked. "Historians? Native American Indian chiefs? An ornithologist, perhaps?"

I spun back to face him, regaining my senses. Regardless of how good he looked, I hated him.

"No, just my sister. And Mamma and Daddy. You know, the ones you're putting out of business?"

He took the champagne flute from my hand and set it on a nearby table.

"Dance with me."

"What?" I said.

"The band has started playing. Dance with me."

"Why would I want to dance with you?"

"Because I hate coming to these things. And dancing with you will give me something else to think about besides how much I'd rather not be here."

"Wouldn't it be easier to just leave?" I asked.

"Touché," he said good-naturedly. "It would be easier, although not as pleasurable as a dance with you. Pop insists on coming to these charity things. He says they're great for community relations and networking."

I retrieved my glass of champagne and downed it. "Especially for an organization that's giving you an *award* for preserving a piece of wall."

The band was pumping out Glenn Miller's classic big-band tune "In the Mood," and the swanky beat reverberated through my rib cage.

"A piece of wall that you found." He took my empty flute and set it back on the table. "Now that you've finished your champagne, will you dance with me?"

"No," I said. "I don't want to dance with you. Frankly, I can't stand you."

Before I could walk away, he caught my bare arm, stopping me. His hand was refreshingly cool, like the flip side of a bed pillow on a sweltering July night. It slid along the inside of my forearm until it found my fingers, and suddenly we were holding hands and I was forced to look into the indigo eyes that were fixed on mine.

"Just one dance, Carly. A simple dance for the sake of politeness among acquaintances. It's what you're supposed to do at these things. Besides, you don't want to let the ballroom dancing lessons Pop made me take when I was twelve go to waste, do you?"

He had a commanding presence and people moved out of our way as he led me to the dance floor. And when one of his hands found the sensitive spot at the base of my exposed spine and his other hand gripped mine palm to palm, a single, explosive shiver formulated at my midsection and traveled in every direction as we moved together in orchestrated circles around the open floor.

He danced with the ease of a seasoned expert, and I followed his lead without thinking about where my feet were landing. Couples around us dissipated into nothingness and neurons in my brain fired impulses at lightning speed.

He spun me away from him and, keeping a firm grip on my hand, pulled me back to his chest on the exact drumbeat that ended the song. With barely a pause, the band members smoothly transitioned into another song. A slow song, accompanied by a sultry female vocalist. I moved away from Trent, but he pulled me back against him.

"One more," he said, and I didn't have the willpower to resist. I thought of Lori Anne's "epiphany." Her advice to flirt with the enemy. I didn't know if dancing constituted flirting, or if anything was being gained. But for a few minutes, I didn't care.

The electrical impulses that had inflamed my nerve endings slowed during the second dance until I felt nothing but the sensation of my body pressing lightly against his. The music was loud, but I didn't hear it. The air was cool on my bare back, but I didn't feel it. Three inches of high, spiky heels elevated me to the point where my chin fit perfectly into the warm notch at his collarbone. I imagined exploring the sweet spot on the side of his neck and wondered what his skin would taste like. I wasn't sure if an hour or a minute passed, but when I opened my eyes the song had ended and Trent was smiling at me.

"See? That wasn't so bad, was it? Just one simple little dance."

"It was two dances. And it was awful. I'm going to go find an ornithologist or historian to talk to."

He laughed, just once, making me want to hear the sound again.

"My God, you're beautiful," he said quietly, and the words emerged as an afterthought he hadn't intended on verbalizing.

An awkward moment passed before we decided we were thirsty and maneuvered through the crowd in search of a bar. Before we found one, we came across Daddy talking to Mister Protter in what appeared to be a heated conversation. I could tell by his stance that Trent's father was agitated. Both men stopped in midconversation when we approached.

"Why, you're looking quite beautiful tonight, Carly," Mister Protter said.

"You clean up pretty well yourself."

"What's going on, Pop?" Trent asked, skipping the pleasantries.

"Jack just got here and delivered some news," his father said evenly. "But it's nothing we need to discuss right now."

"Who's Jack?" I asked.

"Our company attorney," Trent answered. "You've spoken with him on the phone before. He'll be at our table for dinner."

"Oh, *that* Jack," I said sarcastically. "Of course you'd bring your attorney to a social function. You just never know when you might need emergency legal counsel."

A man walked up behind me, chuckling, and introduced himself. It was Jack. He'd overhead my comment and assured me that he was at the charity ball purely in a social capacity. We chatted for a moment, and I found myself liking the man, despite his choice of clients.

"What's the news, Jack?" Trent said.

Jack shook his head to tell Trent that he'd rather talk in private, but Trent didn't give up that easily. "Pop? Tell me what's going on."

Mister Protter sighed and lowered his voice. "We just got word that one of the anchor stores will have to be scaled down in size. It just so happens that it's the west corner. Handyman's spot."

"That won't work," Trent thought aloud. "They have a minimum-size requirement. We'll be in breach of our contract with them."

"Well, we can leave the square footage as it is, but move the west corner anchor into the parking area. But then, we'd have to buy some adjacent land, if it's available. We can't move it in the other direction because of the wetlands. Or, we could add a parking garage."

"But do people really want to park in a garage when they're hauling building supplies or a new washing machine back to their truck?" Jack said. "This could get ugly."

Trent's gaze grew volatile enough to pierce a hole through me, although his single-word question was directed to Jack. "Why?"

"The woodpeckers. I found out they don't qualify for translocation right now. And even if we can convince the U.S. Fish and Wildlife Department to move the birds, we'd still have to wait until after the nesting season. That's more than two months away."

Trent's eyes never left my face as he absorbed the news and took a deep breath to control his anger.

Staring back at him, I tried not to gloat. While I wasn't normally happy about someone else's misfortune, I was elated for Daddy. If Handyman's Depot had to find another location, his store could stay open and it would be business as usual.

"Are you happy now, Carly? Is this what you hoped to accomplish with your childish games?"

"Yes."

He took a step toward me, nostrils flaring. "So you'll stay the hell out of my life, then?"

Daddy stepped in before tempers could escalate further. "Look here now, son. Carly didn't put the birds there. A law is a law, and it's not her fault that some endangered woodpeckers decided to make a home on your piece of land. Perhaps you should have done a more thorough inspection of the acreage before you bought it."

Trent's mouth tightened, and without another word, he shook his head in disgust and walked away. Mister Protter apologized for his son's rudeness and explained that eliminating an anchor store from the original plan would not only create some major problems with the other tenants but it would also cost his company a lot of money.

I couldn't say I was sorry for the situation, so I excused myself to get a cocktail. Jack walked with me, and asked how long I planned to stay in Charleston. Forever, I told him. It was my home. He told me that it was his home, too, and we agreed that neither of us wanted to live anywhere else. We stood in the line at the bar, chatting like friends, and I was surprised to find that we shared several common interests. And, despite the problems I'd created for his client, Jack was cordial. When we got our drinks, he told me that it was nice to meet me, and gave me a fatherly pat on the shoulder along with a handshake before leaving to find Trent.

Sipping my dry vodka martini, I noticed that Daddy and Mister Protter remained huddled in conversation while the joviality commenced around them. From a distance, they appeared to be friends rather than adversaries.

Like Jack, maybe they were taking things in stride. Business was business. But Jack's announcement had certainly cemented the rivalry between me and Trent. There would be no more spins around the dance floor for us.

Half an hour and two martinis later, my family joined the two hundred people who sat down to eat an exquisite meal of cucumber salad and she-crab soup followed by a pork and shrimp dish with a lemon-ginger sauce, served with rice. Aside from the rich ambiance and Victorian styling, the best thing about having a function at the

Mills House was that the chef custom-designed a menu for each group. The delicious food was followed by obligatory speeches of thanks and recognition from the Historic Charleston Foundation.

Although there were numerous linen-covered tables spread about, we were just a few tables away from the Protters. Though it was beyond eavesdropping distance, I had a clear view and couldn't help but notice that Trent, his father, and Jack left together immediately after they ate. The rest of their guests remained at the table to see the outcome of the silent auction and hear some more jazz. But the Protter men hadn't even waited for their key lime cheesecake.

Although I'd just finished a fabulous three-course meal, I felt strangely empty as I watched couples migrate to the dance floor when the band resumed playing.

By the time the charity ball wound down, Mamma had been the high bidder for a beautiful oil painting of the coastal wetlands by local artist Betty Anglin Smith, Jenny had managed to sign several autographs, and I'd gracefully sidestepped eight or ten inquiries as to the status of my husband and job and life in New York.

21

I thought the ringing phone and Daddy's voice and the *click-click* of Taffy's nails on the hardwood floor was just commotion in my dreams until a knocking on the bedroom door forced my consciousness into the present.

"Carly?" Mamma said. Wrapped in a satin robe, she was a silhouette in the doorway. "Honey, are you awake?"

I looked at the digital readout on my nightstand. It was not quite five o'clock in the morning, and it seemed as though I had just gone to bed. The sensation of gliding around the dance floor with Trent, feeling like a princess, remained fresh in my memory.

"What's going on?" I pushed the covers back and rolled over.

"There was an explosion and now there's a big fire! The land across from our store. Your daddy has already headed over there."

I sat up in bed. "A fire? At the Protter development?"

"Yes." Worry filled her voice. "And because it's been so dry, all the underbrush is catching fire. Plus it's gotten windy and your daddy is worried that the fire could jump the road. They're wetting down our store, just in case."

I was instantly alert and out of bed. "Is anyone hurt?"

"Not that we know of."

"How did it happen?"

"We don't know. Chief Jim, the fire chief, just called. He said it could have been some smoldering coals that weren't completely out from where the workers burned some brush. Or someone could have thrown down a lit cigar or cigarette butt."

I pulled on a pair of blue jeans, deck shoes, and sweatshirt, not bothering to look for a bra or a hairbrush. "That doesn't make sense. Why would somebody be walking around at five o'clock in the morning, in the dark, smoking a cigarette? And what caused the explosion?"

"I don't know why somebody would be out there, but Chief Jim said the fuel truck caused the explosion."

"Fuel truck?"

"I asked the same thing. Your daddy said they often keep a small fuel truck at construction sites to refill the tanks on the tractors and equipment. So, the diesel in this one spilled to the ground and caught fire. Chief Jim said not to repeat this, but he thinks it was intentional."

"Arson?" I asked, grabbing my car keys off the dresser.

"It doesn't make sense," Mamma said, shaking her head. "There's nothing there except a construction trailer, and the fire hasn't gotten to it yet. Who would want to burn up a piece of land that's going to be cleared anyway?"

Trent Protter would, if he could make it look like an accident.

"Somebody who had something to gain by destroying trees," I answered.

"Give me a minute to get dressed," Mamma said. "Jenny can stay here with the kids and your granny. I'm going with you."

Approaching the store, we could see flashing red and blue lights at about the same time a huge cloud of smoke became visible in the first glimmers of daylight as the sun prepared to rise over the awakening city of Charleston.

We talked our way through a roadblock and found Daddy standing in a puddle of water in front of Stone Hardware and Home Supply, watching the turmoil across the street. Two massive fire trucks and ten or fifteen men in firefighting gear milled about while a couple of police cruisers kept the roads clear and an ambulance remained on standby in case of injuries. The smell of burning timber, pine needles, and scorched earth swirled in gusts around us, but the fire hadn't managed to cross the pavement that separated it from Mamma and Daddy's business.

We watched the organized efforts of the firefighters and listened to the orchestra of sounds that an assault on nature makes and breathed the bonfirelike odor until dawn gave way to early morning.

Although the fire appeared to be under control by the time we left, an angry concentration of yellow and orange flames kept flaring up in one area, where the fuel truck had been emptied. It was the west corner of the plat. The same spot where some red-cockaded woodpeckers had made their homes in the trunks of eighty-year-old longleaf pines.

"They found a body," Daddy told me after I'd served him and the fire chief a cup of coffee on the back porch.

It was early afternoon, and the morning's fire was still fresh in my mind, but hearing a person had died made my heart stop. My first panicky thought was that it might be Trent.

"It wasn't Trent," Daddy added quickly, reading my mind. "It was a man, but they don't know who yet. Possibly one of the construction workers."

"I just didn't want ya'll to learn about it on tonight's news," Chief Jim told me.

Stunned, I sat down.

Sensing dramatic news, Mamma and Jenny joined us. Taffy followed them, and the kids followed her. My family jockeyed for a position around the fire chief and settled in, crowding the otherwise roomy porch.

"I want ya'll to know that what I say goes no further than this, because the limited version of events the press gets will be much different."

"Different how?" Jenny asked.

"I'm telling you what I think. We only tell the press what we know."

We all nodded our agreement. Precious growled. Jenny picked the dog up and deposited it in her lap, which reduced the growling to something intermittent that sounded like canine belches.

"What's wrong with that dog?" Chief Jim asked.

"It has bipolar disorder," I said.

"She does not! There's nothing wrong with my little Precious," Jenny said.

"It growls," Sherry said.

"At everything," Stacy finished.

"Even its own poop," Sherry added.

"Poop!" Hunter said.

Mamma hushed everyone with a single wide-angle look.

Chief Jim explained that after the flare-up spot fire burned itself out, an investigator found the charred remains of a man by a cluster of trees.

He told us the burn patterns indicated the fire was intentionally set. Plus, it looked like somebody had broken the lock off the fuel truck, opened a valve, and let the diesel flow. What's more, they found some empty toluene containers around the cluster of trees making him think that, in addition to dumping the fuel, somebody had carried a flammable chemical to the area where the man was found. Perhaps to set fire to the underbrush around him. If evidence showed the dead man was not the arsonist, then a murder charge could be pending against whoever set the fire.

"This is unbelievable! First there's a fire on my set," my sister said, thinking everything revolved around her world, "and now there's a fire here."

We chatted into lunchtime, and the conversation migrated toward who could have done it. While I couldn't fathom Trent to be a murderer, I fully believed he had to be behind the fire. He'd been furious about the woodpeckers and left the charity ball early. Then the fire had mysteriously erupted hours later. And it just so happened the toluene containers had been found near the nesting birds. The bottom line was that, without the birds, there would be no violation, and Protter's project could proceed as planned. I guessed that Trent put one of his employees up to starting the fire, and the man had gotten himself killed in the process. I doubted that Trent actually lit the fire himself, because he wouldn't have been so careless as to leave the toluene containers behind.

I felt sick to my stomach, wondering how I could have enjoyed dancing with a man who would do such a thing. A man who put making a profit above the law, above endangered wildlife and above an employee's safety. Mamma took the kids into the kitchen to help her make sandwiches, and I explained my theory to the fire chief.

"So the plan backfired," I concluded. "The fire was to destroy the birds and make it look accidental. Or maybe make it look like vandalism. But those toluene containers you found by the dead man?"

"Yes?"

"That flammable solvent wasn't carried there to pour on the brush around the dead man. It was used to pour into the cavities where the woodpeckers make their nests, in the trunks of the trees. To burn them out, even if the trees didn't actually catch fire. I'm sure of it. Ask the investigators to collect samples of wood around the nesting cavities, because I'll bet they find residual toluene. They should look for a small hole in the trunk, about fifteen feet up. My ornithologist can help them locate the cavities."

He made some notes in a small spiral notepad. "It sounds a bit far-fetched, but okay. We'll check it out."

"I don't think it's far-fetched. Somebody burned out the birds so the development can go ahead as planned," I said. "But, if you prove the fire was arson, that's not going to happen, right?"

"Well, theoretically, there's nothing to stop the development from moving forward, unless criminal charges are brought up against the landowner. And criminal charges won't be filed unless we can prove arson."

Daddy sighed. "And, even that wouldn't prevent the development from happening. Chances are, Protter would just take their losses and sell to another developer. The new developer would go ahead with the existing plans and honor all pending tenant agreements."

"But that's not right. The Protters break the law by setting fire to their land and get off without even a slap on the hand? Who else besides Trent Protter had a motive?"

"Well, Carly," Chief Jim said slowly, "after listening to everything you've told me, any number of people could be a suspect, including you."

"Me? That's crazy!"

"Carly would never break the law!" Jenny jumped to my defense. "She doesn't even break the posted speed limit!"

"She's been fighting the Protters," the chief said. "Trying to stop the development. So she certainly had motive to set 'em up and make it look like they did it."

"Not to be disrespectful, Chief," I said, "but that's ridiculous. It's true I hate the Protters, but I would never resort to arson. Or murder. Good grief."

"My point is, in a situation like this, there's always a slew of suspects."

I looked at Daddy, and he was nodding. He'd known where Chief Jim was going with the conversation all along. It's why he hadn't jumped to my defense along with Jenny.

"We add 'em to the list as new information becomes available," the fire chief continued, "and remove 'em by process of elimination. Your theory about Trent Protter is reasonable, I reckon, but I wouldn't jump to any conclusions."

Daddy agreed with his assessment. "Arson and destroying an endangered species are both serious offenses with serious penalties, little girl. Not to mention murder or involuntary manslaughter. As much as our business philosophies differ, the Protter men are good people."

"I don't know what'll become of the development," Chief Jim said. "But my department has seasoned investigators, and we'll do our damnedest to find out what went on that night."

"And you," he told Jenny, "need to sign on a safety coordinator for your TV program."

Properly reprimanded, my sister and I thanked the fire chief for his advice before everyone gathered around the kitchen table for grilled cheese sandwiches. Nobody ate much.

22

"I didn't have anything to do with the fire, Carly," Trent said. "My immediate concern right now is to find out who did. I need to know how one of my men ended up dead."

The charred body retrieved from the debris belonged to Jerry Stillwell, one of Protter's heavy-equipment operators. And while Trent presented a strong front on the surface, he appeared genuinely distressed by the man's death. Nevertheless, I wondered if he knew more than he was telling me.

We were having a late lunch on the rooftop terrace of the Vendue Inn in the historic French Quarter. From our table, we had an incredible view of the city with its trademark church steeples and could see a slice of the nearby harbor.

Lunch was my idea. Prodded by Lori Anne, I'd called Trent to ask if he would meet me to discuss a few things. I wanted to get him away from the construction site for an hour or so. I wanted to feel him out, with hopes that I'd learn something to use against him. Jenny accused me of playing Nancy Drew, but Lori Anne told her I could get more information out of him than the fire chief could.

Trent was hesitant but agreeable, and suggested his favorite Charleston lunch spot. I didn't tell him the rooftop terrace was one of my favorites, too.

I could smell thriving estuary life in the breeze and knew from the fertile scent that it was low tide. People who didn't know always marveled at how those of us who lived on the South Carolina coast could tell whether it was high or low tide simply by sniffing the air.

"He's been with the company more than four years and has never missed a day. He was a hard worker . . . always taking overtime jobs because he had a wife and two little boys to support."

I cringed, thinking of the innocent man.

Trent looked from his plate of food to me. "You've lost a few bird nests. But they've lost a husband and a father."

"That's not fair," I said. "Don't lay a guilt trip on me. I'm terribly sorry a man died, but I had nothing to do with it. I'm not going to let you put me on the defensive."

As soon as I said it, I knew what Trent was thinking: that inadvertently, I was responsible. I'd been the one to bring in the ornithologist who identified the red-cockaded woodpecker nests on Protter's land. Indirectly, I'd spurred an ugly course of events into action. On the other hand, if Protter's new development hadn't been about to put Mamma and Daddy out of business, I never would have entered the picture. I was simply pushing back so my family wouldn't be pushed down, and I had Newton's third law of physics to back me up.

Despite an empty stomach and the shrimp salad in front of me, my appetite was evasive. Trent didn't appear to be hungry either. Watching him play with the pasta on his plate, it dawned on me that we were both just trying to satisfy our curiosity. Just like me, he was there to gather ammunition for the battle. Wait for the other to slip up and say something incriminating. Sort out feelings, maybe.

I forced myself to look at the water so Trent wouldn't catch me staring. Breathing in the view through my eyes, I decided that the physical attraction I'd felt toward him—since encountering him for the very first time, when I was hungover and fetching breakfast— was finally dead, smothered by circumstance.

But sitting across from the man whom I alternately despised and dreamt of, I wasn't sure how he felt. I had no idea if my body's response to his on the dance floor two nights ago had been reciprocal. Although he had said I was beautiful, his mannerisms were entirely appropriate for any black-tie social affair. Perhaps he simply danced with me to be polite, and perhaps the compliment was just that: a compliment.

To Trent, I was probably nothing more than a business setback.

No different than an uncooperative inspector or inclement weather. To Protter Construction and Development, Carly Stone could simply be an annoying speed bump. And if that turned out to be the case, at least I was proving to be one hell of a huge speed bump.

I returned my attention to the man who'd created havoc with my emotions. He stared at me with a calculating expression, possibly deciding whether he should slow down to go over the speed bump—or simply find a way around it.

Had the situation been different, it would have been a delightful way to spend the afternoon. I knew if we'd met before Robert and I married, Trent and I would have been friends and maybe much more. I suddenly felt guilty about wasting the savory food in front of me. I began to feel like I was wasting the view instead of relishing it. And I was no longer positive that Trent was the bad guy. But I had to find out.

"I'm not trying to lay a guilt trip on you," he finally said, piercing a strip of chicken with his fork but not eating it. "I guess it's just important to me that you realize I wouldn't do something like that. You may think I'm a horrible person because I'm a good businessman and a successful developer . . . and that's fine. Hate me if you want to. I like what I do. But I am *not* an arsonist and I am *not* a criminal."

"Why did you leave the charity ball early?" I said, but answered my own question without giving him a chance. "Because you were angry. So mad, you went out and eliminated the problem."

A patio umbrella shaded his side of our table, and I couldn't gauge the reaction on his face.

"We left the ball early because I wanted to get all the details about the damn woodpeckers. I wasn't even going to stay and eat, but Pop insisted. So we ate and then we left. Me, Pop, and Jack. We went to Jack's house and talked for about an hour. This whole bird thing of yours had really turned into a huge problem." He spoke slowly and cautiously, as if trying to keep his anger in check.

"Had?" I said.

"What?"

"You said *had* turned into a huge problem. Past tense. As though it was a problem but you've solved it, so now it's not."

"Do they teach you that in law school? How to twist somebody's words to make something out of absolutely nothing?"

"Okay," I said. "So you had a meeting at your attorney's house. Then what?"

"Then Pop went home. And I . . . went out for a drink. Then I went home."

"You live alone?"

He nodded.

"So you don't have an alibi."

Annoyed, he put down his fork and forgot about trying to eat. "Now who's trying to put whom on the defensive? I don't know what you hoped to gain from our little lunch rendezvous, but I'm not going to sit here and take crap from you, Carly."

"I'm not *trying* to put you on the defensive," I said calmly, plowing recklessly ahead. "If you're feeling that way, you must have a reason. I'm simply stating a few facts. You found out one of your anchor stores had to be eliminated because of the birds. You left angry. There was a fire hours later. You don't have an alibi."

"Jesus Christ. You don't know when to stop."

"Well, who besides you would have a motive to set the fire? I don't care what Daddy or the fire chief says, I think you did it," I said and paused to take a drink of pinot grigio. But the mood I was in made it taste flat. I didn't feel triumphant like I thought I would.

"Well, maybe you didn't actually light the match, but after your meeting at Jack's house, you got Jerry to do it for you. He needed the money, after all. He figures it's like overtime pay. So you give him a few hundred dollars to torch some trees that he would have cleared anyway, if the woodpecker nests hadn't been found. You probably didn't expect him to kill himself in the process, but since he did, you'll make it work to your advantage."

I knew I was pushing way too hard, destroying Newton's theoretical scale of balance, but I couldn't stop. I wanted to force an admission out of him. Or perhaps I just needed to hear a denial.

"I'll bet Jack is already putting together a convincing case that Jerry had a beef with the company," I said. "Like . . . maybe you were going to fire him or something? And he wanted to torch some equipment to get back at you. So he proves to be the unlucky arsonist, and you get to finish putting up your development as planned. You're happy. Handyman's Depot is happy. Everybody's happy. Except Mamma and Daddy. And of course, Jerry, who's dead."

Trent abruptly stood up but leaned over and held on to each side of the small table as he delivered his next words in a low, incensed voice.

"First of all, if you want an alibi, I'll give you one. I ran into a good friend at the pub that night. We had a few drinks together and went back to my place. Terry didn't leave until the next morning."

Trent pulled some bills from his wallet and threw them on the table to pay for our food. It occurred to me that, even though I'd asked him to lunch and even though he was leaving angry, he was paying the tab. Southern manners aren't precluded by circumstance.

"And second, Jerry Stillwell was one of the most genuine, honest, and hardworking men I've ever known. Say what you want about me, but don't disrespect him."

Trent disappeared, leaving me sitting at the table with two plates of uneaten food and the feeling that I'd just been slapped, hard.

Of course he wouldn't use the death of an employee to his advantage, whether he'd been involved in the plan or not. As much as I disliked Trent, I really didn't believe he would stoop so low, even though I'd just voiced such an accusation.

And of course Trent would have a girlfriend. To imagine otherwise was stupid.

I'd been outclassed and felt foolish. The effect stung. I remained on the rooftop terrace for another hour, sipping the same glass of wine, staring at a view that had instantly become meaningless and wondering what Terry looked like.

23

I was still in a pensive mood when I got home from my disastrous lunch with Trent, and Mamma's maternal radar immediately picked up on it. I gave her a condensed version of my afternoon.

"That man just riles me up," I told her. "I lose my cool around him. If I was still working and he was a client, I'd have to pass the case to someone else. It's ridiculous."

Mamma nodded.

"I've worked with a lot of good-looking men before, and I didn't get stupid around them."

She nodded some more.

"He's trying to put my family out of business, for God's sake. Besides, legally, I'm still a married woman. And besides that Trent has a girlfriend named Terry. Not that I care. I hate him."

Mamma just nodded once more, her mouth forming an expression that was half grin and half frown and kept her reply to herself.

She had this way of nodding—solicitously yet silently—that rivals the most advanced interrogation technique. Under its influence, people felt compelled to talk and would often blurt out a confession. Without ever saying a word, Mamma could make an embezzler not only declare his guilt but also return the money plus interest.

Growing up, Jenny and I had admitted to numerous minor youthful offenses that should have been saved for adult "remember-when" storytelling decades later, like burning out the toaster by dropping buttered bread into it. Somewhere around age eleven or twelve, we decided to combat the effect of Mamma's nod by closing our eyes until the subject matter changed and the urge to blurt out a confession had passed. Jenny and I held to our don't-look-at-the-nod strategy for a month or more, until she got beaned in the head at a soccer match when the ball flew into the bleachers. Mamma was just trying to find out what happened to her jar of expensive face cream, and Jenny ended up with a bruised nose.

Even Lori Anne's mother used to take advantage of Mamma's nod. If she thought Lori Anne was hiding something, she'd give Mamma a call and send her child over. It usually took about twenty minutes before Mamma would call back with a full report.

"Okay, *hate* may be too strong of a word," I said. "I actually really like him. Under different circumstances, he's the type of man I could fall for. But it's all moot anyway," I confessed and shut my eyes, willing myself not to open them until the nod was likely over.

"Why don't you come with me on a drive?" she said after a few seconds. "I want to go over Mary Beth and Paul's place."

I opened my eyes. "They're home?"

"I'm not sure. They still don't answer the phone, and the machine isn't picking up. I called Robert on his mobile number to ask if they were out of town, but he didn't know. He was awfully vague. All he wanted to talk about was you, and how you're doing. But I figure if he wants to know how you are, he can call you."

"I'm not going to keep Robert informed of what's going on in my life. He lost that privilege. I just want to be rid of him for good. Incidentally, where is he living now?"

"He didn't say."

Wanting some attention, Taffy pushed a wet nose into my hand. I rubbed the spot behind her ears and thought about the two people Mamma was going to visit. People who must have loved Robert like he was their own son. People who, like me, deserved much better.

"I wonder if he's even bothered to tell them we're getting a divorce?"

"I don't know," Mamma said. "I just wonder how he can be so distant with the people who raised him."

"I don't know either," I told her. "Robert never talked about them, even back in high school. I'm beginning to think I don't know Mary Beth and Paul *or* my husband very well. How could I ever have married him?"

"Because you thought you were in love."

I shrugged, not wanting to dwell on my rotten decision.

"Hopefully, I can catch Mary Beth and Paul at home," Mamma said. "Let them know there're no hard feelings over selling the land."

"There aren't?"

"I'm sure they had their reasons. Your daddy and I don't know them very well, either, but I don't think they meant to harm us."

"You're quicker to forgive than I am," said the new me, the one who was tired of compromise. "A deal is a deal, whether it's a hand-shake or a signature scrawled on paper."

I decided to join Mamma for the drive because I hadn't seen Robert's stepparents since our wedding day.

Since Daddy was working and Jenny, Granny, and the kids had gone to the beach to hunt for shells, we were on our own. We left the two dogs behind, one happily chewing on a rope toy and the other one growling at it, as we headed out in Mamma's Cadillac.

I offered to drive, but she declined because driving helped her to clear her mind. For her, any trip longer than fifteen or twenty minutes was meditation on wheels.

The downside for a passenger was that Mamma only drove one speed: forty miles an hour. She wanted to get where she was going, but saw no need to be hasty about it. It had always been that way. Growing up, it wasn't much of a problem, because Mamma's pre-ferred speed limit worked well throughout the city. But as time progressed and Charleston grew, its road system didn't adhere to Mamma's one-speed theory. As a result, she was on a first name basis with several Charleston police officers. She'd been pulled over for a variety of reasons: speeding through construction zones, driving too slow, suspected drunken driving, and, once, a helpful officer had pulled her over to see if she was lost and needed assistance.

The twenty-five-minute drive was surprisingly uneventful, and as we approached the house, Mamma's instinct told her something was wrong.

I wasn't sure if anything was wrong or not, but I needed to find out why they broke their promise and sold the land to an investor in-stead of Daddy. Maybe I'd fueled the course of events leading up to the fire by recruiting a few people to help me examine the property, but Mary Beth and Paul Carpenter had started it all by selling their land out from under Daddy.

In the driveway, we sat in shocked silence for a minute before getting out of the car. The grass was tall and dotted with weeds. The shrubbery hadn't been groomed in a long time. The house revealed gutters heavy with pine straw and leaves.

When she opened the door, Mary Beth looked as unkempt as her yard. She wore a tattered housecoat and slippers. Her hair, although clean, was not styled, and her eyes were as dull as the surfaces of the living room furniture behind her. Her skin looked as though it hadn't seen the outdoors in many months. But upon seeing us, she smiled brightly and delivered strong hugs before ushering us inside.

Mary Beth served glasses of ginger ale and a plate of store-bought peanut butter cookies while we settled on the sofa.

We learned that she hadn't answered our phone calls because the ringer was normally turned off so as not to disturb Paul, who was in bed recuperating from chemotherapy and a series of radiation treatments following a recent surgery for colon cancer. I was shocked to learn of his condition, but then they did live outside of town and their neighbors probably didn't know to call us.

"I'm so sorry!" Mamma told her. "We had no idea or we'd have come sooner. How is he?"

"Right now, he's just real tired. He can't eat much, so he's lost weight. He doesn't have the energy to do the things he normally does. His vegetable garden is a mess. But taking care of him takes all my energy, and my arthritis keeps me from gardening," she said.

"Good grief, Mary Beth. I had no idea. I could have been helping you with the yard and the garden. Why didn't you call me? Or call Mamma and Daddy?"

"We don't like to burden people, hon."

She looked at me, and a wrinkle of confusion formed between her eyes.

"Besides, Robert said he told you. And that you sent your regards."

Mamma put a hand on my arm to keep me from responding.

"And he explained that you and Lloyd," she said to Mamma, "were real busy with your store. But that you sent your regards, too."

Robert wasn't just a cheating, selfish husband. He was also a rotten stepson.

"Has he been around to see you lately?" I asked. Surely if Robert realized the condition they were in, he would have done something to help.

"Oh, he's been by." Mary Beth's eyes glazed in an effort to keep tears from popping out. "But he's so busy trying to get his brokerage firm going, he barely has time to think of anything else, the poor dear."

Mamma and I looked at each other, thinking the same thing. Robert didn't have any plans to open his own firm. At least none that we'd been aware of. I was beginning to think my husband led a secret life, and I wondered how I could have lived with a man for almost a year and know so little about him.

He didn't love his aunt and uncle, but they were the closest thing to a family he had. I couldn't believe he'd let them exist in such a downtrodden condition. And why had he kept his uncle's illness a secret? It didn't make sense.

My mind spun the information it had been fed, like a centrifuge, trying to get down to the substance of the situation. And when it stopped spinning, a thought started to form deep in the core of my subconscious.

"Mary Beth, why did you sell the land across from Stone Hardware to an investor? Remember when you told Mamma and Daddy a long time ago that you'd give them first dibs if you ever got ready to sell?"

Genuine surprise registered on her face, and she blinked several times in Mamma's direction.

"Why, we did give you the chance to buy it, Doris! I know we haven't been as neighborly as we ought to, especially since the kids got married. It's just that Paul has been so sick. We've been fighting this cancer for a year now. But we would never go back on our word!"

"So you called Daddy, then?" I asked.

She rubbed a hand, forefinger and thumb spread in opposite directions, over closed eyes.

"No, not in person." She thought back. "You see, we really didn't want to sell the property, but we didn't have a choice. We don't have medical insurance, and Medicare wouldn't cover the experimental treatment Paul's doctor wanted to try."

I got the impression that Mary Beth hadn't spoken with anyone in a long time.

"I called Robert to see what we should do. I figured he'd know what the land was worth."

"And?" Mamma said.

"And Robert knew exactly what it was worth. He's the one who called Lloyd to see if ya'll were still interested in buying it."

Mamma and I looked at each other, and my face felt as pale as hers had become.

"When was that?" Mamma finally said.

"Why, it was just before the kids got married. Right after Paul's cancer was diagnosed and we knew we'd need the money."

"If you knew about the cancer at our wedding, how come you didn't tell us? And why didn't you talk to Mamma and Daddy about selling the land when you saw them?" I rapid-fired.

"It was your special day," Mary Beth said. "We didn't want to put a damper on things by talking about cancer! And, as far as selling, there was no need to bring it up again." Her expression was confused. "Robert had already said Lloyd turned down his offer because the price was too high."

"I don't recall that, Mary Beth," Mamma said. "How much was the offer Lloyd turned down?"

"Fifty thousand dollars."

The land was worth ten or fifteen times that.

"So, who *did* you sell to?" Mamma asked slowly.

"Why Robert of course! Didn't he tell you?"

I heard a buzz in my head and felt sick to my stomach.

"I know he doesn't love us like real parents," my husband's aunt confessed. "He never got over his mamma and daddy dying on him. But he's such a sweet boy, really. Fifty thousand is more than the property would have brought on the open market. Plus we didn't have to worry about paying commissions and all that rigamarole. And since we don't have any children, he would have inherited it someday, anyhow."

My ears grew hot with anger and disbelief.

Unaware of my reaction, Mary Beth shook her head from side to side. "I told him we didn't want to take advantage of him like that, but he insisted. He didn't want us to have to mortgage the house to pay bills."

"So he bought it from you and then he sold it to Protter Construction and Development," I thought aloud.

Probably for something close to a million dollars.

"Can you believe the luck? The timing was perfect."

I'd never seen Mamma gulp anything before, but she suddenly downed her glass of soda. Probably as a way to buy some time, to think. To try and make sense of something that didn't. I guzzled mine at about the same rate, wishing it was a beer or something stronger, and we set down empty tumblers at the same time.

We declined Mary Beth's offer for a refill.

Although the Carpenters had been robbed, they'd gotten something out of the property. So where had the money gone? After paying the medical bills, there should have been enough left to hire a gardener and someone to help with the housecleaning. Enough, at least, for Mary Beth to buy a new housecoat and get her hair done at the salon.

"So then, all your medical bills are paid from the sale," I probed. "That must be a relief."

She sighed. "Not entirely. When Robert bought the land, he gave us ten thousand dollars, and said he'd pay the rest as soon as he found a buyer. But then, to close the deal with those developer folks, he worked out some sort of contingency arrangement. He said he wouldn't get the money from them until the center was finished, and as soon as he gets his money, we'll get the remaining forty thousand."

I found it hard to believe that any seller, especially one as greedy as Robert, would simply turn a piece of land over to a developer without getting his money up front.

She shrugged her shoulders. "Robert says it won't be much longer now. We just need to hold out a few more months. Mainly, I just want Paul to get better. I want us to get out and do stuff again, like we used to."

A shuffling noise caught our attention, and we looked up in time to see Paul amble out. His physical appearance was worse than I had imagined. His skin was thin and transparent and hung on a previously robust frame like soggy clothing that had gotten wet in a sudden downpour. A colostomy bag was visible beneath pajamas.

"Paul! You're awake . . . Doris and Carly are here," Mary Beth jumped up to help him.

In a practiced move, she held his arm and he held her shoulder for support. He shuffled along because lifting his feet took too much effort. Their progress was painstakingly slow, and when they finally reached the recliner, he refused to sit. Mamma and I took turns giving him a hug, lightly, so as not to topple him.

"We didn't know about your cancer," Mamma told him. "We'd have come sooner."

"I know. I heard."

"Oh," I said, going for cheerful. "We thought you were asleep! It's so good to see you."

"He never offered the land to you, did he?" Paul asked, skipping the small talk protocol. His voice was surprisingly strong and familiar, despite his shrunken appearance. He wobbled but still refused to sit, awaiting an answer.

Mamma shook her head from side to side. There was no reason to lie.

"So Lloyd did want the land."

Mamma nodded again, up and down this time.

"And it's worth five times what he says he's going to pay us for it."

"Fifteen." I felt horrible for them. "Maybe more."

His legs lost what strength they had, and Paul folded into the chair.

"I knew it," he said. "If I'd handled things myself, this wouldn't have happened. But I've been so sick, I haven't thought of much other than getting out of bed once in a while. And, how I should have planned better for retirement. Something like this happens, and all of a sudden everything becomes strikingly clear."

"You've done good for us," Mary Beth said. "There's no way you could have seen this coming."

"I should have bought supplemental insurance. I should have

saved more. And I should have put that boy into a military academy and gotten him some counseling while he was still young."

"Robert?" Mary Beth looked confused, still not getting it.

"He's never thought of anyone but himself," Paul told us. "It's always been that way. Oh, he's smart and clever and charming. But that boy doesn't have an ounce of decency in him."

"Paul! Don't say that! It's not true!"

"The first time I noticed it, Robert was eight. We bought him a puppy. Two days later, we saw a crowd of boys around him in the backyard. He was taking money to drop the dog from the tree. We found out that he started at just a foot or so, but he kept going higher as long as someone would give him another dime. To see how far the puppy could fall and still get up."

Paul stopped to make sure we were listening. Me and Mamma. The closest thing to in-laws he had, sitting side by side on the sofa, appalled.

"Any other boy would have loved that dog."

"Boys will be boys," Mary Beth said. Perhaps she was so forgiving of his actions because Robert was her brother's son. "He didn't know how fragile puppies are."

I was about to ask if the dog lived, but decided I didn't want to know.

"That was just the beginning, Mary Beth," Paul said quietly, "and you know it. We just kept thinking he would grow out of it."

"I . . . I'm sorry," I said. "I don't know what to say. I'm finding out Robert isn't the man I thought he was when I married him."

"I'm sorry, too," Paul said. "I'm sorry for you. I thought since he was marrying such a beautiful and bright girl, maybe he'd grown up. But the two of you aren't together anymore, are you?"

So Robert hadn't told them about the divorce. Nothing could surprise me now.

"No, we're not."

Mary Beth shook with suppressed sobs and ran from the room. Mamma started to go after her, but Paul stopped her.

"Leave her be, Doris," he said. "She needs to face the fact that Robert has swindled us."

Mary Beth eventually returned to the room to bring her husband some pills and a glass of water. He thanked her. She kissed his cheek. He patted her hand.

She poured more ginger ale for Mamma. I told them I was divorcing Robert and had moved back to Charleston for good. Mary Beth declared that it was awful news, but Paul said I was better off.

The next minutes were uncomfortable as emotional debris from dropped bombs slowly settled, but in the aftermath, we caught up on each other's lives and even shared a few laughs. I told them I was going to become a litigation attorney and Paul said I would certainly liven up any courtroom. Mamma extended a dinner invitation, and they agreed to come when the chemotherapy treatments ended.

"Please get better, and soon!" I told Paul. "I feel so badly that I haven't done anything to help."

"It's not your fault that Robert lied to everyone," he said.

I was doing some research on the property, I told them, and asked if they had copies of the paperwork from the sale. Mary Beth rummaged through a rolltop desk and produced an envelope, which she told me to keep as long as I needed.

They thanked us for coming, and we promised to visit again soon. Cocooned by individual thoughts, neither of us spoke as Mamma drove us home at forty miles an hour.

"They're a strong couple, honey," she finally said, halfway home. "They'll make it."

I hoped so, but my thoughts had already gone elsewhere. I mentally urged her to drive faster. I had a lot to do.

I needed to hire the divorce lawyer that Lori Anne had recommended. She'd dated him briefly and said he was incredibly sweet—unless he was suing you. Although I had a lot of friends from law school, none of them specialized in family law and divorce. Lori Anne's fellow was a divorce guru. His peers had nicknamed him Gator because once he had a grip on something, he didn't let go.

I wanted to get a look at the documents in my hand as well

as the purchase agreement between Robert and the Protters. I had to go to the courthouse to get copies of the tax maps for Protter's plat of land. And I wanted to find out why Robert had lied to everyone.

24

"I think the aroma-gizmo is working," Daddy said from his lookout point at the kitchen window. If he stood just right and leaned sideways, he could observe the fortress he'd built around the garbage cans and check for furry intruders without alerting them to his presence.

"You mean on the raccoons?"

"It's been over a week now, and they haven't gotten into the trash once!" It was a declaration of triumph. Man over beast. Or, human over four-legged, mischievous mammal.

"I still can't believe you dumped the Aroma-magic Ionizer and Environment Enhancer in the trash." Jenny poofed up her lips and tried to look indignant.

"It's *by* the trash can," Mamma clarified for Daddy. "Not *in* the trash can."

"Whatever."

"I have relaxed them into passivity," Daddy announced, and I wondered if, somehow, the machine had worked on him, too.

His anxiety attacks had stopped, despite the fact Handyman's Depot was still on track and the future of his store uncertain. Although the arson and potential murder investigation was under way, detectives had collected all the evidence they could from the site and saw no reason to hold up construction any longer. No arrests had been made, and there was nothing to keep Protter's heavy equipment from rolling again. For the time being, my arsenal was empty.

It was Jenny's last night in Charleston, and we were going out for supper, so I had the run of the kitchen table until breakfast time. I'd spread out enough stuff to cover nearly half of it. Tax records, a dossier on the Handyman's Depot chain, reference books. I knew there was a simple solution, a way to tie everything up into one neat package. I was playing detective, trying to figure out who had motive to set the fire besides Trent Protter. I just had to keep poring through information, keep examining the possibilities, keep turning the squares of the Rubik's cube until something came together and made perfect sense. I knew Robert was a piece of the puzzle, and my first priority was to figure out where he fit in. Which presented a challenge since I was also suing him for divorce.

"It's been so much fun being home and being pampered," Jenny said. "I almost hate to leave."

The set of *In Home Now* was repaired and, according to my twin, was even bigger and better than before. It was time for her to get back to work and time for the girls to get back in school. They'd be out for summer in a few weeks, but the homework they'd brought with them had already run out.

"I know what you mean," I agreed. "Mamma has a way of making you feel like you don't have a care in the world and could stay here forever."

I dropped a fountain pen, and it landed with a clatter. Precious contorted her body into a menacing arc to growl at it.

"Jesus," I said, retrieving the pen. "You really need to get that dog checked out."

"Checked out for what?"

"I don't know for what. But it's obviously got some kind of a problem."

"She does not!" Jenny plopped into a chair across from me. She was drinking a frozen margarita through a straw and carrying a bag of low-fat tortilla chips.

"One of the exclusive products we sell on *In Home Now* is a well-being evaluation kit for your pet. It's all the rage among upper-class pet owners . . . you know, the ones who don't have children in the home anymore and dote on their dog or cat? Buy health insurance for them and all that? Anyway, Precious passed with flying colors. There's not a thing wrong with her."

We looked down at the quivering, growling, twenty-pound ball of fluffed-up white fur. This visit, the dog sported a yellow bow on top of its head, and folds of the ribbon vibrated with irritation.

"You know, Jenny, you ought to sell some gadgets from your daddy's store on that TV show of yours," Granny said, stepping carefully over Precious. "Not some stupid poodle-dog evaluation kit . . . but something that'll really help folks. Maybe tools or kitchen things."

Whenever Granny said something that made sense, it meant so much more than it had in the past. She'd always been a no-nonsense, down-to-earth, streetwise woman, and people listened to her advice. In retrospect, I'd usually taken Granny's offerings of wisdom for granted. Sometimes, I'd even shoot her an eye roll when she delivered a prophesy. But now, when a clear comment came through her muddled brain, I savored it.

"It is a good idea," Jenny said, "but we try to sell stuff you can't get just anywhere. Unusual and upscale items. Exclusive products."

"Exclusive?" An idea danced in my head.

"Right. *In Home Now* doesn't just sell any old thing. We sell exclusive stuff."

My brain kicked into high gear. Handyman's Depot had become known as *the place* to find exclusive home and and garden products people couldn't get anywhere else. They made deals with the manufacturers of newly patented tools and gadgets to obtain exclusive distribution rights in return for co-op advertising exposure. I'd learned that typically their exclusive distribution agreement term was sixteen months, after which time the product would become widely available at a variety of stores. It was an ideal way for a new product to be consumer-tested on the open market while allowing the manufacturer to gear up for mass production.

As we liked to say in the mediation and arbitration world, it was a genuine triple-win situation. Retail shelf space for the manufacturer, a successful marketing tool for Handyman's Depot, and an exclusive buy opportunity for the consumer.

But even the best of situations allowed room for improvement. What if Handyman's Depot could increase sales of their exclusive products without putting them on the shelves of competitors?

"So how do you choose what goes on the show?" I asked my sister.

Granny appropriated the bag of tortilla chips and crunched into one with raised eyebrows. She wanted to know, too.

"We have a team of buyers for all that," Jenny said.

"What about the carpet cleaner machine that blew up?"

Jenny aimed a short sigh at me and, taking the chip bag back from Granny, popped half a triangle into her mouth.

"It didn't *blow up*; it caught on fire," she said, as if it was a huge difference.

"Right. But wasn't it you who got the show to carry the carpet cleaner?" I asked.

"Well sure," she said. "If I come across something I think would be a good seller, I'll turn them on to it."

"I wouldn't think the on-air talent had that much pull."

"Well, not normally. But in my case, I do," she said. "I get ratings, so they want to keep me happy. Plus, my husband *is* the producer of the show!"

I grinned. She was right. Stephen was indeed the producer of *In Home Now*. And she had him wrapped around her product-selling pinkie finger.

"Why?" she said. "Do you know of something exclusive that people would buy?"

"I just might."

"Well, let me know. You want something on the show, I'll make it happen."

I suddenly had a newfound respect for her and for what she did. "You know, I poke fun at you sometimes, but I'm really proud of you. And it's very cool that you could get something on the show just because I asked."

"Hey," she replied with a nonchalant wave of her hand. "What's family for?"

I was invigorated and empowered. I still wasn't sure how the whole puzzle fit together, but I knew I'd found another piece of it. A bargaining tool, at least, for when the time came.

"You rock," I said.

"Rock!" Hunter said.

Amused, we watched him play with Taffy on the floor.

"Rock!" he tried again, since he hadn't been hushed the first time.

"*Rock* isn't a bad word, little guy," I told him. "Good try, though."

"Rock?"

"Rock," I smiled. "Rock on."

He frowned, trying to dig a word out of his memory that would get a better reaction. Before he could manage to draw one out, his attention was diverted by the squeaky toy that Taffy pushed into his little hands. She wanted him to throw it so, as her genetic makeup dictated, she could retrieve it.

I thought about my genetic makeup and decided I was retrieving something, too. My dignity.

25

"What do you want this time, Carly?" Trent said, and it was not the greeting I'd anticipated.

I'd caught up with him at the project site, but instead of greeting me with a friendly smile or even a neutral stance, he faced me with folded arms. His biceps, accentuated by the pose, caught my attention. They pushed out, sculpted and solid, from beneath a short-sleeved shirt.

"I just thought I'd stop by to say hello . . . see how things are progressing," I said sweetly, but he didn't buy it and apparently wasn't in the mood to humor me.

"Look, you've made your position very clear. If you think I'm going to help you gather a case against me to prove I set fire to my own land, you're crazy."

I shook my head. That wasn't why I was there.

"Well then, you must be here to take another look around. See if you can find anything else to stop construction for a few more days."

He removed his sunglasses, hung them over the collar of his shirt, and squinted at me. "But the problem is, if you try that again, security will ask you to leave. We've got a man on duty twenty-four/seven now."

I took a step closer and touched his arm in a move of sincerity that I usually reserved for female clients involved in dispute. Trent didn't move. His demeanor didn't soften.

"Trent, I'm sorry."

A short laugh escaped him. "You're sorry?"

"Yes," I said, dropping my hand.

"For which offense? The legal problems you've caused me? The money you've cost me? The accusation of arson and murder? Or just the verbal attack?"

"For all of it," I said and paused to think. "Well no, I take that back. For most all of it. Everything except the legal problems. I can't apologize for trying to save Mamma and Daddy's business."

"Oh. Well then. I feel much better," he said. "Thanks for dropping by." The words were sharp with sarcasm, but I detected a hint of a smile. Just a flicker of upturned skin at the edges of a wide, full mouth. Lips that my eyes locked onto, like a radar-guided missile, despite my command for them to look elsewhere.

With some effort, I managed to blink. "Honestly. I am sorry for the things I've said to you. A lot of it was uncalled for."

"A lot of it?"

"C'mon," I pleaded. "I'm trying to apologize here. This kind of thing is new to me."

A darting squirrel caught my attention, and finally I was able to look at something other than Trent's mouth. The animal scurried across the ground and disappeared up a nearby tree.

"How so?"

"Well . . . in the past, I've never behaved in a way that left me needing to apologize to someone."

He raised one dark eyebrow, barely. It contrasted nicely with the lighter color of his hair. "Never? You're kidding."

At some point during the conversation, we'd started walking, side by side, and I was unsure where we were headed. It was late morning, and the playful spring air carried a musky-sweet scent of wild wisteria blooms laced with damp earth. As it did every year between late spring and summer, a super-thin layer of pine pollen dusted the surface of everything, like pale yellow powdered sugar sprinkled through a sifter from above.

"I've always been the one to get other people to apologize to each other," I told him. "Or if not apologize, at least come to an agreement. First as a kid. Then as a volunteer counselor in college. And then as a career."

I explained to him how I'd always been the mediator, moderator, and sometimes cheerleader. How I'd always avoided conflict in my personal life. How people would inevitably describe me as laid-back or easygoing, right after they'd declared I was pretty and smart. How people would sometimes take advantage of me because I'd never say no. And how I'd exchanged my hometown, the city I loved, for unfamiliar territory in New York. Just because Robert had asked. Because I didn't want to be disagreeable.

"I guess I've always wanted to please everyone else," I confessed, "without ever focusing on what would please me. I mean, I'm very good at what I do, so I don't mean to sound like a martyr. But trying to keep everyone happy doesn't make me a saint, either. In fact, the way things have gone for me lately, I'd probably classify my affinity for peacekeeping as being a complete pushover."

"Carly," Trent said, pausing until I looked at him. "I can personally attest to the fact that you are not, by any means, a pushover!"

I laughed. From his point of view, I was anything but.

We arrived at the piece of historic city wall whose discovery had altered the original shopping center blueprints. A temporary chain-link fence encircled it, and two specialists of some sort busily worked.

Following Trent's lead, I sat on a makeshift bench that consisted of two-by-fours and concrete blocks. He explained that the chain link would become white-picket vinyl fencing, and the blocks and boards would become cast-iron benches when the shopping facility opened. Everyone at Protter Construction and Development agreed the wall area would make a wonderful gathering place for customers. In a roundabout way that was almost gratitude, Trent admitted he was proud of the artifact.

And then he asked what had changed in my life. Why I had taken a hundred and eighty degree turn. Started seeking out conflict instead of avoiding it.

I answered without hesitation. "Because my husband is a piece of shit. I couldn't keep letting him walk all over me, so I left him and moved back. And because your development, with its Handyman's Depot, will destroy everything Mamma and Daddy have worked to build up over the last thirty years. We're talking a store that's been in my family, in the same location, for almost one hundred years! I couldn't watch it happen without trying to do something."

We sat close to each other and, real or imagined, I could feel the energy radiating from his body. I looked into his eyes, focused on me, and took a deep breath. "I guess it was just time. To start fighting back."

Trent nodded his understanding and looked away, toward the sky, at a group of doves flying above us. Out of his usual uniform of jeans and work boots, he was wearing a sage green golf shirt, light tan cotton slacks, and leather loafers without socks. He looked clean and fresh and ready to spend a casual afternoon doing something other than working at the construction site where I'd found him.

"And?" he said, somehow knowing there was more. His gaze still followed the erratic flight path of the birds. His short sideburns emphasized an angular jaw. I could see the muscle in it working, flexing. I didn't know if the movement was a result of anger or contemplation.

"And it feels good," I answered.

Trent nodded again, and I decided that I saw contemplation, after all. He was focused on listening to me and was thinking about what I said.

In my experience working mediation cases, few people genuinely *listen* when other people talk about themselves. But seeing that Trent cared enough to really *listen*, I had an odd rush of admiration for his character. It stirred me in much the same way catching a whiff of his scent did. Or sneaking a glance at his wide shoulders. Or feeling his body against mine during a slow dance.

Looking again at the casual clothes he sported, a sinking feeling moved through my stomach as I wondered if he was meeting his girlfriend for lunch. Or something more. I sighed, knowing there wasn't a chance of anything happening between us anyway, regardless of whether he was available or not.

We sat quietly, appreciating the day, and the meticulous work being done on the wall. And perhaps, each other.

"What you can see is only a portion of what's there," Trent said after a while. "They tell me there is a lot more underground. And it probably was connected to a bastion, because they found some cannonballs."

"Really? Wow. Are they going to dig out around the buried part?"

"No. But the informational plaque will tell our shoppers it's there. It will even have an artist's rendering of what the original wall might have looked like."

With one graceful move, he turned sideways and straddled our makeshift bench to face me. I tried not to stare at him.

"This entire area will be covered by an open-air shelter," he continued, not seeming to notice my roaming eyes.

One of his knees brushed the side of mine. My nerve endings at the contact point jumped to attention and eagerly waited for more stimuli. When none came, they calmed, but I couldn't shake the tingling sensation that settled in every sensitive part of my body.

I angled myself to face Trent and tried to remember what I wanted to say to him. The conversation I'd rehearsed in my car on the way over was evading me, and, sitting so close to the man that wouldn't stay out of my thoughts, I nearly forgot what I was doing there.

"I need your help," is what came out.

A gust of wind blew my hair into swirls around my face, like a veil to hide my emotions. I pushed it back and tucked one side behind an ear.

"Help with what?"

"I need to see a copy of the original purchase agreement on this land. A copy of the contract. The closing papers. A copy of the most recent survey and plat map. And I'd like to know as much as you can tell me about the man you bought the property from."

"Anything else, Carly?" Trent said, amused by my audacity.

I shook my head. "That'll do to start with."

"Why should I help you? And why are you so interested in the seller?"

"To answer both questions, because I believe the seller was—still is, actually—my husband."

There was a stunned pause while Trent considered what I'd just told him.

"The same husband who tried to punch me out at your folks' house?" Trent asked, one eyebrow skeptically arched higher than the other.

"Believe me," I said, "I was as surprised to learn about it as you are. He may have sold you the property under the name of some bogus company, but he's the man behind it."

Trent gave me a look, very much like one of Mamma's powerful looks that demanded elaboration.

I explained the entire situation. I told Trent about how Robert's parents died in a car accident when he was young and how Mary Beth and Paul raised him. How he'd never respected, much less loved, them. How he'd gotten out of Charleston as quickly as he could after graduating high school. And how he'd deeded the property into his name, Ellis, under the pretense of helping the Carpenters by doling out a meager ten thousand dollars. And then turned around and sold it to Protter Construction and Development for an outrageous profit, the amount of which I did not yet know.

I finished by adding that Daddy wanted to buy the land twenty years ago, and that Paul, with a handshake, had promised to give him the first option to buy if they ever decided to sell. But Robert had lied to his ailing uncle, insisting that Daddy had passed on the offer he never made to begin with.

Like me, Trent was a born and bred Charlestonian and understood the honor behind a handshake agreement, not to mention the legality of it.

"Jesus Christ," he said and stood up.

I followed his lead. We started walking.

"I never actually met the seller in person," he said. "His attorney handled the closing."

"That's why you didn't recognize him when he tried to punch you out," I mused.

"But you know what? Something about his voice that day was vaguely familiar. I just never placed it," Trent said. "So your last name is Ellis? I thought it was Stone."

"It is Stone. I kept my maiden name," I said, looking at my bare toes as we walked in the direction of the construction trailer. I wore black flat sandals and was glad my brightly painted toenails still looked good from the pedicures Jenny and I had gotten the day of the charity ball.

Although the fire had destroyed most underbrush and the land was leveled for development, a fine layer of leaves and pine straw covered the sandy ground. We stopped to admire a beautiful live oak tree that had to be two or three hundred years old. It would have taken six, maybe seven, adults, hand to hand, to encircle the trunk. Thick curving limbs created inviting archways in every direction, and some almost touched the ground.

Protter's architect made allowances in the blueprints to preserve several clusters of trees, and three of them held a single, magnificent live oak. I had to give the Protter men credit for that. It cost money to leave anything standing on a plat of land. It would have been much easier to clear-cut.

"So then, Robert sold it to you in his own name?" I said.

"The seller was actually a company. At least on paper. But, yeah, an R. Ellis was the man who was doing business as Vive Investments. If he'd changed his name to Carpenter when his aunt and uncle adopted him, I'd have realized there was some sort of connection between him and the original owners, because Jack pulled the tax map information to get an ownership history of the land. There's no record of this land ever having been owned by anyone else, other than the Carpenter family. And then, Vive Investments."

"I think they wanted him to take their name after he got old enough to consider it, but he refused. Carpenter sounded too . . . blue collar for his taste. And besides that, he's always been bitter about being cheated out of growing up with his 'real' family."

"Well, Jack said the low selling price to Vive Investments was unusual. But then again, people commonly work out all kinds of deals under the table especially when family is involved. More than once, I've seen a selling price of one dollar for a parcel of land."

We'd stopped walking and were back where we started, at the construction trailer. Trent nodded at my BMW, parked next to his truck.

"Any more tire trouble?" he said.

I shook my head no and started to explain that the flat had been successfully patched and was performing flawlessly when he grinned. He was just teasing me.

It was the same grin I'd first experienced nearly two months ago through a foggy, alcohol-saturated brain at seven-thirty in the morning. Wearing crumpled blue jeans and the previous night's makeup. Over a dropped country-ham biscuit, in Diana's at the espresso bar.

I took a deep breath to help me claim the memory. By the time I exhaled, the biscuit encounter was so vivid, it felt like it had just happened yesterday. I forgot about Robert and Daddy's store and Handyman's Depot and my uncertain future, and allowed myself to wonder about the man who had changed my flat tire then and was grinning at me now. To wonder what he would do if I just moved straight into his arms and kissed him. Boldly, full on the mouth.

"You know, I don't remember if I even thanked you for changing my tire. That day seems like it was forever ago!" I lied, attempting a light-hearted laugh.

"That day seems like yesterday, Carly Stone," Trent said in a voice an octave or two lower than normal.

In that moment, I almost did move in to kiss him, boldly, full on the mouth. But before I could act out my fantasy, Trent let out a small laugh and got his normal voice back.

"I'm headed to the office to see Pop for a few minutes. Why don't you ride along, and I'll have Sophie get you copies of everything you wanted."

I agreed and let him open the passenger-side door for me before hoisting myself into his truck. He called his secretary on a two-way radio and asked her to make the copies.

Lost in our own thoughts, we were quiet during the drive, but it was a comfortable silence. When we pulled up to the office of Protter Construction and Development Company, Trent turned off the engine but didn't immediately get out of the truck. He cocked his head and looked at me. He'd just realized something important.

"What?" I said.

"You can read everything for yourself," he began, "but there were some unusual contingencies and clauses in the contract. The up-front purchase price, four hundred and twenty thousand dollars, was a good bit less than the true market value, but Robert will receive seven percent of the gross tenant lease income for the next five years. He has absolutely no ownership or management involvement, but he does get seven percent off the top."

"Why not just go for a higher purchase price to begin with?"

"Any number of reasons. There could be a tax advantage for him. It could be a way to show income over the next five years for his bogus investment company. Who knows?"

I nodded. In the world of real estate and land development, everything was negotiable. If you owned a desirable piece of property, you could sell to a buyer on your terms.

"We agreed because we wanted that particular piece of land. The location is prime. But our attorney—"

"Jack," I interjected.

"Right. As a safeguard for us, Jack put in a clause that the seven percent would only be paid if the center were completed to the exact usable retail square-footage specifications and number of tenant slots as outlined in the original master plan. Or it could be higher but not less. In other words, based on lease income per square foot, we could give up seven percent, and the numbers worked. But if the plans changed for any reason, as they sometimes do," he shot me a you-certainly-know-how-that-could-happen look, "that seven percent could become a problem."

A crease appeared in Trent's forehead as he thought back.

"They didn't realize the safeguard was in the contract until closing, when the attorney questioned us about it. She was flying back to New York that afternoon but said she'd stay an extra day if we would reschedule the closing to give us a chance to negotiate the clause. She thought that a sliding scale should be determined, instead of the percentage being paid on an all-or-nothing basis. For example, say the retail square footage dropped by ten percent from the original plans. Then, instead of Robert getting seven percent for the next five years, he'd only get six percent. That kind of thing."

"So what happened?"

"She contacted him on her mobile phone and explained the situation. But he was adamant about proceeding with the closing that day. He told her to go ahead and close and not to miss her return flight to New York."

"And?"

"And we closed. That was that. I guess your husband just didn't want to wait. Although, if something happened, he'd forgo the seven percent. Which, over five years, could add up to about five hundred thousand dollars."

"How did you pay?"

"We prefer to directly deposit funds into a seller's account, but in this case, he insisted on a certified check for the full amount. The attorney took the check back to New York with her."

"Do you remember what day it was? The closing?"

"Well . . . let me think." He looked up, through the sunroof of the truck. "It was June of last year. I remember because it was the day after Pop's birthday."

He told me the date. It was a date that gave me the same sickening feeling of betrayal as when I'd discovered Robert in my bed with Corin Bashley.

Needing fresh air, I opened my door, as the implications of what Trent had just told me sunk in.

"That was the day before we left for our honeymoon," I mumbled. "See, we got married three weeks before, during the first week of June, but took a delayed honeymoon because of his work schedule. Robert demanded you close that day because he wanted to have the check in hand when we left for Belize, and he couldn't very well reschedule the honeymoon."

"You obviously didn't know about the sale," Trent said. "But what difference did the honeymoon make?"

"He opened an offshore account. You closed on Wednesday and the attorney brought him the check that night. We flew to Belize the next day but got in late. So, the first day of our honeymoon was Friday, and I remember thinking how odd it was that Robert disappeared to the bank to cash a check for three hours while I was sunning on the beach. But now I realize he must've opened an offshore, untraceable account. To hide the money from me."

A throbbing ache emerged at the base of my skull, and I subconsciously rubbed it to ease the tightness. The sensual part of my brain, the part that could care less about the unfolding drama, imagined Trent's strong hand massaging the back of my neck.

"See," I told him, "I just wanted to go somewhere quiet in the Florida Keys for our honeymoon. But he convinced me that we needed to go to the Caribbean. Then at the last minute, he surprised me with airline tickets to Belize. And when I spoke about my upcoming honeymoon at work, one of the clients, a banker, mentioned that Belize is one of the best places to hide money right now. Of course at the time, I thought nothing of it."

"So he planned your honeymoon around hiding money from you. And maybe Uncle Sam, too."

"Right. And what you just told me about the seven-percent all-or-nothing clause?"

Trent nodded, frowning. He'd already come to the same conclusion.

"If the Handyman's Depot spot were axed because of the red-cockaded woodpeckers, Robert would have lost his seven percent. Which you said would amount to half a million dollars."

"Yes."

"The fire . . ." I began before my sentence melted into nothingness as I envisioned a jumbled mass of horrific possibilities, all involving Robert and greed and arson.

Trent reached across the console and found my hand.

He gave it a squeeze. "We'll figure this thing out together, Carly. Okay?"

It was my turn to nod.

26

The first thing I needed to know was whether or not Robert had been in Charleston at the time of the fire. Mary Beth said he hadn't visited them, but then he rarely ever did. My next plan was to start checking hotels near the site. I'd pose as Mister Ellis's secretary calling to see if anything had been turned in to the front desk, as my boss believed that he'd left his Palm Pilot in his room. They'd want to know the date he checked out, which I'd say was the day after the fire, and they would want to know what room number he'd been in, which I'd talk my way through. Over and over again. Charleston was home to a lot of hotels, not to mention the bed-and-breakfasts and vacation condo rentals.

It suddenly dawned on me that Robert would have most likely flown from New York and checking with the airlines would be much easier. After all, there were only two that flew into Charleston. He usually flew the same airline everywhere he went, and at social events, he liked to brag about how many frequent flier miles he'd racked up. A good travel war story was his second favorite ice breaker, right after the day's stock market activity.

I retrieved my frequent flier card from my wallet and made the toll-free call. My member number was imprinted into the plastic, and I'd written in Robert's number on the back.

After being put on automated hold for ten minutes, I got a bored customer service representative who I thought would be easy to manipulate.

"I'd like to find out how many total points my husband and I have because I'm planning a surprise vacation for our one-year anniversary. Can you help me with that?"

"That information would be on your current statement, ma'am."

"Right, but he's real close to having enough points for two first-class tickets. And he just took a recent flight that isn't reflected on the statement."

She sighed, as though my call were an intrusion to her workday.

"I'll need his frequent flier number, mother's maiden name for security purposes, and the confirmation number of the last flight."

I gave her the first two answers and tried to talk my way through the last.

"I can't help you ma'am, if you don't have the confirmation number. You can have your husband submit a request in writing to get an updated points statement."

I hung up and hit the redial button. This time I only had to listen to oldies music and intermittent recordings about my call being important for eight minutes. I got a much friendlier representative. I gave him the same story but ended it with "My husband will be so surprised! I really appreciate your help with this."

When we got past the initial questions, I told him, with as much contrition as I could muster, that I didn't have the confirmation number or flight number because my husband's secretary handled all that. For good measure, I added that she was having a baby and was out on maternity leave.

"Well, let's see what I can do," he said, apparently studying the computer monitor in front of him. I could hear the clicking of his fingers hitting a keyboard. "Yes, you're right. There are a couple of recent flights that aren't reflected on the most current statement. And you'll be pleased to know that your husband has earned enough points for two roundtrip airfares in the U.S. or Puerto Rico."

"Oh, that's super!" I said with forced enthusiasm. "The round-trip to Charleston must have added just enough miles!"

"Yes ma'am, that was the last one," he said happily. "If you have his password, you can go ahead and reserve your flight right now."

"What a good idea, but I'll have to reserve the hotel first. You've been so helpful. Can I ask for you when I call back?"

"Sorry, no. You just get the next representative. But anyone can make your reservations."

"Oh, well then. Thanks again," I said, dismayed that I still didn't have the information I needed. "Just one more thing. That flight from LaGuardia to Charleston . . . what were the dates on that?"

He hesitated.

"I just want to write it down on my frequent flier statement, so I'll know I've already counted those mileage points."

He told me the departure and return date to LaGuardia.

Robert had spent only one night in Charleston. The night of the fire.

My next call went to the fire chief, and I didn't dance around the fact that I'd called seeking information. Had he not been longtime friends with Daddy, he would have politely told me to get lost. But instead, Chief Jim agreed to pass along what he'd learned so far, after I agreed to keep it confidential.

"The fire was set, using the diesel from the fuel truck. And you were right about the toluene and the woodpecker nests. The cavities were completely burned out, but we did find some traces of residual chemical in the wood. It could have been two men—one standing on the shoulders of another to reach the nests—but, more likely, a single man or woman just used an extension ladder. For that matter, someone could have driven an SUV up to the trees and stood on top of it."

The news confirmed what I already suspected. I asked Chief Jim if he could tell me anything more, especially pertaining to the man whose body had been found. There was a long pause while the fire chief decided how much to tell me.

"Well, you'll be reading about it in tomorrow's paper anyway," he began. "The Charleston Police Department is involved, and they've requested assistance from SLED."

SLED was the acronym for the South Carolina Law Enforcement Division. They were the elite of the cops and handled special situations and unusual occurrences.

"So if the police and SLED have been brought in, then the autopsy report must indicate murder?"

"Let's just say that Jerry Stillwell was injured before the fire started," Chief Jim said.

"But what is the evidence of actual murder?"

"Well, either Mister Stillwell just happened to die with a head injury, sitting against a pine tree on a construction site sometime in the middle of the night, and then a fire mysteriously broke out. Or," the fire chief said, "someone dragged his unconscious body across the ground, propped it against a tree, and set the fire."

"He had a head injury? And what was he doing out there in the first place?"

"Who knows? His wife says he left right after dinner to check on the storage shed that he forgot to lock up, where they keep the chemicals. That's the last she saw of him."

"It doesn't make sense," I said.

"The entire situation doesn't make sense," Chief Jim agreed. "That's why we called in SLED. We're talking arson, murder, and purposefully destroying an endangered species . . . all wrapped into one tidy package."

"So how did it go down?"

"There was debris inside the back pockets of what was left of his jeans to indicate he had been dragged along the ground. He'd also been hit across the side of the head with something heavy, and it wasn't falling debris." Chief Jim paused to take a drink of something. "And his lung tissue had smoke damage, so he was still breathing when the fire broke out."

I wondered if Robert had broken into the storage shed in search of chemicals and stumbled upon Jerry Stillwell. Even if Robert had knocked the man unconscious, he could have let him live. Had he really dragged the man to the cluster of trees, lit the fire, and left him for dead? The thought that I married a possible murderer sickened me.

"Does his wife know?"

"Yes," Chief Jim said. "She knows her husband may have been murdered. But she is somewhat comforted by the knowledge that, in all probability, he didn't suffer."

We both thought about that for a moment, seeking some solace in a circumstance where there really wasn't any.

"Now, it's your turn, Carly. I know you found the woodpeckers, but what's your continued interest now?"

"I'm just trying to figure a few things out," I said, evading his question. "If I come up with anything that will help, I promise to pass it on."

"You do that," he said. "And give your daddy my regards."

Driving to the Stillwell home, I thought about the murdered man. Trent had described him as a hard worker and a good father. But I had to wonder why he was at the site so late. Had he really gone to lock up a building?

I didn't know if his widow would talk to me, especially unannounced, but I was on an investigative roll and figured it worth a try.

Entirely unlike what I expected, Alecia Stillwell opened the door with a toddler clinging to one leg. Another slightly older boy watched from the hallway. Despite having given birth to two children, she had a dainty frame and appeared fragile.

With an apologetic smile, she told me she wasn't interested in buying anything but thanked me for stopping by.

Before she could shut the door, I explained I was researching the construction site fire and wanted to talk to her. Just for a few minutes.

"I've already spoken to the police. And the fire investigators. And two SLED officers. And three reporters. Please, leave me alone."

"Look, I can't begin to imagine what it's been like for you. Losing your husband. And I'm sorry to barge in on you. But I really need your help. I'm trying to find out who killed your husband."

I didn't tell her I already had a pretty good idea who'd killed her husband.

"Who are you?"

"My daddy owns the hardware store across the street from the construction site where Jerry worked. Stone Hardware and Home Supply?"

Something dawned in her eyes. "You're that bird lady. You're like a lawyer or something? Jerry told me about you. He said you stopped construction because of some woodpeckers in the trees? He lost five days' pay over that. Luckily, Mister Protter gave him some work at another site, painting, until he could start clearing again."

I nodded. That would have been me. The bird lady.

"Look, I may have a lead on who did it, but I can't go to the police until I get more information."

Extracting the young boy from her leg, Alecia sighed and invited me inside.

With the click of a remote control, she turned on a cartoon to occupy the boys in front of a small television and served me a glass of apple juice, apologizing that it was all she had on hand, besides milk. I loved apple juice, I assured her, and asked her to tell me about the night of the fire.

"There's nothing new that I haven't already told everyone else."

"Alecia," I said, "from the police department's point of view, I'm just a concerned citizen. They're not sharing their information with me. So, I have no idea what you've already told them. All I know is your husband left home that night because he forgot to lock up a building."

"We had supper," she began, sounding tired. "Mashed potatoes and chicken. It was left over from the night before, but the boys will always eat mashed potatoes and fried chicken. That was around six o'clock, or maybe a little after. Then Jerry played with the boys for a while . . . they were working on one of those big puzzle things." She gestured toward a child-sized wood table that Jerry had probably built from scratch. It held some books and toys and pieces of a giant puzzle that appeared to be an orange and green turtle.

"Then we were watching TV, and right in the middle of the show, Jerry remembered he forgot to lock the shed. He said he had to go lock it, and he'd be right back."

"The shed?"

"On the construction sites, they always put up a temporary storage building. A shed. It's where they keep oil and stuff for the heavy equipment. There's always a fuel truck on site to fill up the diesel tanks, but anything in containers or drums goes in the shed. And also supplies and chemicals, I guess, like adhesives and stuff."

"So he left to check on the shed?"

"Yeah. They keep it locked up just for safety, really. I don't think people would try to steal anything in there. But, like, kids or something could be out messing around, and some of that stuff could be dangerous if it were out in the open."

"So Jerry always locked up the shed?"

"No, several of the guys had keys to the shed. All the supervisors. And all the heavy-equipment operators, like Jerry. I think whoever was last off the site for the day made sure the shed was locked up."

I nodded. "So then what happened?"

"Jerry called me half an hour after he left. He said there was something suspicious going on. That the shed doors were open."

"Open as in wide open?"

"Yeah. Normally the doors would stay shut. Even if the shed wasn't locked up."

"I wonder why he didn't call the police when he found the doors open," I said.

"That's not Jerry's style. He is a—I mean, he was a pretty self-sufficient man. He would've walked the site, checked the heavy equipment, taken a look around to see if anything was missing. Then he might call his boss if something was really wrong. But see, he just called me so I wouldn't worry because he'd driven the motor-cycle and he knows how much I hate him driving it. Those things are like, so unsafe. But our car is in the shop because the transmission went out. So anyway," she took a deep breath, heavy with burden, "he called to let me know he wouldn't be right back. But that's all he said. The shed doors were open and something wasn't right and he was going into the trailer to get a flashlight so he could look around the property. And I never saw him again."

Her voice quivered, and she wiped away a tear with the back of a balled fist.

"So it was dark, then? If he had to get a flashlight?"

"Well, yeah. It was already getting dark when he left the house."

"So, he called to tell you he would be a little longer than he thought and not to worry."

"Yeah. It was no big deal. But, then it was like an hour and a half later, then two hours later. And I really did start to worry. I called his mobile phone, but he didn't answer. I wanted to drive to the site but couldn't, with the car in the shop." She sighed and drank some apple juice. "It's still in the shop. It's just old. So I was going to ask one of the neighbors to drive me, but by then it was already getting near eleven o'clock, and I didn't want to wake anyone up. So I called the police."

"You didn't call anybody at the company?"

"No. Jerry would have been mad if I'd called one of his bosses at home, late at night."

The comic whoops and bangs and crashes of cartoons filtered into the small dinette area where we sat, and I could hear one of the boys laughing. They were probably too young to comprehend death and understand that they'd never see their daddy again.

"I guess I should have. Called Jerry's boss. But I'm told Jerry was probably already dead by then anyway," she said matter-of-factly.

I nodded. That fact I already knew.

"So instead of calling the Protter family, I called the police and told them what happened. The dispatcher said she would have an officer drive to the site and check things out. But I knew she figured that Jerry had just stopped off at a bar for a drink or something. They probably get calls from concerned wives all the time."

One of the boys let out a yelp and began crying. Alecia left the table to check on her children. I drank some more apple juice. After a couple of minutes, the crying stopped, and she returned to the table.

"Some more time passed. I checked on the boys; they were sound asleep. I read a few chapters of a paperback. I tried Jerry's mobile number a few more times. Then I did call my upstairs neighbor, Lisa, and ask her to drive me out there. But when her husband heard what was going on, he said for me to stay here with the boys and he went. If nothing else, he told me, he'd look for Jerry's motorcycle to see if it was there. So Lisa sat with me while we waited. And then the phone rang. It was Matt, her husband. He told me there was a fire. The next morning, Jerry's boss knocked on my door. That's when I knew. Jerry was only twenty-eight, you know."

"Who came by your apartment that morning?"

"Trent Protter. One of the owners. He's the one who hired Jerry. He told me they found Jerry's body, and I got sick and I think I screamed at him and he helped me to the sofa and asked if he could call someone. My mother came, but she had to go back yesterday because she works. Me and the kids are going to move in with her in a few weeks. She lives in Savannah."

Before now, Jerry Stillwell had simply been an unlucky heavy-equipment operator who worked for Protter Construction and Development Company. But as I sat across from the young mother and watched her two boys playing on the floor in the next room, Jerry Stillwell became the husband and father that Trent had spoken of when we'd met for lunch on the rooftop terrace. When I'd accused him of being responsible for Jerry's death.

"Alecia?" I said. Her attention had drifted, and she stared at something on the tabletop that I couldn't see.

She looked up. "Yes?"

"You don't know me, but this is a genuine offer, okay?" I took a notepad out of my purse and wrote my mobile number and Mamma and Daddy's home number on it. "If there is anything I can do to help you, I want you to call me. I just moved from New York, and I'm living at Mamma and Daddy's house, but they would welcome you into their home. I don't even have to ask. Even if you and the boys would just like to come over and have supper with us one night before you go to Savannah."

Alecia took the paper. "Thanks."

"And, if you happen to think of anything else that could be important, would you call me?"

"Okay."

I pulled a photo of Robert out of my purse. Originally it had been a shot of me and him at my company Christmas party, but I'd cut myself out of it. I laid it on the table in front of her.

"Do you recognize this man? He might have come by the house sometime to talk to Jerry?" It was a long shot but worth a try.

She shook her head. No. I put the picture back in my purse.

"Just one more thing," I said, "and you can tell me to mind my own business if you want to. Are you okay with the finances? Do you need any help paying your bills?"

She shook her head again. "We'll be okay. Mister Protter gave me three month's of what Jerry's pay would have been. It's enough to get us by until I find a new job in Savannah. And the company paid for Jerry's funeral. It was a real nice one, too."

I didn't need to ask which "Mister Protter." I knew it was the same one who'd knocked on her door to deliver the news in person. The same one who'd held my hand across the bulky console of his truck and assured me that we'd figure this thing out together.

27

Robert found me before I had a chance to track him down. Stretched out on the back porch, I took up the majority of a well-used wicker and throw-cushion sofa and pored through all the information I'd accumulated about the land, the fire, and the investigation.

I'd been engrossed in a tax map printout, trying to figure out what bothered me about it. Public record, it contained a property description, the seller's name, the buyer's name and address, the purchase price. Nothing out of the ordinary. But I kept going back to the single sheet of paper that I'd obtained from the courthouse and was rereading it for the third time when the cordless phone rang. I answered it without sitting up.

"Carly, it's me."

"Me" was Robert. I sat up.

I hadn't been able to find out where he was living, and his mobile number had gone unanswered. I'd tried his office, but they said he worked mostly from home and wouldn't give out the number. In fact, my divorce lawyer hadn't been able to track him down to serve the papers. When a New York process server went to Robert's office, she was told that he no longer worked there and they didn't have a forwarding address.

"Where are you?" I said. "I've been trying to call you."

"Sorry about that. I changed cell phones and got a new number. And I did get the message you left at my office, but I wanted to talk to you in person."

"If you wanted to talk to me in person, why are you calling on the phone?"

"I'm outside," he said. "In the driveway."

Shaken, I confronted him immediately, outside, with Taffy on my heels. I didn't invite him in. Daddy was working and Mamma and Granny had gone grocery shopping, and I didn't want to be alone in the house with him.

"Tell me about the land deal, Robert. I'd like to know what motivated you to screw your own aunt and uncle out of a fair price at the same time you screwed Daddy out of a chance to buy it."

"Whoa, slow down," he said. "It's been a long flight. I got stuck in Atlanta. And then when I finally got to Charleston, the rental car place lost my reservation. You could at least say 'hello.' Offer me a beer or something before you start interrogating me."

He made a little motion, as though waving an invisible white flag in surrender.

"Tell me about the land, Robert."

He sighed, then smiled. "Okay, Carly. We'll play it your way. But can we at least sit down first?"

I moved to a lawn chair in the backyard, near Mamma's fragrant garden. Robert followed suit and sat across from me.

"I assume you're talking about the land Protter bought for the shopping center? Mary Beth said you and your mother stopped by."

"Yes. To both."

"What do you want to know?"

"Well, you can start with why you bought the land from them for the ridiculously low price of fifty thousand dollars. And then, only gave them ten thousand. And you can finish by telling me why you didn't let me or Daddy know they were ready to sell the land. Or why you didn't even tell me that Paul was so sick."

Robert took a deep breath and ran both hands through his hair before looking at me. I noticed that beneath the handsome, salon-tanned exterior, he look tired.

"Okay. The fifty thousand dollars. It was simply a price on paper. If Mary Beth told you any different, then she's confused. I think she's been getting into Paul's pain medicine and drinking too much wine, and she's not thinking right."

He reached out to pet Taffy. But perceiving what I felt toward Robert, the dog sniffed his legs, backed away, and sat by my feet. We both looked at him, awaiting answers.

"Putting just fifty thousand dollars on the paperwork saves them a lot of money. Think of how much capital gains taxes they'd have to pay on four hundred and twenty thousand dollars! They've done little to zero retirement planning. They have no tax shelters," his arms stretched out in a semi shrug. "I thoroughly explained to Mary Beth that I'd give them the full purchase price as soon as the money came through. But, I'd give it to them in a way that wouldn't cost them any capital gains or income taxes."

"Okay, so where is the money? Other than the lousy ten grand you gave them, which didn't even cover the outstanding medical bills. And speaking of medical bills, why didn't you tell me what was going on with them?"

"Please. Carly. I'll tell you everything you want to know, but one thing at a time. First of all, the ten thousand was all I had in liquid savings, and I gave them that as earnest money. Second, I had to do some creative financing on another project, so the rest of the money was tied up for a while. I planned to surprise you with this, but I've been working on opening my own agency. In fact, I've left the firm, and I'm already working for myself."

He managed a bright smile, and the charm that had convinced me to walk down the aisle a year ago reappeared. But now, it seemed forced, like the smile of a veteran used-car salesman trying to cement another deal. And besides, I already knew that he'd quit his job. My divorce lawyer had been unsuccessfully trying to track him down.

"And, third, I just gave Mary Beth and Paul the money. The entire purchase price, less closing costs and my expenses. That's why I came to Charleston. That, and to talk to you."

"Yeah, right."

"Carly, if you don't believe me, pick up the phone and call them. I drove Mary Beth to the bank. She opened a money-market checking account. I'm not the monster you seem to think I am."

He leaned forward, as if to take my hand.

Reflexively, I leaned back, out of his reach, and readjusted my chair so that I sat even further away from him. A pained expression crossed his features, but I felt no sympathy. Talking to the man I'd professed to love till death do us part was one thing, but having physical contact with him was another.

"You think I'm a monster," he announced and then waited for me to disagree or offer some words to soften his conclusion.

I didn't.

"We both know I hurt you and really screwed up our marriage. I acted selfishly, and I'm sorry. And we both know that I'll never think of Mary Beth and Paul as real parents. They took me in like a stray dog and made sure to put food in my bowl every day, but it wasn't enough."

I started to disagree with him, but it wouldn't have done any good. He had issues about being orphaned and subsequently raised by two people he wouldn't have chosen if the decision had been left up to him. He'd always considered himself suave and refined, while they were embarrassing rednecks.

"But just because I don't call them Mom and Dad," he continued, "doesn't mean I'd steal from them."

I thought he was lying. I dialed their number, and Mary Beth answered on the second ring.

"Hi, Mary Beth. It's Carly. I just wanted to see how Paul is feeling," I said.

"Oh, he's much better! Right now, he's sitting outside to get some sun."

Before I could inquire further, she told me the good news. "And guess what? Robert came by earlier and brought us a big check! Almost four hundred thousand dollars, the money he got for our land!"

She happily rambled on about what a good boy Robert was and how proud she was of him for getting his own business started and how Paul had gotten himself all worked up about nothing, probably due to all the drugs he'd been taking.

"That's wonderful, Mary Beth," I said. "I'm very happy it all worked out for you."

"Well, it could all work out for you, too, honey," she said. "I know Robert hasn't treated you right, but you should think about giving him another chance."

I asked her to tell Paul "hello" for me and hung up without commenting on giving her son another chance. He'd already had enough chances from me.

He watched me place the handset on a small table.

"Satisfied?" he asked.

I looked at the man sitting across from me, outlined by clusters of bright pink azalea blooms in Mamma's garden, suddenly unsure if he was the villain I thought him to be. My arson evidence against him was circumstantial. He had been in town. And he had motive. But had he been the one to hit Jerry? Or light the match?

"Congratulations on Vive Investments," I said and his eyebrows shot up in surprise. "I'd like to hear more about it, but what I really want to know is what you're going to do with the seven percent of retail gross. That's a lot of money."

The eyebrows moved up another fraction of an inch, and his head began to nod slowly up and down, as if confirming something to himself. "So you already know the name of my company. And the terms of the property sale."

"Tell me about the seven percent. Are you going to pass that along to Mary Beth and Paul, too?"

Robert said he had to hand it to me and threw out a compliment about how smart I was and how my intelligence was one of the things that had initially drawn him to me.

"New York women are all pretense, Carly, but you are so . . . real. You've got the beauty and the brains! And you're going to make such a wonderful mother. I just know you are."

Ignoring the flattery, I repeated my question.

"Since you asked, no, I'm not. The seven percent is my fee for handling the transaction, and it's the money to jumpstart my new business," he reasoned. "Look, if I didn't buy the land from them, I would have gotten it anyway. When they died. This way, they get enough money to live comfortably for the rest of their lives, and I get the opportunity to make a good future for us!"

I started to tell him there was no "us," but he interrupted.

"Yes, Carly," he said. "For us. We can still have a good life together as husband and wife. I'm getting my act together. My business can be based anywhere. I'm even willing to move here. Move to Charleston, for us."

There it was again. *For us.*

The second time the phrase rolled off his lips, it wasn't any more appetizing than the first. There was no "us." And looking back on the past year of my life, I realized there never had been. I couldn't believe I'd ever thought I loved him.

"I want us to work things out," he pleaded. "I want us back together. I won't give you a divorce."

I just smiled. This wasn't the eighteen hundreds. He didn't have the option of not giving me a divorce. In South Carolina, adultery was certainly grounds. And his mention of divorce reminded me I needed to do something. I excused myself, telling Robert I would get him that beer he wanted, after all.

Once inside I called my attorney and asked if he could get a process server to Mamma and Daddy's house immediately. Yes, I told him, Robert was there.

"I don't like this, Carly," he whispered, as though Robert could hear our conversation. "You be careful. I'm going to tell Guy to hang around until Robert leaves. He's a retired cop and one of the best process servers in the business."

I grabbed a beer and headed back outside. Still in his chair, Robert tried to get Taffy to play ball, but she kept her distance.

I handed over the beer. "So then, why did you tell them Daddy didn't want the land?"

"You're not having one with me?"

"Maybe later," I said, to appease him. I didn't want him to leave before the divorce papers were served. It was a crucial part of the lawsuit process, and if we couldn't find Robert to serve him, I'd be stuck in unwanted matrimony for longer than necessary.

"Now, what about the land? You knew Daddy wanted the option," I continued.

Robert frowned, as though trying to think up a viable excuse.

"I screwed up. I mean, I remember you saying something about it, but that was back when we were still in high school. When Mary Beth mentioned to me that they needed to sell the property, I just figured out the best way to do it. I didn't even think about calling your father. And as far as Paul being sick? They never told me. I had no idea until just recently. Mary Beth told me they wanted to sell the land because it was time for them to start traveling and enjoying their retirement. She never said anything about the cancer."

"That's not what she told me and Mamma. About Daddy's first option to buy, or about Paul's cancer."

"I told you, Carly. Her mind hasn't been right. She's confused."

Robert was full of explanations, yet something wasn't quite right. He'd said Mary Beth *needed* to sell the property, then seconds later that Mary Beth told him they *wanted* to sell. A slight change in vernacular but an inconsistency nonetheless. And Daddy always said that inconsistencies were like single-edge razor blades: they would cut through a fabric of lies, one thread at a time, until the truth was revealed.

I still had unanswered questions, like why Robert was in town the night of the fire, and why he had initially put the money in a Belizean account. But my head was suddenly pounding, and I needed some time to think. I wanted to ask him to leave, but I needed him to stay until Guy arrived with the divorce papers. Whether or not he was a criminal, I had no intention of remaining married to him.

"So tell me about your new business," I said. "It sounds really interesting."

He brightened and went into a thorough explanation of how his investment and financial planning agency would be different from all the others. How he envisioned managing portfolios of all sizes and how he would have four or five branch offices open within two years. He droned on, finished his beer, and asked for another.

I went inside to get it, and when I returned, another man was striding through the yard. Dressed casually, he approached Robert in a friendly manner.

"Robert Ellis?"

Startled, Robert stood up. "Yes?"

The man handed him a thick manila envelope. "You've been served."

"What the hell?"

"The divorce papers," I said smugly. "In case you forgot, I am suing you for divorce. But my lawyer had trouble tracking you down in New York to serve the papers, since you didn't leave a forwarding address and you quit your job. So I'm glad you paid me a visit today."

"I told you, we're not getting a divorce," he said flatly. "You are going to make me some children, and we are going to be a happy family."

I was going to make him some children? Maybe Lori Anne had been right when she surmised that Robert wanted to invent the childhood family he'd been cheated out of.

"I think you should leave," Guy said to Robert.

Robert threw the envelope at Guy's feet. "Get lost. And you can take your damn papers with you."

Guy didn't care what Robert did with the envelope. Whether or not he actually opened and read the contents didn't matter from a legal standpoint. He'd been served, and the divorce could proceed. But since my lawyer had asked him to look out for me, Guy wasn't going to leave me alone with Robert, either.

"I said, get lost," Robert repeated.

Guy let his sport coat fall open, revealing a shoulder holster and large-caliber handgun. Robert looked from the weapon to Guy and back to the weapon before turning to me.

"I'm going to stay in Charleston until you make up your mind, Carly. We can have a good life together. Think about it. I'm at the Days Inn on Meeting Street," he said and walked back to his rental car.

28

When the breeze shifted, it carried with it the fragrance of Mamma's confederate jasmine vines. Dotted with small white blooms, they spiraled up the trunks of several trees in the backyard. I took a sip of perfectly chilled chardonnay and inhaled deeply. The light vanilla flavor of the wine complimented the perfumey smell of the flowers. The combination elicited sensory bliss.

Mamma, Granny, Lori Anne, and I shared the bottle of wine for cocktail hour. Daddy enjoyed a beer and had begun the ritual of lighting his pipe. Taffy chewed on a peanut butter–flavored dental bone. We talked about Robert, and they let me call him as many disparaging names as I could think of. It made me feel a tiny bit better, so I spewed out a few more descriptive nouns for good measure.

"Don't hold back, Carly," Lori Anne teased. "How do you really feel?"

"Actually, I feel like a fool having married him," I said.

"He could be very charming when he wanted to be, and he fooled a lot of people besides you." She distributed the remaining wine evenly between our four glasses. "So quit blaming yourself."

"If it was me, I'd dirty up the sheets with that Trent boy," Granny said, examining her nails. "Heck, if I was younger, I'd go for a roll with him myself."

"Good Lord." Mamma shook her head.

"Maybe I oughtta go to that spa of yours," Granny told Lori Anne, pushing her cheeks up with her palms, "and get my face all lifted up." She cupped her breasts and shook them. "Or get me one a those tube jobs. Men like the big titties."

Lori Anne burst out laughing. "My spa doesn't do cosmetic surgery, but we sure can tighten you up!"

"What needs winding up?" Granny asked.

"Not your mouth," Daddy said. "That's for sure."

I passed around a bowl of pistachio nuts while he filled us in on the latest news from the fire chief. With still no solid leads in the investigation, progress had come to a standstill. They'd questioned all the workers on the construction site. They'd questioned past employees. They'd questioned contractors. They'd looked into Jerry's background. They'd pursued the possibility that one of the Protters had planned the fire to eliminate the woodpecker habitat. And to be fair, they officially questioned me, Mamma, and Daddy, since we didn't want to see the Handyman's open. They'd even questioned Robert and the Carpenters, as the two prior owners of the property, to see if there had been any unusual occurrences on the land in the past. But for all their efforts, they had nothing.

"This wine is right good," Granny said. "I bet the dog might like a little nip."

"I don't think Taffy likes wine," Daddy said.

Hearing her name, Taffy looked around but didn't see any people food coming her way. She turned her full attention back to the half-eaten bone.

Instinct told me that my soon-to-be ex-husband was involved with the fire, but I had no way to prove it. And hypothetically, even if Robert was guilty, it wouldn't change the outcome of the shopping center. It looked like my stalling tactics had been in vain.

Meanwhile, construction of Protter's newest shopping center clipped along at a rapid pace. Most of the underground infrastructure was complete and soon buildings would emerge from the ground. Although I made periodic visits to satisfy my curiosity, Daddy was forced to view the progress every day as he went to and from work. Whether he wanted to or not.

I asked him if he was still going to shut down the store.

"I think so," he said. "Yes."

"This wine is right good," Granny said. "I bet the dog might like a little nip."

"I don't think Taffy likes wine," Mamma said.

"I'm sorry my plan didn't work. I figured Handyman's Depot would get fed up with delays and find another site for their Charleston store," I told them.

"I think your plan was pretty ingenious," Daddy said. "You certainly got their attention."

I nodded. I had done that. Lori Anne raised her glass to toast to me.

"And, if it weren't for you, that section of Charleston city wall would have been bulldozed!" Mamma said, trying to cheer me up. "Now, people can sit and look at it, and ruminate on Charleston's past." Her Southern drawl gave "ruminate" five, maybe six syllables, each of them soothing.

"And as far as Robert goes," Daddy said, "anybody can be fooled once. We're just glad you got out of the marriage early on."

"Exactly," Lori Anne said. "I mean, look at me. I was fooled once, too. I got married when I shouldn't have. You live and learn."

"This wine is right good," Granny said. "I bet the dog m—"

"I don't think Taffy likes wine," Mamma and Daddy and Lori Anne cut her off in surround sound.

Granny shrugged her shoulders and sipped.

"I just feel foolish. And disappointed that things aren't working out like I'd envisioned."

"Hey," Daddy said. "Remember what I always told you and your sister about looking at the stained-glass window from the end of the church pew?"

I did, and smiled. As kids, Jenny and I loved to sit at the very end of the church pew, next to the wall, midway between the pulpit and the door. She liked the end of the row because she could stare at the handsome teenage usher-in-training whom she had a crush on. And I liked to sit there because all the freshly sharpened miniature pencils were there, and I could draw on the back of Mamma's Sunday program to my heart's content. Plus, our pew was next to the very best window.

In the historic district, the church had giant stained-glass windows on both sides of the chapel. When I tired of drawing, I'd gaze through the colorful glass while the preacher's booming voice rattled my rib cage. I could see all the intricate details of the handiwork, and I'd pick out one single piece of uniquely shaped glass and play a game by imagining all the different animals that it resembled. But, as Daddy pointed out, sitting so close to the window prevented me from seeing the entire scene. To fully appreciate the artist's vision, I had to view my favorite stained-glass window from a distance.

Growing up, if my focus on something became too narrow, Daddy would simply remind me of the stained-glass window. It was his way of saying that I needed to take a few steps back and distance myself.

"Okay," I relented. "I probably do need to look at the bigger picture. But that won't change the fact that Stone Hardware and Home Supply is being forced out of business. What's in the bigger picture I'm missing?"

"Well, for one thing, you're back home, in Charleston," Lori Anne said.

That was true.

"For another thing, you've got a wonderful future ahead of you, loaded with options and opportunities. You can do anything you want to do," Daddy said.

"And besides that," Mamma interjected, "your daddy has been thinking it just might be time for him to slow down a little."

I shot Daddy a look. *You? Slow down?*

He finished packing his pipe and lit it with a wooden match, puffing a few times before answering my look.

"We've paid a wonderful tribute to your great-grandfather Wade and your mamma's side of the family by everything we've accomplished at the store. And by taking care of all the people we've served over the years."

"We're going to buy a big motor home and do some traveling around the country," Mamma said. "We've always said we'd do that someday."

"You have?" I was incredulous. It was the first I'd heard about it.

"Sure. We just never got around to it," Daddy said. "Owning a business, even with good people working for you, you can't just up and go traveling whenever you want to."

I think my jaw dropped an inch or two because I felt my mouth open.

"Oh, we're not going to get one of those huge things that look like a giant luxury bus," Mamma said with a dismissing wave and sipped some wine. "But something with a full-size bed and a slide-out. We'll start with short trips here and there. Maybe just a week-end at a campground in Myrtle Beach. Then some week-long trips to state parks in Georgia. By next year, we might be ready to do a cross-country loop."

I looked at Granny.

"I'm going, too," she said. "I like cookin' weenies over a campfire."

I looked at Mamma.

"Sure, your granny can go with us when she wants to. Or she'll stay next door with Miss Rose while we're on the road. Even Taffy can travel with us in the motor home."

The way Mamma casually dropped the lingo, she already sounded like a seasoned RVer.

"Wow." It's all I could manage.

"And the final part of the bigger picture is that you have met some interesting people since this whole mess started," Lori Anne said. "One person in particular comes to mind."

"Really?"

"You know who I'm talking about," she said, knowing full well that I knew exactly who she referred to. Trent. My gorgeous, polite, compelling, and infuriating construction worker.

I almost reminded Lori Anne that he had a girlfriend but decided it didn't matter anyway. The idea of anything happening between Trent and me, after all that had happened at the construction site, was far-fetched.

"If it was me, I'd dirty up the sheets with that Trent boy," Granny repeated.

Mamma rolled her eyes and went inside to fix supper. I told Daddy I felt a little guilty about letting Mamma do all the cooking.

"Are you kidding?" he said. "She loves fussing over you. I haven't eaten this good in a year. Hell, you ought to have come home sooner."

"I'll second that," Lori Anne agreed and drank some more wine.

Watching the cherry tobacco smoke dance lazily around Daddy before escaping through the screens, it dawned on me that he looked relaxed. The panic attacks, or what he referred to as the "pulse thing," had stopped. I asked him what had changed in a few weeks' time. Why he was no longer upset at the prospect of closing the business.

He smiled. "I made myself look at the bigger picture."

Daddy had taken his own advice. I laughed and drank some wine and laughed some more. It felt so good to be in the company of my family and my best friend. Looking back, I couldn't believe I'd left Charleston in the first place.

Granny, making a show of situating herself on the ground, proffered her glass of wine to the half-snoozing dog. Taffy picked up her head to investigate the offering, sniffed it, licked the rim once, yawned, and went back to sleep.

"This dog don't like wine!"

Granny climbed back into her chair and began flipping through a magazine.

"It's like I said," Daddy continued. "Wade would be proud of everything your mamma and I have done with the business that he started. And our employees won't have a bit of trouble finding something else. They're all good people, and any company would be lucky to have them."

"You certainly are looking on the bright side of things."

He nodded. "Oh, if I could influence exactly how this whole thing would go down, I'd choose my own version. But your mamma and I will take the hand that we're dealt."

"What would your version be?"

"Well, slowing down and spending more time with your mamma is certainly appealing. But I'd like to keep working, maybe part time."

"Doing what?" I couldn't envision Daddy selling T-shirts or greeting people at Wal-Mart.

"Good question. Hardware and home supply is what I know and love."

Mouth-watering cooking smells wafted out from Mamma's kitchen and mingled with pipe smoke as the evening slipped into dusk. A chorus of crickets began to make their rhythmic music. Taffy snored contentedly.

Mamma returned to announce that her famous plantation hash was ready and we could eat anytime. Whenever she prepared a meal out of rice and whatever she happened to find on the refrigerator shelves, it was dubbed Plantation Hash. The term originated before the Civil War years, when South Carolina's rice plantations thrived and slave families would often mix cooked rice with whatever else they had on hand.

Relaxed by the comforting scents and sounds of home, I suddenly figured out what had been nagging at me about the tax maps and closing paperwork. Like a persistent mechanic, my subconscious had finally repaired the loose connection in my brain, and I sat up so abruptly that some wine sloshed out of my glass.

"Son of a bitch!"

"What?" everybody said.

"The dates!" I said.

"What about the dates?" Daddy said.

"When he bought the land from Mary Beth and Paul, Robert made sure the closing took place before we got married. The date on the settlement statement was the day *before* our wedding. A Friday."

"Right," Daddy said.

"But the title wasn't recorded until the following Monday, *after* we were married. That's what bothered me about the date, but I didn't make the connection until just now!"

Mamma and Daddy looked at me, not understanding my excitement.

"Do you know what this means?!"

"What difference does a day or two make?" Mamma said.

My heart pounded with the discovery. "It means that, technically, the asset wasn't acquired until *after* Robert and I married. And South Carolina is an equitable-distribution divorce state. Which means, I can ask for half of that seven-percent income and half of the gain from the sale to the Protters."

"That money is probably already gone," Daddy said.

"Or it's hidden offshore."

"So then, what are you so excited about?" Mamma asked.

"I can make a strong case that the entire transaction was illegitimate, because Robert had no right to sell the land to the Protters to begin with! Since, theoretically, the investment was acquired after we became husband and wife, I can claim it was jointly owned property! I can make an argument that construction should be stopped because I want my half of the land back. Of course it won't hold. Any judge in her right mind would work out an equitable solution. But I sure can slow things down in the interim. It could be a major setback for the Protters, time wise."

"You can do that just because the title deed wasn't recorded the same day of the purchase?" Mamma said.

I smiled. "Yes."

"How did it happen?" Lori Anne asked.

"Well, after a real-estate closing, a courier takes the paperwork from the attorney's office to the courthouse. That's why most closings are scheduled to take place in the morning or early afternoon. The sale, or transfer of the property from one owner to another, is not technically complete in South Carolina until the deed is recorded at the courthouse. But in this case, something must have happened to the courier."

I paused to eat a pistachio nut. "Who knows what? He could have had a flat tire on the way to the courthouse. Or a personal emergency. The bottom line is that he didn't get to the courthouse before it closed that Friday, so the title wasn't recorded until the following Monday. Meanwhile, Robert and I had gotten married during the weekend."

"Good Lord," Mamma said.

"Exactly," I said.

"Amazing," Daddy said.

"Is supper ready?" Granny said.

We went inside and ate and pondered the possibilities.

Robert had bought the land before we got married, or so he thought. Then just weeks later, right before our honeymoon, turned it for an outrageous profit. And to top that, he'd stashed the money in Belize. But, despite the fact that he'd done it all without my knowledge, I now had another way to stall Protter's development.

Mamma concocted tonight's version of plantation hash with chicken, sausage, tomatoes, onions, and yellow squash. It was delicious.

"God, I miss this cooking," Lori Anne said through a full mouth. "If Carly leaves town again, can I still come over to eat?"

"I'm not going anywhere!" I said.

"And even if she does, you're welcome to come eat anytime," Mamma said.

As I thought about the Protter family business and Stone Hardware and my newly discovered ammunition to once again halt progress at the construction site, I had a revelation. Forcing my mind to contemplate an even bigger picture, it dawned on me that I could fight and negotiate simultaneously. I didn't have to give up one for the other. I didn't have to avoid conflict to work out a win-win situation.

I had additional ammunition in my arsenal. And I had the ability to sweeten Handyman's pot with the lure of *In Home Now* as a marketing avenue for their exclusive products. I could do what I did best—negotiate—and fight!

I told everyone what I had in mind.

"Oh, man," Lori Anne said. Her eyes glowed with anticipation. "This is going to be good."

"Exactly what will you negotiate?" Daddy asked.

"That's for you to figure out!" I said. "You're the businessman."

"I'm not following you."

"Okay," I said. "This is what we've got. The Handyman's Depot is going to happen. But, it can happen smoothly or it can happen with delays. It's in their best interest for the store to open on schedule. That's our ammunition. That's how we strong-arm our way to the table. Then, we work out a deal to market their exclusive products through *In Home Now*. That's the incentive we bring to the table. The third part of this equation is your demand. How does the deal benefit you? For example, maybe you'd want to work part time for them as a local consultant. How would you paint your version of this picture?"

Daddy nodded, thinking. After a minute or two, he asked for the dossier on Handyman's Depot.

We finished eating, and Daddy and I retired to the drawing room while everyone else stretched out on the back porch. For the next hour and a half, Daddy read the information I'd given him and intermittently scribbled notes. I followed him to the screened porch when he got up to smoke his pipe and call Stephen with questions about *In Home Now*. When he hung up, he was grinning.

"An exclusive products distribution warehouse and public showroom for *In Home Now*."

"*In Home Now* doesn't have any public showrooms or stores," I said.

"Exactly!"

When he finished explaining it, I realized Daddy's idea was genius. It made good business sense all the way around.

During his phone call, Daddy learned that *In Home Now*, in a trial move, was going to open three retail locations across the country. The stores would sell most everything featured on the show and give consumers the opportunity to do on-air reviews. Two of the locations were already targeted for New York and Atlanta but the third was open.

Although *In Home Now* had not considered South Carolina, Daddy convinced Stephen that Charleston was a perfect choice. And Stephen was confident that he could sell the idea to the partners and his boss. Not only was it Jenny's hometown, but the charismatic city drew a brisk tourist business year round. Between the locals and visitors, and Jenny's support with frequent appearances, the site was sure to be a hit.

Daddy also learned that *In Home Now* would entertain the idea of forming a partnership with Handyman's Depot to sell their exclusive products on the air, which was the key to making my idea work. Meanwhile, the existing building Mamma and Daddy's store occupied would make a perfect warehouse from which to inventory and ship Handyman's products to *In Home Now* viewers. Daddy could oversee both the retail store and the warehouse. And, if he hired the right people to manage them, he could travel with Mamma as often as they wanted to go.

"That's brilliant!" Mamma told Daddy.

"Can it work?" Lori Anne asked.

My mind forged ahead, preparing lists of what I'd have to do to make it happen. "Of course it can work. Mamma's right. It's brilliant."

Lori Anne wished me luck, thanked Mamma, and headed home to

get a good night's sleep. I thought about going to bed early but decided I'd never be able to doze off. There was too much activity inside my head. Energized, I headed to the kitchen table with my laptop, and by the time I called Trent an hour and a half later, it was past midnight.

"Hello?"

It was a sleepy greeting. I tried not to think about what Trent's perfectly proportioned body looked like stretched out in bed. I wondered if it was a king-sized bed. I wondered if he slept nude.

"It's Carly Stone. I want you to arrange a meeting with Joseph Jones and his people. Preferably here, in Charleston. Sometime soon. I have a proposal."

"Carly?" he asked, quickly gaining full consciousness.

"Yes?" I said sweetly.

"Can you repeat whatever it was you just said?"

"Sure." I did.

"And what makes you think that Joseph Jones, president and CEO of Handyman's Depot, has any desire to drop everything and show up for a chat with you?"

I told him exactly why.

"Son of a bitch," he muttered.

"That's what I said when I realized the possibilities."

I heard the rustling of sheets and imagined Trent sitting on the edge of the bed. Wearing only boxer shorts or, better yet, totally nude. He sighed heavily into the telephone, and I knew he was no longer in bed. I had a mental image of him pacing, back and forth, on his bedroom floor.

"Can't you just have the divorce lawyer work something out between you and Robert?"

I didn't say anything.

"You're not going to just let this drop, are you?"

I still didn't say anything.

"No, of course you're not," Trent answered his own question.

I silently agreed.

"Jesus Christ," he said.

I nodded through the phone.

"Can you at least tell me what you plan to propose at this little meeting?"

I did. When I'd finished, Trent began laughing. It was a soft chuckle at first but escalated to a genuine, full-blown laugh.

"You're a jewel, Carly Stone."

I wasn't sure if the comment was a compliment or an insult. "So will you set up a meeting with Joseph Jones and his entourage next week?"

"Sure. I'll get Jo Jo to the table. He's already scheduled to be in town because we're having lunch Wednesday. Perhaps we can do it at Jack's office."

I detected a mix of humor, frustration, and resignation in Trent's voice.

"Look," I told him. "This thing can turn out to be a good business decision for everybody involved. Good for Mamma and Daddy, good for *In Home Now*, good for Handyman's, and good for you, because you get to finish your shopping center on time. It's a winner all the way around."

"But isn't this negotiation?" Trent asked. "What happened to the new Carly Stone? The fighter. The one who told me she was tired of compromise?"

"She decided to get off the end of the church pew."

29

"Is this Carly?"

The sweet voice coming through the telephone sounded familiar, but I didn't immediately place it.

"Yes, it is."

"I'm Alecia Stillwell, Jerry's wife? Or, Jerry's widow, I mean," she said.

"Alecia, how are you doing? I'm glad you called."

"You told me that you're trying to find out who killed my husband."

"Yes, I am," I told her. "But right now, all I have are suspicions. And the police won't listen to suspicions."

"Can I come over?"

Alecia arrived half an hour later. She looked as young and innocent and fragile as she had when I'd gone to her house, except this time she didn't have the two youngsters hanging on her. She told me that she was moving in two days and her mother had come up from Savannah to help her drive the U-Haul back. We got two glasses of lemonade and sat on the piazza. She asked if I still had the photo I'd shown her before. I found it at the bottom of my purse and handed it to her. She studied it and frowned.

"That could be him," she announced.

"Could be who?"

She took a deep breath, deciding where to start. "I went by the construction site to see Mister Protter this morning. To say good-bye and to thank him. And because . . . I don't know . . . I guess I just needed to get a feel for where Jerry died. To say good-bye to him, too."

She reached down to pet Taffy, who nuzzled her knees, probably detecting the scent of two small children on their mother.

"There was this guy there? He was leaving when I got there, but Mister Protter introduced me anyway. So when the guy finds out I'm Jerry's wife, a real strange look comes over him. And then he says something about giving me condolences, or whatever, and gives me a hug? That's when I smelled it."

"You smelled what?"

"The chemical. It's a solvent they use with the adhesives. The same stuff the arson people found traces of in those bird's nests. The cavities in the trees?"

I nodded.

"Well, I smelled it on his jacket when he hugged me. It was kind of windy and drizzly this morning? And he was wearing this red windbreaker jacket? With, like, a country club logo on the front?"

Although she was talking in questions, they didn't require responses.

"So the smell was on the sleeve, I think, or maybe the collar? I don't know. But I definitely smelled it. I have a real good nose, and this stuff has a unique odor. Sort of like an oily plastic but kind of sweet?"

"When did you smell it before?" I asked. "How did you know what the chemical smelled like to begin with?"

"Jerry didn't work with that stuff, but once, him and a crane operator got it all over themselves by accident. I had a heck of a time trying to get the smell out of Jerry's clothes? Anyway, he explained to me what the stuff was and what they used it for."

"So you smelled this adhesive solvent, the same one used in the fire, on this man that Trent Protter was talking to on the site?"

"Uhm huh."

"And you think it might be the man in this picture?" I said holding up the small photo of Robert, my heart racing. "Are you sure?"

She studied the picture again. "Pretty sure."

"You said Trent introduced you. Do you remember the name?"

"Randy, maybe? Or Roger? I can't remember. But I asked Mister Protter who the guy was after he left? He said some investor. I already knew from looking at the man's hands that he wasn't in construction, you know? They were manicured."

Something jumped in my stomach, and I had to put my glass of lemonade down before I dropped it. Robert had always taken pride in the way his hands looked, and got a manicure every two weeks.

"Was the man's name Robert?"

"Yep, that was it. Mister Protter called him Robert."

"Did Trent tell you who the man is?" *That he is my husband?*

"Yeah, I just told you. He was, like, an investor."

I told Alecia that I knew the man she was talking about and that I'd suspected his involvement in the fire.

"Well, you tell me. Why would some investor have this chemical on his jacket? It's not something you'd use around the house or anything. And besides that, there was a spot on his shoe."

"What do you mean, a spot?"

"He was wearing these preppy-looking brushed-leather shoes? Like the kind with the white rubber soles that you're suppose to wear on a boat? So one of them has this spot over the toe. Almost like a bleach spot, with a dark ring around it?"

I nodded my understanding.

"Well, it was exactly like the spots on Jerry's boots when he got that toluene stuff all over himself."

"So you smelled it on his jacket and saw it on his shoe."

"Yep," she said.

"Was there anything else?"

"I didn't like the way he looked at me when he found out I was Jerry's wife. It was a little creepy? I got good instincts about people."

I asked Alecia if she'd told the police what she was telling me. She hadn't told anyone else, she said, because they would think she was imagining things. And besides that, she said, she had a good feeling about me.

"With you being a lawyer and all, I figured you'd know what to do," she said.

I knew exactly what to do. "What color were the shoes?"

"Tan?" she said. "Like, maybe a caramel color? With dark brown shoestrings."

"And you said the jacket was a red windbreaker with a country club logo on the front?"

"Yeah."

I knew the jacket she was talking about; I had bought it for him.

I explained to Alecia that she would need to give a statement to the police before she left for Savannah and that she may need to appear in court at some point to testify if Robert was charged with arson, or murder.

"So you really think this man did it?"

"Yes, I do. I was suspicious before, but now I'm almost certain. If investigators find out who started the fire, it'll lead them to Jerry's murderer. Most likely, it's the same person."

Realizing I shared a home and a year of my life with Robert made me nauseous.

I called the fire chief, who called the lead investigator, who said they'd be right over. While we waited, I explained to Alecia that Robert was my husband and gave her a condensed version of events. Her reaction began with shock, turned to anger, and ended with sympathy.

"I'm so sorry," I said, taking her hand.

"I'm sorry for you, too," she told me, squeezing mine.

We drank our lemonade and played ball with Taffy in the backyard until the fire chief arrived along with a Charleston police officer and a SLED officer. Alecia repeated her story. When she finished, I gave the men a copy of the land purchase agreement between Robert, doing business as Vive Investments, and Protter Construction and Development Company. I showed them the safeguard clause pertaining to the seven percent of retail gross and explained what it meant. It proved motive. And then I gave them the airline information and flight number indicating that Robert had been in town the night of the fire and flown out early the next morning.

"When we questioned Mister Ellis by phone to see if anything unusual had ever happened on the land when he or the Carpenters owned it, he said 'no.' And then he joked that maybe the fire was just a redneck way to clear it, you know, instead of using heavy equipment? It was an inappropriate thing to say, but then, we hadn't told him a man had been killed," the SLED officer said.

"Did you ask him where he was that night?" Alecia said.

"I don't believe so. He wasn't a suspect."

"Well," I pointed out, "somebody with Robert's name and frequent flier number most certainly did fly to Charleston the night before the fire and leave the morning after."

Chief Jim shook his head. "You gonna be okay, Carly?"

I told him I would. Then I told the men that Robert was in town, in a hotel, and planned to stay until I agreed not to divorce him.

"We'll get a warrant to search his hotel room and car as well as his residence in New York. The New York thing could take a few days, since we have to find him first to obtain a primary residence address. But we can get into his hotel room as early as tomorrow morning to look for the shoes and jacket," the Charleston cop said. "Maybe even tonight."

"If he calls, you just make sure he doesn't go anywhere, Carly. Can you do that? We need to keep him in that hotel, at least through tomorrow."

I nodded.

We decided that, as soon as the cops had the search warrant, I'd call Robert on his mobile number and ask him to meet me at his hotel. That would ensure that Robert, along with his shoes and jacket, would be there. And even though I had no intention of going to Robert's hotel, all three men warned me to stay away from my husband. He could very well be dangerous, they said. I readily agreed.

30

"You've got your meeting," Trent told me when I opened the back screen door.

Had he been a minute earlier, he would have caught me sunbathing, stretched out on a chaise lounge, lazily reading a paperback. As it were, I'd gone inside in search of a snack and had grabbed one of Daddy's long-sleeved button-downs before answering the knock at the door. Although it was big and baggy and I had to roll up the too-long sleeves, it wasn't buttoned, and I was suddenly self-conscious of my exposed navel.

"That's good news," I said in my most businesslike voice.

We stood awkwardly in the doorway. Mamma and Daddy were at the store preparing for their liquidation sale, and Granny was napping. Taffy ambled up to greet our visitor and nuzzled Trent's hand.

He gave her an absentminded rub behind the ears. "It's next Tuesday."

"Excellent."

"In the morning, ten o'clock," Trent said.

"Ten o'clock works well," I agreed.

"At Jack's office. He has a nice meeting room."

"That's great."

We looked at each other for a few expectant seconds, waiting for the other to say something else, but neither of us did. I invited him in. He agreed. I moved aside to let him through the door. But instead of passing me, he grabbed my shoulders and pulled me toward him until my body was just shy of touching his. His back pressed against the screen door, preventing it from slamming against us. I looked up and he looked down and our faces were so close, I could feel the moisture in his breath.

He held me that way, close but not touching, for what seemed like an eternity as he studied my eyes.

"Kiss me," he finally said. His voice was commanding, and I forgot about my exposed belly and bare feet. "Kiss me, Carly. It's making me mad, thinking about it. Thinking about kissing you."

I was too close to see his whole face at once, so I opted for his lips and focused on the way they formed words.

"One minute I want to kiss you, and the next minute I want to strangle you. But mostly I want to kiss you," he continued.

"You do?" I asked, still inches away from him.

"Yes. Kiss me."

"Okay," I said and kissed him.

It was tentative and soft, at first. Until I put an arm around his neck and he took my other arm and placed it around the other side of his neck, and I stretched up to better reach him, and his hands found my face before traveling to the sensitive spot at the back of my neck, and his fingers entwined themselves with my hair. Then, the kiss became needy and sweet, and we tantalizingly explored each other's mouths, slowly.

Feeling left out of the game, Taffy wedged herself between our legs and woofed. Trent released me and smiled. It was a brilliant smile.

"My God," he said. "That was just as I imagined it would be. Well, except for the dog."

"Would you like to come in? Or sit outside on the piazza?" I asked pleasantly.

He pulled me back to his chest and thoroughly kissed me again, not caring that we still stood in the doorway. The taste of his mouth was addictive, like chocolate, and I instantly wanted more.

When I managed to pull myself away from him, we retrieved a couple of sodas from the fridge and moved back to the piazza. We sat for a few minutes, admiring Mamma's garden and the sunny day. Taffy dropped a tennis ball into Trent's lap. He tossed it high into the air; she expertly caught it and ran a victory lap around us.

"The lead investigator told me they're going to arrest Robert as soon as they find him," Trent said, confirming what I already suspected. "They found toluene on the jacket collar and sleeve."

I'd called Robert's mobile number once the search warrant was obtained, but it was no longer a working number. I also tried his motel room several times, but he wasn't there, even though the motel had no record of him checking out.

Officers wanted to search his rental car but hadn't been able to track it down. And not wanting to chance losing evidence, they went ahead and searched the room even though Robert was absent. Luckily, the red jacket was hanging in the closet.

"There's no record of him flying out of Charleston, and he's not at his aunt and uncle's house," Trent said. "And the check he wrote them for the land? It bounced. Nearly four hundred thousand dollars' worth of bounce. The account it was written on has since been closed."

"Damn." I wasn't shocked. Just sad for Mary Beth and Paul. They deserved so much better.

"Yeah," Trent agreed.

"He told me it was certified funds."

"He lied."

"I feel really bad for them," I said.

"I know."

"I wonder if he went back to New York?"

Trent frowned. "Carly, you need to be careful."

"He may be pond scum," I said, "but he wouldn't try to hurt me."

Trent shook his head, disagreeing. "We're talking about a possible murderer."

"I bet he took off," I said.

"The cops think he bolted, too. In fact, one of their profilers believes he will head for the West Coast or possibly leave the country. But I'm not so sure. He could still be in Charleston. And he could want revenge. You're the one who busted the case wide open. There's no telling what he might do."

"Thanks for your concern, but it's unwarranted."

"Just be careful, okay? Keep your eyes open. Keep your cell phone with you whenever you're out of the house. Keep the doors locked when you're in the house. And if he does show up here, just call the police. Don't let him in."

I wasn't worried but nodded my agreement anyway.

In addition to the evidence from the hotel room, Trent told me, investigators also found a concrete block with droplets of Jerry Stillwell's blood on it, along with just a smidgen of someone else's. It was the weapon used to knock him unconscious. Whoever hit Jerry in the head with it had scraped one of his hands in the process. If DNA testing showed that the blood belonged to Robert, the prosecutor's case against him would be solid. They'd collected his shaving kit and a comb, which should carry some DNA evidence. But to make a solid case, they had to find him and get a sample directly from his body so there was a positive source to match.

"What was Robert doing at the site when Alecia came by to say good-bye?" I asked Trent, suddenly thinking of Jerry Stillwell's widow.

"He said he wanted to make sure there were no hard feelings about the time he tried to punch me out at your folks' house. I told him there weren't. Then he said that he's moving to Charleston and that the two of you are going to work things out," Trent said. "I wished him luck. Then he asked about the possibility of doing an amendment to the original purchase agreement. He said he'd forgo the entire seven percent in exchange for a flat two hundred thousand dollars, but he would want to do the deal soon. Before the end of the week. He said Protter would come out ahead of the game by paying an additional two hundred grand now instead of half a million over the next five years."

"So what did you say?"

"I told him I'd talk to Jack and that he should give me a call in a few days," Trent answered. "But that was just to get rid of him. I'd already decided that Robert will never get a dime of that seven percent. We're going to take advantage of the safeguard clause. Plans for one of the anchor stores were modified. Cut by a thousand square feet."

"You're kidding. Were you planning to do that all along? Even before you found out about Robert?"

"No, not at all. Protter Construction and Development is all about integrity, Carly. Ask anyone we've dealt with. But pay a man who murdered one of my employees, for the next five years? No way. No way in hell."

His eyes narrowed with anger at the thought, and I had to wonder how he could stand to be around the wife of that same person. Even though I had no control over Robert's actions, I felt shamed by mere association.

Trent read my mind. "I don't hold anything against you, Carly. You were just another of Robert's victims. Anybody can be fooled once."

"That's exactly what Daddy said."

"Well, it's true," Trent said, and leaned back in his chair to stretch. "You know, the fact that you could stake claim to half of that seven percent he was supposed to get has occurred to me," Trent said.

It had occurred to me, too. "Yes."

"Well, like I said, he's not getting a dime. To be fair though, I'd still like to give you your cut. In ways other than cash."

"Such as?"

"For starters, lots and lots of dinners. Maybe some of them aboard my sailboat. Did I tell you I have a boat? I haven't been out on it in more than a year, which makes me think that I've been working entirely too much," Trent said.

"I like food. And boats."

"And, I'm thinking a vacation will be in order as soon as the new center is finished. You think we could spend a week or so together without annoying the hell out of each other?"

"Of course."

"Well then, we'll have to go to that little place you like in the Florida Keys."

I couldn't help but laugh. And feel like a cherished princess.

"Sure. Why not?"

Trent smiled, and for the first time, I noticed that a tiny dimple formed at each corner of his mouth with the expression. The realization made something flutter in my chest. I was saturated with anticipation, and the sensation was intoxicating. The man sitting in front of me was a newly discovered treasure, with a history and a future, both waiting to be unveiled.

"And the main way I'd like to pay you your share of that money is with a signing bonus."

I didn't understand. "Pardon?"

"The way I figure it, seven percent over five years would amount to, and this is ballpark, but half a million dollars going to Vive Investments. Your half, assuming you would have gotten it, would be a quarter of a million dollars. And let's face it, even if we hadn't taken advantage of that safeguard clause and did give Robert his percentage each quarter, the chances of you seeing any of it were slim."

"True."

"So I propose you take Jack's offer and—"

"Jack's offer?"

"Oh, he must not have called you yet. Jack is going to offer you a position in his law firm with a signing bonus of fifty thousand dollars paid by Protter Construction and Development, since you'll be on retainer for us."

"What? He doesn't know a thing about me!"

"Oh, but he does. Jack's first rule in any encounter is to know your adversary. He insists on that. And, my beautiful Carly, you were our adversary. Jack was quite impressed with your track record of corporate mediation in New York. An astounding closure rate. He says if you can do that good out of court, you'll kick ass in court. And, graduating from law school at USC summa cum laude? Impressive. Mostly, though, he wants to hire you because he said you have balls."

"Balls?"

"Well, Jack's not always politically correct. But I can say this about him: he is the shrewdest, most calculating, intelligent, compassionate, and caring man I've ever known."

"You've just described a complete paradox."

Trent gave me another smile. The one with the nearly imperceptible dimples designed just for my viewing pleasure. "Jack says you remind him a lot of him when he was your age. If you truly want to work as an attorney, Carly, you won't find a better mentor."

I felt like I was dreaming. My fingers and toes went numb, and for an instant, I wondered if my body might have been experiencing a mild form of shock. I was totally blindsided. And happy. But what right did they have to do a background investigation on me?

"Don't be mad about Jack looking into your background, Carly. It's what he does. And, as much as I wanted him to turn up something to make me hate you, the opposite happened."

"Dammit! Would you please stop it?"

"Stop what?"

"Reading my mind!" Not knowing whether to be irritated or flattered, I glared at my tea before plucking out an ice cube for Taffy. She chewed it exactly three times before swallowing.

Trent put an envelope on the table. "I'd like you to give this to Paul and Mary Beth Carpenter."

It held a check for a hundred thousand dollars.

"There's another one, for the same amount, being delivered to Alecia Stillwell."

Overwhelmed, I felt my eyes dampen with emotion. "Why are you doing this?"

"Let's just say I'm bypassing Robert and putting the money to much better use."

"What does your father have to say about all this?"

"Pop about had a coronary at first when I told him what I was doing," Trent said. "But, I showed him how we're coming out ahead in this deal. He's always trusted my judgment before."

Deep in thought, I made doodling patterns in the condensation on my glass and occupied the present part of my mind by watching Taffy sniff her way around the base of the bird feeder. I jumped when Trent's hand took mine.

"So are you okay about Robert?" he wanted to know. "The possibility of his going to prison?"

"I'm very okay with that," I said. "He's a total stranger to me. I really don't have any idea who he is or what he's all about. And at this point, I don't need to know. I just want the divorce to be finalized. Maybe I can persuade the judge to speed things along, once we satisfy the mandatory waiting period."

"With your powers of persuasion, Carly, I'm sure you can convince a judge to see things your way."

It was another compliment that may have been an insult. I moved my hand from beneath his.

"Thanks. I think."

"It was a compliment," he confirmed.

"Okay."

Watching him swirl the ice in his glass of tea, seeing the muscles in his forearm quietly ripple, taking in the bigger picture of the man sitting across from me, I decided that he could compliment or insult me as much as he wanted to. As long as I knew another kiss was forthcoming.

And as long as I knew things were over between him and Terry.

"You know, it could be bad, this thing happening between you and me," I said. "Being faithful is important to me."

"What do you mean? You just said you want the divorce to be over with as soon as possible."

"I'm not talking about Robert. I hope never to lay eyes on him again. He's old news," I said, trying to control the flood of possibilities that danced through my overstimulated brain. Me surprising Trent with a picnic lunch at the construction site, or snuggling up to him on the sofa while watching a movie. Us, all dressed up, going to a charity ball. Together. Him cooking me breakfast at his house after a night of physical bliss. The two of us walking and talking and sharing complaints and thoughts and ideas and dreams.

"I'm talking about your girlfriend," I said. "Terry."

Trent put down his glass of tea and smiled. Taffy brought him the tennis ball. He tossed it straight up into the air a few times and caught it, teasing the dog without meaning to.

"Well," I began, since he hadn't responded. "You said she spent the night at your place. She was your alibi, remember? I assume she's an old girlfriend you happened to run into. Or maybe she's your current girlfriend."

He tossed the ball into the grass and started laughing.

I got angry. "Look, maybe your social life isn't any of my business. But you can't just go around kissing people like you just kissed me while you have a girlfriend that you sleep with on the side!"

Taffy pushed the ball into his hand and Trent threw it again and laughed some more.

"What's so damn funny?"

"I was just imagining," he managed, "me and Terry sleeping together! He's bald, has a scraggly gray beard, and weighs about two-fifty. Wait until I tell him about this!"

"*He?* Terry is a *he?*"

"Yes, Carly Stone. Terry is a *he*. He owns a heavy-equipment rental company, and we've been friends for years. We went back to my place that night because I wanted him to look at some blueprints for a parking garage and we ended up drinking ourselves silly. I wasn't about to let him drive home, so he crashed on my sofa."

"Oh."

Relief outweighed the embarrassment that drew a blush to my cheeks, and I didn't care if he was laughing at me. I just wanted him to kiss me some more.

"I'm not laughing at you," he said, reading my mind again, the laughter still erupting in spurts. "And as soon as I stop laughing I want to kiss you again."

He did and we did and I suddenly felt as beautiful as my evening had become.

We drank our tea and watched Taffy chase a butterfly and tried not to think too much. I asked Trent who would be at the big meeting, and as I listened to his answer, I struggled to think about business instead the lingering taste of his mouth on mine.

"Jo Jo will be there, along with a personal assistant, the vice president of marketing, and one of their attorneys. Of course, Pop and Jack will be there. I spoke to your brother-in-law to see if Tuesday worked for him. He'll be there with your sister and his boss—the top dog at *In Home Now*. I'm sure your folks will be there. So that's, what, twelve people? Not including us."

"Good grief! I've got to get busy! I've got a lot to do before then!" I said, a mental list forming. "I'll have to put together a draft of the proposal and a benefit sheet for each party. Run some projections of sales numbers and the estimated value of publicity and goodwill. Get a clean drawing of the existing layout of Daddy's store. Arrange for a caterer to bring in some pastries and juice and coffee . . ."

"Carly."

"Yes?"

"Kiss me."

31

Except for a chase scene taking place within the confines of the television set, the house sounded quiet as I made the first trip from my car to the kitchen toting bags of groceries. It was *too* quiet, and I wondered where Granny and Taffy were. I knew Mamma and Daddy were working at the store, taking a final inventory before the liquidation sale. But when I'd left them, Granny and Taffy were watching a movie.

I called out to Granny but got no response and clapped my hands to call Taffy, but she didn't come. I wondered if the two of them had gone next door to Miss Rose's house and decided to walk over after I finished unloading the groceries. Even though all of the neighbors knew Granny, I wasn't comfortable with the idea of her wandering around the neighborhood.

Mamma had told me it was okay to leave Granny by herself for short periods of time, and I'd only been gone a half hour. In the past, when she was by herself, Granny had always stayed at home. But since her disease could progress, we had to be on the lookout for changes.

I made a second trip to my car and was returning with a large watermelon when a feeling of unease rippled through me. The fine hairs at the nape of my neck stood upright. Before I could set the heavy melon down on the kitchen counter, I sensed someone else in the room and spun around.

"Hello, Carly," Robert said.

Shock and a jolt of something foreign that may have been fear ran through my midsection, and I dropped the watermelon. It hit with a thud just inches from my toes and split into pieces, splattering sticky juice and seeds.

He stood several feet away with his feet spread and his arms crossed over his chest. His stare was locked on me like a laser on a target, and he radiated an aura of sheer anger.

"Robert," I said. "You startled me."

He'd appeared out of nowhere, and it occurred to me that he had been hiding, waiting. There wasn't another car parked in the driveway or the street. And even when we were on good marital terms, he would never just help himself to Mamma and Daddy's house if nobody was home.

"Looks like you won't be eating that tonight."

Although he was referring to the sticky mush of watermelon, his eyes never left mine. His face was cold and blank and devoid of expression. But his eyes fumed.

I forgot about the complaining hunger in my stomach, the fact that I had to pee, and the melting ice cream in the backseat of my car. My heart pounded in my chest and time slowed as my senses zeroed in on the situation.

Instinct told me to make a dash for the door and run to a neighbor for help. But Robert stood between me and my escape route. And on top of that, a sinking feeling told me Robert knew where Granny was.

"Where's Granny?"

He stared at me, not moving.

"What are you doing here?" I hoped my voice sounded calm.

"I'm your husband," he said and moved closer to block me against the kitchen counter. He reeked of booze, bitter and stale. A residual odor that resulted from a night of solid drinking was leaking from his pores.

But the man before me acted entirely sober. "You suddenly have a problem with talking to your husband?"

"I don't have a problem talking to you, Robert. But I don't appreciate you sneaking up on me like that. And just for the record, I wish you'd quit referring to yourself as my husband. You've never been a real husband to me. It was a mistake to marry you."

Robert kept advancing toward me, seemingly without moving his feet, and I quickly found myself sandwiched between him and the counter. I sidestepped out from between the two. But in a move that matched mine, he kept my body trapped between him and the counter.

"That's where you're wrong, Carly." His words were without inflection. Flat, like the expression on his face. "You didn't make a mistake when you married me. I made the mistake in marrying you. I thought you would make the perfect mother for the son I am going to have. I thought you were good breeding material. But it turns out you're a stupid small-town girl, happy to be born and bred in this piss hole. I got you out of here and was going to make a good life for us. But you had to keep taking the damn birth control pills . . . because you didn't want to make my baby!"

I tried to calm him by talking sensibly. "The timing wasn't right for a baby. I wanted to wait a few years."

He ignored me. "And then you went and really screwed everything up. You started it all by making a big fuss over the woodpeckers. And then you went and blabbed to the police. But, see, it's going to end with me. I'm going to end it."

"End what?" I asked and immediately wished I hadn't.

"*It*, Carly. I'm going to end it. Or should I say end you?"

A chill traveled the length of my spine. He wasn't making sense, but his voice was drenched with venom and I got the general meaning. I'd seen Robert angry a few times before, but the anger had always been directed at his job or his boss. Never at me. I'd always been the one to console him. And I'd never before witnessed the evil look emanating from his pupils.

I tried to reason with him. "Robert, if you had bothered to tell me what you were doing, I would have known what was going on. Instead, I had to find out through research. I had no idea you were the landowner until it was too late. And as far as screwing up your business plan, I didn't do that."

I sidestepped away from him, just a few inches, hoping he wouldn't notice. Again, his move matched mine, and I was still trapped between him and the kitchen counter. I couldn't reach anything to hit him with, and he stayed just far enough away so I couldn't knee him in the crotch like I'd seen at a self-defense demonstration in New York. I thought about quietly trying to dial nine-one-one, but the cordless phone was atypically in its handset across the room, and my mobile phone sat uselessly in the front seat of my car.

I took a deep breath and forced myself to stay calm. Robert was angry and hostile, but would he really try to hurt me? In answer to my question, the instinctive part of my brain responded, *Yes, he would*. He was already wanted for murder. He had nothing to lose. I tried to think. And prayed to God that Granny had simply taken Taffy for a walk.

"You didn't screw up my business plan? You didn't screw up my business plan!" He laughed, and the sound was crazed. "You didn't screw up my business plan," he repeated, then stepped forward and shoved me, hard. I stumbled backward into the counter but stayed upright. The center of my chest stung where his hand hit.

I tried to stay calm and sound authoritative. "Don't touch me again, Robert."

The next shove came with amazing speed. I jumped sideways to deflect the blow but slipped on a chunk of watermelon and went straight down. I landed on my hip and scrambled away from him.

"I swear, Robert. You touch me again, and you'll regret it."

"Baby doll, I regret the first time I ever touched you. You wouldn't make me the child I deserve, and on top of that, you stuck your nose into my financial business. You've ruined my life."

I got to my feet and backed away, putting some distance between the two of us.

"Robert, where is Granny? She hasn't done anything to you. It's me you're mad at. Tell me where she is."

"They're after me, you know. I'm on the run because of you. You make me kill the birds. You blab to the cops. You set me up at the hotel, which by the way, didn't work because I saw a cop scoping out my room." He shook his head with disgust. "You're not being a very good wife."

I heard a muffled bark but couldn't be sure if it was real or imagined.

"Is that Taffy I just heard? Is she with Granny somewhere in the house?"

Although his glare remained locked on me, it seemed as though he couldn't hear. He ignored my questions.

"Robert, I didn't make you do anything. Now, please tell me where Granny is."

"Forget about the old woman already, you stupid bitch. She just kept going on and on about you and your boyfriend. I told her to shut up, but she wouldn't." He shrugged his shoulders. "And then she has the nerve to say I don't have any manners? So I shut her up with my fist. She's back there in the bathroom, with the yapping dog. I put her in the bathtub. She looks kind of funny. Passed out, with her feet sticking up and all. Kind of like something out of *Beverly Hillbillies*."

Over the noise from the television, I definitely heard muted barking. I turned and sprinted toward the bathroom where the barking seemed to be coming from, but Robert was quicker and tackled me before I even got out of the kitchen. He slammed me into the tile floor, and the instant I rolled over to get up, a white explosion blew through my vision. Pain reverberated in my skull as though a jackhammer had punctured it. Blood ran from my nose or maybe my mouth, and I realized he'd punched me in the face.

"Yeah, baby doll, you did. You did make me do it," he said, kneeling over me, one hand gripping the collar of my shirt and the other poised for another punch. "And now they think they're going to bust me for arson. I should have just poisoned the birds. The only reason I set the fire was to cover up the burned-out nest holes."

The raised fist dropped slightly. "I'm busting my ass, climbing a ladder in the dark, trying to find the freakin' holes. And setting them on fire. Then I say to myself, how will that look? Smoke just shooting out the sides of trees? Something like that could keep burning, slow, for a long time. It could smoke for days. So it occurs to me to set a ground fire. Brush fires happen all the time. Sparks could have easily gone into the holes and caught the nests on fire."

I shoved his hand away and scooted backward on my hands and feet. I tried to get up but slipped again and actually saw the second punch arcing toward my head before I felt the impact. This time his balled fist made contact with the side of my jaw and my head rocked back as pain exploded through my face. I felt blood squirting somewhere inside my mouth and my teeth rattled against each other.

When my eyes came back into focus he was squatting beside me, shaking his head from side to side, seemingly talking to himself.

"It would have worked just right, too, except for that dumb ass who came poking around with a flashlight."

"Jerry," I said, struggling to keep from panicking. Or blacking out. I had to stay calm and get help. I had to find Granny.

"What?" Robert demanded, distracted from his rant.

"His name was Jerry." I swallowed a mouthful of blood before I gagged on it.

"Who gives a shit what his name was? He didn't have any business being out there in the middle of the night."

"But did you have to kill him?" My tongue was thick, and I had trouble getting the words out.

Robert cocked his head to think. A maniacal gleam appeared in the eye I could see. I looked around, hoping to locate something to grab and use as a weapon. But the nearest thing was a kitchen chair, and it was out of reach.

"No, I don't suppose I *had* to kill him," Robert said finally. "But once I knocked him out, I figured I could make it look like he was the one who set the fire. So I dragged him over by the woodpecker trees. And then I let the diesel run from the truck. I had to bust the lock on the valve, but it was easy."

"You killed a man, Robert."

"You made me do it." He stood, jerking me up with him. "You're the one who stuck your nose in my business."

I tried to pull away, but his grip on me tightened. "It was your fault and his fault, too. He shined a light right in my face. I couldn't take the chance he would remember what I look like."

I didn't need to hear anymore. I didn't want to hear anymore. If I didn't do something, he would kill me, too. I needed to keep him talking.

"What do you want from me?" I couldn't feel the right side of my face, and my ears were ringing. I willed myself not to show fear.

"What do I want from you?" he said, pulling out a kitchen chair and shoving me onto it.

I considered fighting back with kicks or punches or scratches but knew I'd lose. He was heavier and stronger and quicker. My best chance was to keep him talking as long as I could.

"What do I want from you," he said again and pulled the coffee maker off the kitchen counter by its cord. The glass pot fell to the ground and shattered. But all he'd wanted was the length of electrical cord.

With a single jerk, he ripped it out of the appliance and threw the coffee maker into the sink. I figured he was going to tie me up with the cord, or worse, try to choke me. I jumped up and drove my head into his gut.

The blow took him by surprise, and I managed to dash around him. But not away from him. The impact of a chair slamming into me was lightning quick and low down. My legs buckled and even though I couldn't feel it, I sensed that my right knee had been seriously damaged.

He pulled me off the floor as though I were weightless and dragged me into a fresh kitchen chair. I noted with a sense of detachment that my knee was twisted at an odd angle and I didn't struggle when he busied himself tying my wrists together with the electrical cord, behind my back. I had to figure out a way to buy some time.

"What I want from you, bitch, is, I want you to suffer. I want to show you what happens to people who mess with Robert Ellis." He yanked the cord tighter with each word. "I want to repay you for ruining my life."

My hands felt fat and numb. When I tried to move them, I discovered that he'd not only tied them together, but had woven the cord through the back of the chair.

"Let's talk, Robert," I managed to say through a puffy bloody mouth, still thinking my only way out was to keep him talking and hope that someone would come home. "You don't have to be here, doing this. People make mistakes, and we have a legal system that gives you certain rights. There is another way."

"Another way to get even with you?! Oh, there are plenty of ways I could do that! Maybe I should just take you somewhere and keep you locked up, like they want to keep me locked up."

Using my hair as a handhold, he yanked my head backward, and in that instant I saw a flash of something through the window that looked like Trent's white work truck. It had to be. It had red lettering on the sides and a big toolbox in the back. And it was pulling into Mamma and Daddy's driveway.

"That's not going to happen," I said, energized by the sight of Trent. "I'd sooner die than be locked up by you."

He sighed, and the feel of his breath was revolting. "That can certainly be arranged. I mean, they want to send me to the clink for killing some jerk who was out nosing around in the middle of the night anyway. So what if they pin another one on me? Besides. Even if I get off the murder rap, they'll put me in jail for wasting a few birds. Hell. I didn't even get them all." A corner of his mouth went up in thought. "I should go back and finish the job."

"There's no job to finish, Robert," I said through gritted teeth, the back of the chair cutting into my neck. "You burned out all three nests before you killed Jerry."

"Wrong again, bitch!" He released my hair with a jerk. "I saw another hole when I was up there, but then that asshole showed up asking questions before I could get to it."

He grabbed my lower lip in a vicelike grip and moved it as though I was a puppet and he was making me talk. "Say it, bitch! Say, 'I was wrong!'"

I jerked my head sideways to get his hand off my face. Enraged, he left me to rummage through Mamma's kitchen drawers until he found a weapon. It was a carving knife. He tested the blade's sharpness against the side of his thumb, as though he were going to cut slices of meat from the breast of a roasted bird.

The situation was out of control, and I was helpless. I mentally begged Trent to hurry, wondering if I really had seen his truck or just wished for it. I was thinking that I might have imagined it when the door to the back screen porch opened with its signature squeak.

"Carly?" Trent called.

Cocking his head, Robert moved out of Trent's view and stood silently with his back against the wall. When Trent walked into the kitchen, he'd see me but he wouldn't see the knife coming at him.

"Carly? Where are you?"

By his footsteps, we could hear Trent approaching the kitchen. Robert raised the carving knife above his head.

"Trent! Watch out!" I yelled and lunged at Robert, dragging the chair with me. My knee collapsed, and I fell to the floor.

Barking filled my ears, and Taffy sailed over me at the same time

Trent came into view. His attention diverted by the dog, Robert was a second late in swinging the knife, and Trent deflected the pointed blade with the palm of his hand.

Cursing, Robert swung the knife back and forth in front of him as he advanced toward Trent. I scooted across the floor like an inchworm, trying to move into a position to be of some help, but Taffy was protectively keeping herself between me and the fighting men.

"It doesn't have to be this way, Robert," Trent said, barely jumping out of the way each time the blade arced in front of his gut.

"Yeah," Robert snarled, lunging forward with the knife. "It does."

Trent dropped into a squatting position and came up ramming his shoulder into Robert's crotch. When Robert staggered, Trent threw an uppercut that caught him on the jaw, and followed it with another punch to the side of the face.

Robert was dazed, but his grip on the knife didn't loosen and he lunged at Trent yet again. Dodging the blade, Trent slipped on a piece of watermelon rind and went down. He tried to roll away, but his back was against the dishwasher, and there was nowhere to go. With an evil grin, Robert raised the knife high above his head.

"Don't do it, Robert!" Granny shouted, stepping over me and the chair I was attached to. She held a side-by-side shotgun waist high, pointed in front of her.

Registering the gun, Robert froze for a fraction of a second.

"Screw you all!" he yelled and spun around until the knife was poised above me.

An explosive shot rang out and echoed through the house. Robert screamed and went down, landing just inches away from me.

The aftermath of silence lasted only a second but seemed like minutes passing in slow motion as I took inventory of the situation. I was alive and hadn't been stabbed or shot. Granny and Trent were okay. And Robert was going to jail, where he could never hurt me again.

Taffy's wet nose was the first thing I became aware of. I was still in a tangle on the kitchen floor and she was licking the blood off my face. And then suddenly Trent was beside me, cutting my hands loose and picking me up and carrying me to the sofa. And before I could ask if she was okay, Granny was there too, peering into my eyes, asking if any of my bones felt broken. She still gripped the shotgun, and a barely visible trail of smoke curled out the end of the barrel that was now pointed at the ceiling.

"The knife . . ." I sputtered. I didn't trust Robert. Wounded or not, he was crazy enough to keep coming after us.

"The knife is in the kitchen sink. And you don't need to worry about him anymore," Trent said, pushing the matted hair out of my face to get a better look at my injuries. "She about tore his shoulder and arm off."

"I shot him good," Granny said.

Robert moaned and called for help.

"I was goin' for his chest, but Taffy got in the way," Granny apologized. "I didn't want to put any pellets in her!"

I had to smile.

Trent immobilized my knee with some pillows and retrieved a bag of frozen peas for my face before calling nine-one-one. Despite being battered and bloody and the pain that was rapidly settling in all over my body, I felt deliriously good.

Granny sat on a chair next to the sofa and arranged the shotgun across her legs with the end of the barrel pointed at Robert.

He moaned some more.

"You shut your trap or I'll shoot you again," Granny said. "I've got a shell in the other barrel, and I'll bet I could blow a hole smack through your belly now that Taffy's out of my way!"

The moaning stopped.

Granny was lucid, and I'd never been happier to see her. She saved my life. And quite possibly, Trent's.

Since I was having trouble talking through my rapidly swelling mouth, Granny gave Trent a condensed version of events while we waited for the police and ambulances to arrive. Her explanation ended with an indignant "I woke up in the bathtub! He hit me on the side of my head and threw me in there like some drunk at a barn brawl."

Even though Granny insisted she was fine, Trent convinced her to go to the hospital with me and let the doctors take a look at her head.

As I wondered about Granny's head, a curious thought entered mine. "How did you get the gun? I thought Daddy keeps them locked up."

"Of course he keeps 'em locked up. But that don't mean I don't know the combination to the gun safe!"

"I love you, Granny," I said through a puffy face. "You're the best."

"I love you, too," she told me. "You just be sure an' pick you out a better one next time. Somebody like this here Trent boy. Now, he's a keeper."

Trent gave my hand a squeeze and smiled at the compliment. "Yes, Carly Stone, your grandmother is right. I am a keeper. And I can't tell you how thankful I am that you came into my life."

The sound of distant sirens entered the room and slowly grew louder.

Listening, Granny harrumphed. "Those fireman boys sure do have tight butts," Granny told Trent, staring curiously at him. "Have I met you before, dear?"

"Yes ma'am. And you liked me, too," he answered as he gently took the gun from her and switched the safety on.

32

"You did it, little girl," Daddy said.

"*We* did it!" I corrected. Even though a brace ran from my ankle to my thigh, I had the same sense of elation an athlete might experience after crossing the finish line of a marathon—in first place.

Mamma's kitchen table was full, and my sister was busy washing dishes. She had flown in the day before with her entire family, a publicist, the president of *In Home Now*, and Precious.

Cheryl had accepted my invitation to fly down for a few days and meet my family, and was engrossed in a conversation with Jenny about a new do-it-yourself permanent makeup system that one of the *In Home Now* interns tested. The college student declared it a failure after her permanently blushed cheeks turned green, and was threatening to sue the manufacturer.

Lori Anne had taken the day off work to be my 'personal assistant' at the big meeting and was trying to convince Granny that becoming a brunette would not make her look younger.

And, Jack, Mister Protter, and Trent were at the table discussing the details of the partnership.

After the meeting with Handyman's Depot, the three of them had accepted Mamma's invitation to join us for a late lunch of grilled hot dogs with pineapple slaw and homemade banana pudding for dessert.

Even though my teeth finally felt solid in my mouth again, I couldn't eat. I was too excited. And I couldn't keep my eyes off Trent. I didn't even care if anyone caught me staring.

The afternoon before, he and I had met up with my ornithologist friend at the construction site and found a fourth woodpecker nest.

And a fifth. Both were much higher up than the first three and active with birds, despite the fire. I had been overjoyed and, jumping around on one leg, hugged Trent. He hugged back, even though the discovery could have meant trouble for him.

We'd driven to the beach afterward, to sit and picnic and be with each other. He explained some things to me about commercial construction, and I explained to him the differences between mediation, arbitration, and litigation. We planned a scuba diving trip to Mazatlán as soon as my knee healed from the orthoscopic surgery; we decided to spend a week in Florida as soon as the shopping center opened; and we set a date to go sailing on his boat the following week. And then we kissed like two hormone-driven adolescents until the sun dropped and the breeze raised chill bumps on my bare arms.

Two days later, wildlife officials determined it was in the best interest of the birds to immediately relocate them because of all the fire damage to their environment. Trent happily agreed to pay the associated costs.

"The meeting was a smashing success," Mamma said to her houseful of guests, radiating joy. "Jo Jo couldn't say enough good things about a partnership with *In Home Now*."

Mister Protter laughed. "And couldn't thank Trent enough for arranging the deal. Little did he know that it was all your daughter's doing and that we were blackmailed into it!"

"*Blackmail* is kind of a strong word," I said, feeling drunk even though my glass only held sweet tea.

"You're right," Mister Protter agreed. "How about *gently persuaded?*"

"That's better," I said. "And anyway, wouldn't you agree that everything worked out for the best?"

"I'll concede that point to you, young lady. You're going to make one hell of a lawyer."

Cheryl joined us at the table. "You're right, she will, because she was one fine mediator. And now that she's gotten a taste of some 'whup ass,' she'll be an unstoppable lawyer!"

I smiled.

"Anyway, I always knew she should have been litigating instead of mediating," Cheryl added.

"Well," Jack said. "I'm very pleased that she accepted the offer to work for my law firm."

"She did?" Lori Anne said, plopping down at the table. Yes, Jack told her. We'd met yesterday and agreed to the terms of my employment.

"Awesome! Of course, we'll need to get her a new haircut before she starts. Maybe some crown highlights with reddish lowlights. We'll go for a sexy, powerful look."

"She could do that look well," Cheryl agreed.

"Would everybody please quit talking about me like I'm not here?" I said.

"Everyone is just happy for you," Jack said through a mouthful of banana pudding. "You're fortunate to have such a great family and such good friends, Carly."

He had a face that could make him anyone's grandfather. It was a face that had probably fooled many of his opponents into believing that he was a pushover. I'd done some research on the man after Trent told me about the job offer. Jack was a warrior. He was also a saint. And in court, he was unbeatable. I couldn't wait to start work.

"You're right, Jack," I said, beaming through all the makeup Jenny had artistically applied to cover my bruises, "I am fortunate."

"Congratulations on your new job," Daddy said, circling behind me and eyeing what food remained on the table in much the same way that Taffy would if she could stand upright.

"Thank you," I said.

He stopped beside Granny and reached for her plate. "Are you finished with this?"

"Yup," she said. "I'm downright full."

He dumped the contents of her plate, a few remaining bites of hot dog and some baked beans, into a pie tin before moving on.

"What is Daddy doing?" Jenny said.

"He's feeding the coons," Sherry and Stacy answered in unison, sounding very grown up.

"Coons!" Hunter said.

"You *feed* the raccoons now?" Jenny asked Daddy. "Like a cat or a dog or something?"

"It keeps them out of the trash," Daddy told her, eyeing a half-eaten bowl of banana pudding that she'd put on the counter to save for later. "Were you going to finish that?"

"Yes!" she said and stuck it in the refrigerator before he could get to it. "Besides, I thought you aroma-therapied them into passivity."

"It was a good theory," Mamma said, "but your Aroma-magic Ionizer and Environment Enhancer didn't stop them from getting into the trash at all. They just took their time about it. They got to where they wouldn't even run off if you caught them. They'd just look at you and grin."

"Feeding them was actually your granny's idea," Daddy said. "Sometimes the simplest solution is right in front of you the whole time."

"Exactly!" I said. "You just have to get—"

"Off the end of the church pew to see it," Trent finished for me.

We grinned stupidly at each other until we realized everyone was watching us watch each other.

"He means that sometimes you have to look at the bigger picture," I explained to Jack, who wasn't familiar with Daddy's stained-glass–window lesson.

"Bigger picture, huh?" Jack said, polishing off his pudding and scanning the table for more.

"Take me and Carly, for example," Trent said, displaying the miniscule dimples I couldn't get enough of. "Before I looked at the bigger picture, all I saw was a royal pain in the ass. Now I see an intelligent, incredibly beautiful woman. One I plan on spending a lot of time with."

I blushed. And felt like a giddy teenager.

Precious growled at something that none of us could see.

"That poodle-dog's done gone and gotten itself bit by a rabid fox, I do believe," Granny said.

Jenny rolled her eyes and managed to look glamorous doing it. "My little Precious doesn't have rabies."

"Who's having babies?" Granny said.

Trent leaned over and whispered into my ear, "I love your family."

"Thanks," I said. "I love them, too."

His next words were spoken loudly, boldly. "And I love you, Carly Stone."

My heart stopped and time stood still and every other cliché that I'd ever heard about romance came true for me at that moment.

"So then, the two of you are having babies?" Granny asked.

"I'll think we'll just date for a while first," Trent told her, "And save the baby thing for later. After we're married."

"Good grief," was all I could think of. That, and me and Trent making love. And making more love. And having babies. One baby, anyway. In two or three years.

Granny harrumphed at a still-growling Precious and left the table.

Daddy opened a bottle of champagne and distributed a flute to everyone, assuring my sister that bubbly did indeed go well with banana pudding.

After filling the glasses, Mamma raised hers high in the air. "To new friends and new beginnings."

"And to Charleston," Lori Anne said.

"And to 'lawyering' instead of mediating!" Daddy said.

"And looking at the bigger picture," Trent and I added.

The room was so full of joviality and promise, nobody noticed when Precious circled the table and stopped at Jack's briefcase to growl at it.

Except Granny. She'd returned to the kitchen and was pointing a pump-action shotgun at the dog. The butt of the weapon was firmly planted against her shoulder and the stock was tight against her cheek as she lined up the bead with her canine target.

"Granny, no!" Jenny and I shouted in unison.

Precious looked up to see the end of a barrel looking back and, amazingly, stopped growling.

"I'd better change the combination on that lock," was all Daddy said.